AWAY

Dove's vision went to white. He felt a hot, blinding wind pass over him. A sound like the banshee's howl. Mixed in it, faintly, were the screams of women and children. The fireball reached out to him, sucked the air out of his lungs, and passed on. Chunks of hot metal and asphalt danced around him.

He looked up. A woman's body was sprawled atop the rear door of the squad's truck, her back bent at an unnatural angle, her clothing smoldering. Behind her, the truck itself lay on its side, crackling with flame.

Then Dove's cellular phone rang. He took it from his jacket pocket. The case was cracked but it still apparently worked. It was a moment before he could hold it steady against his ear.

BLOWN AWAY

Novelization by KIRK MITCHELL
Story by JOHN RICE & JOE BATTEER & M. JAY ROACH
Screenplay by JOE BATTEER & JOHN RICE

AVON BOOKS ◆ NEW YORK

BLOWN AWAY is an original publication of Avon Books. This
work has never before appeared in book form. This work is a novel
based on a screenplay by Joe Bateer & John Rice and a story by
John Rice & Joe Bateer & M. Jay Roach. Any similarity to actual
persons or events is purely coincidental.

AVON BOOKS
A division of
The Hearst Corporation
1350 Avenue of the Americas
New York, New York 10019

Copyright © 1994 by Metro-Goldwyn-Mayer, Inc.
Published by arrangement with Metro-Goldwyn-Mayer, Inc.
Library of Congress Catalog Card Number: 94-94158
ISBN: 0-380-77844-0

First Avon Books Printing: July 1994

AVON TRADEMARK REG. U.S. PAT. OFF. AND IN OTHER COUNTRIES,
MARCA REGISTRADA, HECHO EN U.S.A.

Printed in the U.S.A.

RA   10   9   8   7   6   5   4   3   2   1

In appreciation to Chief Warrant Officer Michael A. Cordoza (USN, ret.) for both his help on this book and his twenty-eight years of Explosive Ordnance Disposal service to the American public.

1

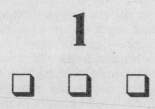

Ryan Gaerity sat before the back wall of his cell, visualizing what lay beyond. The cricket field, of course. And then the high fence. A guard tower stood at the seaward corner. Its searchlight would be probing the night, raindrops shimmering through the beam like strands of Christmas tree tinsel. That would obscure the view of the man in the tower. Belfast radio had been predicting the storm for days. It'd come in off the North Atlantic shortly after supper. Gaerity hadn't seen the rising surf and drizzle with his own eyes, for he didn't have the run of the place—as did the trusties, the quislings who brownnosed the guards. Still, he could see through the grimy, ancient stones of his wall and watch the waves smashing to mist against the rocky headland, the fog wreathing around the castle. Tourists, if Northern Ireland still had tourists, might be struck by the medieval charm of Castle Gleigh. Until they noticed the towers and the fence line strung with concertina wire.

Gaerity checked the small clock on his bookshelf. Quarter to ten.

Years of planning came down to tonight.

Everything depended on his cellmate being re-

1

turned to him from solitary, where Kevin Daidy had spent the last two weeks contemplating the Irish "troubles" from a different point of view. The former laborer was rather stuck on one idea. He wanted the British out of Erin, dead or alive, and tended to smack anyone who disagreed with him.

If the guards brought him back to the block tonight, it would be done only minutes before the lights went out. An added cruelty in that. Naturally, a fellow who'd just spent a fortnight on his lonesome might appreciate a bit of chat to reassure himself that he hadn't gone out of his mind. But no talking was allowed five minutes after lights-out.

Gaerity concentrated on gazing through the wall again.

At that very moment, he could see the small fishing boat threading through the dark mountains of water toward the castle. He only hoped that the spring storm wasn't so violent that the skipper had turned back for his home port, Buncrana on the Republic of Ireland side of the border. Money could rent pluck, but seldom could it buy genuine courage. And in all his years, over all his adventures, Gaerity could count only one man who'd had such courage. Natural. Elemental. He'd been no more than a boy, really. But he'd had grit.

Gaerity checked the clock again.

Three minutes had elapsed.

He resisted scratching his neck. From his collar line to his feet he'd coated himself with a thick layer of petroleum jelly. It made sitting rather uncomfortable, but the insulation would be welcome during his swim out to the boat.

Finally, he could hear footfalls coming down the corridor.

Smiling, Gaerity listened to the block stir, taunts being hurled through the bars at the Protestant guards.

A County Tyrone accent asked, "How's soli, Daidy?"

"Now I know what the ass end of nowhere looks like," Gaerity's cellmate answered, his voice cracking from disuse.

"Didn't touch yourself in there, did you?"

"Why d'you think I'm havin' such a hard time seein'?"

"You're a bloody caution, Kev."

Keys rattled in the barred door behind Gaerity. Slowly, he half-turned in his chair. Kevin, one side of his face covered with a brown stain of dried blood, was already shuffling stiff-legged inside the cell, but the guard decided to hurry him along with a blow along the kidneys.

Kevin collapsed to a knee, groaning, fighting for breath.

The guard was rearing back for another strike when Gaerity rose from his chair and said coldly, "It's a fine stick you have there, Orangeman."

The man checked his swing and met Gaerity's gaze. After a few seconds, he lowered his baton and went out, slamming the door behind him.

Gaerity chuckled under his breath.

It was all right for the zookeeper to tap the glass of the king cobra's cage—but not too often and never too hard. The cobra has eyes that remember. And who knows? One lovely morning years hence, the keeper's wife sets off to Londonderry in her old English Ford to visit Mum—and she's bitten as soon as she turns the key in the ignition. A fat little Presbyterian woman is transformed into a dazzling burst of orange light. Poetry in plastique.

"Ah, Ryan," Kevin said, trying to smile with swollen lips, "I'm done with bein' tossed in the hole."

"No, you're not." Gaerity helped him to his cot. "It's your nature to fight, and it's their nature to lock fellows up for fighting."

Kevin blinked up in confusion from his pillow. "How's that?"

"We're all prisoners of our own natures. It's useless to resist."

"Useless?"

"We are what we are."

"Ah." Kevin nodded, although he was still thoroughly in the dark over what Gaerity was getting at. He turned philosophical only after several pints of black porter, and then his choice of dialectic was how best to stick it to the Brits. "Thanks for waitin', Ryan."

Gaerity's eyes clicked in warning toward the corridor, where he could still sense the guard hovering close by, eavesdropping. He could finger a guard the way a psychic could feel a ghost. Then he said in hushed Gaelic, "Couldn't do it without you, Kevin."

The footfalls clipped off toward his desk near the steel door at the far end of the corridor.

"Let's make you presentable for your public," Gaerity said, lapsing back into English. He went to the sink in the corner and wet his washcloth. Coming back to Kevin's cot, he knelt and began softening the dried blood on the man's face, gently wiping it away.

"How've you done it?" Kevin asked.

"Done what?"

"Survived seventeen bloody years here. All the times in soli for not goin' along with 'em. I done just eighteen months so far, and I'm goin' out of me head."

Gaerity smiled warmly at the man. "I fixed heart and mind on the one thing that'll make me free."

"Bustin' out, you mean?"

"No, these old stones could tumble into the sea and we'd still be prisoners *here*." Gaerity tapped his temple with a knuckle.

"Don't understand."

Of course not. He was a simple Provo. Scarcely

two inches of forehead separated his eyebrows and his hairline. "Why're you here?" Gaerity asked.

"That's easy enough—some bastard sang on me just as I set out to do a lovely little snipe on the Brits down in Armagh."

"Betrayal, then?"

Kevin nodded groggily.

But Gaerity pressed, "Someone close to you?"

"Yes . . . Haggerty. Loved him like a brother."

"Did you think of him in soli?"

Kevin's bruised face hardened. "All the time. I had to scream now and again. Not for bein' alone. But for wantin' to kill him so fierce."

"Why?"

"For puttin' me in the dark."

Gaerity wrung the cloth. A trickle of pinkish drops fell to the tiled floor and drained down a joint from which the grout had been chipped away. "Then you do understand, boy-o. That's the demon. You must kill it before you can go on with your life. Otherwise, it remains a running score inside your guts."

"You're on to something there, Ryan. You have a fine mind, and sometimes you lose me. But I get this."

"I'm glad."

The overhead fixture bumped off twice.

Gaerity said, "Here we go now . . ." All the lights in the block except one went out. A faint green blush from the guard's desk lamp shone down the corridor and filtered through the bars. Gaerity stood, still clutching the washcloth. "Get yourself some sleep. I'll wake you when I'm ready."

He eased down onto his cot and waited. The petroleum jelly made him feel as if he'd been basted for the spit. A fire of icy salt water.

After a minute, Kevin asked sleepily, "But if you get free of that demon, Ryan—what then?"

"You become a bloody god. Sleep."

"Wake me, for sure."

"I will, don't worry."

Gaerity slipped his toothbrush from his shirt pocket. The bristled end had been snapped off, then sharpened to a point on the rough stone wall behind his cot.

The guard started down the corridor on one of his periodic strolls. He probably fancied that he kept to no schedule on his rounds. But he did. He now glided past the bars, phantomlike in the dimness, made his turn in front of the last two cells, and began ambling back for his desk.

Gaerity waited for him to go by again, then crept across the floor to Kevin's cot, the toothbrush shank clenched between his teeth.

The man had fallen into his usual irritating nasal snore. What did he dream of? Certainly not the old world destroyed and a new one rising from the ashes. No, not Kevin Daidy. Glasses of porter and dead Brits were more like it.

Swiftly, Gaerity stuffed the cloth into Kevin's mouth with his left hand and felt for the bottom of the man's rib cage with his right. Finding it, he followed the sternum up to the location over the heart— just as Kevin startled awake and made a muffled cry.

Gaerity brought the shank down. Not with all his strength, for that would have only shattered the plastic toothbrush handle against bone. Instead, he jiggled the shank on impact, allowing the blade to slide between two ribs and angle into the heart.

Immediately, Kevin's body went limp.

Gaerity plucked out his shank and rushed to the sink. Leaning over it, he thrust two fingers down his throat, sucking in his abdomen to strengthen the gag reflex. He vomited, then fished in the remnants of a potato cake for the condom. The cake had been a gift from his "uncle," who'd come all the way from Carrickfergus that morning to wish his nephew a happy May Day. It had been X-rayed but only lightly prodded by Protestant fingers. Lucky no one had given it a good shake.

Gaerity would have heard the blast clear across the castle. The condom was filled with nitroglycerin. For the moment, he set it in his water glass.

Turning, dizzy from his lingering nausea, Gaerity ripped open his mattress cover with the shank and dumped the cotton stuffing onto the floor. A few kicks heaped it up while he went on rummaging inside the mattress. He came out with a cricket ball, careful not to dislodge the spoon that was jammed into its center.

Kevin had stolen it for him. Before his temper had gotten the better of him, Daidy had worked on the cricket field maintenance gang. This had given him access to the garden shed and machine shop. Gaerity himself got out of the cell only for an occasional interrogation.

He was wrenching off one of the iron posts to his cot when the distant groan of a wooden chair stopped him.

The guard had leaned forward to listen. No doubt he'd heard something—but was trying to decide if it was worth a jaunt all the way down the long corridor.

Gaerity waited ten seconds, then finished freeing the bedpost.

It was a lazy man's work: watching the Queen's prisoners. The oppressors become as sluggish as the oppressed. Time to wake them up.

He removed the bedpost cap with the heel of his hand, then poured the grainy liquid inside on his mattress stuffing. A mixture of ammonia nitrate fertilizer from the garden shed and hydraulic fluid from the machine shop. Kevin had nicked both in miniscule increments over months. Gaerity had then added a dash of "uncle's" nitroglycerin to give the blast more bite. A trademark of his.

He covered the pile with his blanket to keep the smell from wafting down the corridor, then squatted with the empty post across his lap. His hands groped over the floor for the loose tile. It popped free under pressure from the shank, revealing a small space he'd cobbed out of the damp-rotted cement.

He kept a bandanna there.

Wrapped in it were nearly a pound sterling of the coin of the realm, possession of which was forbidden in Castle Gleigh, and a vinyl-encased photograph, which he now pocketed. It was burned in his memory— his teenaged self and an even younger boy, angel-faced, clinging as one to a schoolyard "shuggey shoe," a rope for swinging. Almost a quarter century ago. They had parted company on another May Day, so this was something of an anniversary.

Covering the sound with a hacking cough, Gaerity dumped the coins down the open end of the bedpost. Then he snugly packed them with the oil and fertilizer-soaked stuffing, seated the cap back on with a quiet slap.

He laid the post atop his savaged mattress and went to his next task.

Curiously, he felt as if he were only imagining each step, so endlessly had he rehearsed this all in his mind. He'd awaken soon, and another day of waiting would stretch before him like a still, gray sea. Prison was not a square of walls and bars. It was a flat plain of empty hours.

He scooped an armful of stuffing and filled the toilet bowl with it. Tamping and then more packing. He tamped again.

Taking care not to grunt as he strained, he hoisted the stool off the floor—the nuts had already been taken off the bolts—and leaned the mouth of the bowl against the outer wall of the cell.

Yes, this feels like a dream. It is unfolding with that queer, colorless ease.

He took a thin cord from his trouser pocket and tied it around the neck of the condom. It was a flame fuse he'd fashioned from Daidy's rosary bead string and soaked in a solution of pulverized matchheads.

Gingerly, he nested the bulging rubber on the stuffing in the bowl, then threaded the string through the toilet's crookneck and across six feet of tile flooring.

Now, at long last, it all came down to the flaring of a single match.

After all these wasted years ...

Gaerity lit the fuse, then lay down between the two cots and pointed his shoes toward the toilet. As the sputtering flame inched up into the bowl, he pulled Kevin's corpse down on top of him.

The blast came.

He felt the concussion as a caress rippling over his body. For a breathless split second he was suspended in the primal light, moving outward through black space on a wave of searing heat. Expanding with the newborn universe.

Then he rolled Kevin off him and stood up into the swirling smoke.

A hole had opened his cell to the rain and the glare of the searchbeam. Not an enormous gap in the stones, but certainly big enough for a quick squeeze through. Months ago, he had imagined his toilet to be a cannon, and it had become one. He felt powerful once again, not helpless. Not at the mercy of his enemies. He could do anything he could visualize.

Kevin's backside was peppered with chips of porcelain.

Am I hit too? Gaerity rubbed his face, his legs, then his hands together. Just to make sure that he wasn't bleeding. Nothing. Not even a scratch, as near as he could tell.

He grabbed the cricket ball and stepped over Kevin's corpse to approach the bars.

As expected, the guard had hit the alarm button on the wall behind him. An electronic buzzer was rasping with an annoying pulse that reverberated throughout the entire castle. Over the jubilant shouts of his fellow inmates, Gaerity could hear the steel door boom open and then several pairs of shoes scuffling down the corridor.

He plucked the spoon from the cricket ball with his teeth, thrust his arm between two bars, and bowled. The hand grenade he'd fashioned was a crude device, but it detonated with a roar that quieted the block.

Gaerity ran for the hole, snatching up the bedpost along the way.

But he hesitated at the windy opening.

The sea was a dark blur beyond the phosphorescence of the surf. No sign of the boat, but he expected to hear the murmur of its diesels before he ever glimpsed the blacked-out trawler. The searchlight was still sweeping up and down the length of the fence, the guard in the tower somehow convinced that the explosion had been set off along the perimeter to breach the chainlink.

Gaerity braced to jump.

"Hold, mick!" a voice cried behind him.

He froze, then dropped his chin to chest. There was always one who survived the blast. Always. He smiled to himself.

"I have a fine Sten gun," the guard said deliberately, "and if you have any wit you'll turn around as slow as—"

Gaerity whirled and slammed the capped end of the bedpost against the inside wall. The shower of coins caught the guard at the midriff, and he went down with a clatter of keys and gunmetal.

Gaerity flew to the bars and, straining, reached for

the Sten. Just beyond his grasp. Had to have it. The tower had finally trained the light on the jagged hole.

He tried with his leg next and managed to scoot it back to the bars with the toe of his shoe.

"It is indeed a lovely Sten," Gaerity muttered, then tumbled through the hole and out into the squall. Rain stung his face. He plummeted fifteen feet onto the edge of the soggy cricket field, rolled, and came up firing a burst at the tower. A tinkle of shattered glass followed, and the beam winked out.

In darkness, he started climbing the fence. He could hear the boat, the low grumble of its engines.

"Crossmaglen!" he bawled to urge himself on.

2

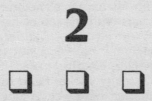

"**H**ere you are, Mr. Dove," the aged music store owner said, "gift-wrapped and all."

"Great." James Dove accepted the package, laid it on the countertop while he dug out his wallet. As he flipped the billfold open, the glint of his badge caught the owner's eyes.

"Ah, why didn't you say so, *Lieutenant* Dove?" A trace of a brogue, suddenly, in the old man's voice.

"Pardon?"

"On the department here in Somerville?"

"No, across the river," Dove said.

"Doesn't matter. My discount applies to Boston P.D. too. Ten percent. I've been givin' it for over forty years now to the men in blue—and gladly too."

"Oh, that's fine ..." Dove handed over a C-note. "Appreciate it, but you've gotta make a living."

The cash register chimed, and the old man winked as he handed back a twenty.

Dove stuffed the bill in a little plastic bank for the Catholic Youth Organization. Twenty years ago the cup would have been for NORAID, the Irish Northern Aid Committee, which helped bankroll the IRA's terror campaign in Ulster. Thank God Ted Kennedy and other American paddies had urged an end to those contributions.

"You're not from around here, are you?" the old man asked as Dove started for the front door. "Originally, I mean."

"Philadelphia."

"Ah. Well, it's a fine town too."

"That it is. Thanks."

Outside, Dove strapped the two-foot-long package behind him on the seat of his Harley-Davidson motorcycle. He sat a moment before starting the engine. The view down the street was uncannily familiar: the short block of commercial buildings, which included O'Farrell's Music Emporium, opened onto row after row of brick houses that stretched off into the muggy haze. Old women were returning in pairs from Saturday morning mass. Kids were playing stickball among the parked cars. Achingly familiar. There was a quiet normalcy to Irish Catholic life here that'd been lacking in his own upbringing.

Dove nursed his Harley's engine to life, then made a U-turn and accelerated for the Charles River.

It was only mid-June, but already the sultry air could be cut with a butter knife. The slipstream cooled his sweat-damp skin. Wind in his hair. That'd been the idea behind buying the motorcycle surplus from the Traffic Bureau—thundering all the way across the continent with a seventy-mile-an-hour wind in his hair. And bugs on his front teeth, no doubt. But a year and a half ago, he'd made up his mind to finally use four months of accumulated leave and strike out for California. He had no real idea how big this country was and had looked forward to being overwhelmed by vast distances.

But then he'd met Kate O'Bradaigh—thanks to the President of the United States, who'd committed to a Memorial Day appearance with the Boston Pops. As the orchestra rehearsed that morning, Dove assisted the Secret Service with the first of two sweeps of Symphony Hall. Each time he passed the first violin section, a striking-looking redhead in a low-cut summer dress whispered, "What're you looking for, paddy?"

At first, Dove just smiled back at her. It was no-no to use the word "device," let alone "bomb." Next thing, everyone would be stampeding for the exits.

But she wouldn't let up. "Find it, paddy?"

"What makes you think I'm a paddy?" Dove asked, shrugging in apology when John Williams, the conductor at that time, shot a killing glance at him.

She waited for the percussion section to come in before answering. "Strong Celtic features. Hazel eyes, which mean a Viking had a waltz in the woods with one of your dark-eyed great-grannies. Bit of capillary damage just beginning to redden up the tip of your nose. If you're not Irish, I'm not." Then she did it again. "What're you looking for already?"

"Condom dispenser."

"Go-wan," she said. That told him she was a Southie. South Boston. "Find it?"

"Nope."

"I've got one at my place." Then she lifted her violin to her chin and made music like an angel.

Now crossing over the muddy Charles into Boston, Dove chuckled to himself, remembering his mild shock that morning—and his strong attraction for the salty-mouthed Southie.

A surprise, by no means unpleasant, had been waiting for him at Kate's house after the performance. A seven-year-old daughter named Lizzy, the issue of a failed marriage with a jazz musician. Dove had gone away that night with nothing more under his belt than three cups of decaf and a promise for brunch the next day at the Top of the Hub. There, overlooking Cambridge from the fifty-second floor of the Prudential Tower, Kate had suddenly turned from the view and asked, "Just where the hell are you from, Dove?"

"What d'you mean?"

"You don't sound Massachusetts."

"Then what do I sound?"

She stared at him, her face cradled in her lightly freckled hands. "I . . . don't know."

"Born in Philadelphia," he admitted. "Spent most of a misguided youth in Somerville. Thank God, my juvenile records were sealed by court order."

"Your folks still there?"

"No, dead."

"How?" Good old Southies. Not exactly shy, as you could ask any bill collector.

"Fire," Dove had finally answered. "My old man was smoking in bed."

Slowing on Kate's street, he kept an eye out for Boomer, his mutt, who'd already been moved in with her and kept excavating holes under the backyard fence. There was no grass anywhere near Dove's downtown apartment. Kate feared prowlers and needed a watchdog. Yet, besides all that, Dove knew the significance of keeping Boomer over there—and the danger if things didn't work out between Kate and him. Lizzy was attached. Good-bye to one dog.

As expected, Boomer darted out into the street just as Dove approached the house. "God Almighty, dog," he said, pulling up behind Kate's Jeep Wrangler, "someday I'll make a scatter rug of you."

Dismounting, he gave the mutt a scratch behind the ears, then glanced over the Wrangler. Heavy salt-corrosion damage to the wheelwells. Even the roll bar was rusted. That was probably the next decision if he stuck it out here: a new car.

He could hear children singing out back.

Hurriedly now, he grabbed the package and jogged down the sloping side yard to the gate. But, coming to the fence, he decided not to spoil Lizzy's big moment with a late entry. He peeked over the top of the boards. Kate was conducting a dozen kids in "Happy Birthday," thin arms jerking to the tempo. He smirked to himself. Only Kate.

He noticed that the house paint was peeling off. Best to call a tin company and let them slap on aluminum siding. He hated to paint.

The song ended, and Kate said, "Make a wish, bug."

Lizzy could be heard spluttering out the candles. Then, lowering her voice to her mother, she said, "I wished Jimmy Dove could be my dad."

Kate said sharply, "Keep your wishes to yourself or they won't come true." Irish mothers. Superstition flowed out in their milk. Only that could account for all the junk Dove himself half-believed.

He crept backwards a few paces, then trod noisily down the gravel walkway and cried out, "Happy birthday, Miss Lizzy O'Bradaigh!"

"Jimmy Dove!"

Coming through the gate, he said, "Birthday girl, you look like a dream." He scooped her up with his free arm and gave her a big kiss. "Is that your Communion dress?"

"No." She giggled. "Mom bought it at the mall. Eighteen dollars." She craned her head over his shoulder to have a look at the package he was concealing behind him. "What's that?"

Dove handed it over, let her down. She made quick work of the wrapping, then turned happily to Kate with the Casio keyboard. "Look, Mom—a little piano!"

Dove flicked on the power, and Lizzy pounced on the keys, raising a wail. "Sounds like the vet hospital just ran out of anesthetic," he said apologetically to Kate. "I can give her lessons, if you don't want to."

"Good—at your place."

"It's a small place, and I'm surrounded by the elderly. Heart patients on the mend."

"*Your* place," she insisted.

He kissed her. Her body felt good in his arms. It'd been a couple days.

"You're late," she said as soon as their lips had parted.

"And you're beautiful."

She looked questioningly into his eyes. He knew that she was waiting for an answer. He didn't have one. Not this soon. So, frowning, she gave him a quick spank on the fanny, then whipped out a blindfold and tied it over his eyes. Something like a feather was thrust into his right hand. "What's this? Ouch!" He'd found the thumbtack in it.

"You should know, Dove—a donkey's tail."

Cheering, the kids rushed him, spun him around. Instant vertigo, which made him stagger and reel. "Where is this poor tailless beast?" Me, he realized. Forty-eight hours without it, thanks to a stubbornness he knew to be wrong.

The kids shrieked with laughter as he tramped around the yard.

Kate warned, "Put a kid's eye out, and the parents will sue." Then he heard her shoes drumming up the short flight of outside stairs to the kitchen. Sharp, angry steps.

He took the blindfold off, handed it to Lizzy, and went up to Kate.

She was filling the coffeepot at the sink.

In silence, he hung his seersucker jacket over the back of a chair and sat. A vase of strawflowers lay at the exact center of the tablecloth. Next to it a holder for saccharine, or whatever the stuff was now. Everything precisely in its place. Yet he liked that about her. It pleased him that she had the universe so nicely under control. Her world had never been blown apart. The only thing close to a disaster she'd ever known had been her divorce, and even that had been handled with the cool efficiency of a spring housecleaning.

"Well, James Dove," she said, with her back still to him, "are you going to talk to somebody?"

"Yes." Then he added rather sheepishly, "You."

She lowered her head. The direct sunlight through the window made her hair look like billows of spun copper. "That's not good enough." The water was running over the top of the glass pot. "I just don't know how to deal with something like this." She finally flipped off the tap and turned. "Don't put it on me. I'll do everything I can, but don't do that to me."

"Didn't know I was such a burden."

She shook her head in exasperation. "No, don't take it that way, Jim."

He nodded, hiding his relief. "I don't know how to start with a stranger, Kate . . ." Too much to reveal even to her. It'd take years to explain something like this—and have anybody truly understand. "Maybe we're both barking up the wrong tree. Maybe there's another way. You know, even try to eliminate the source of the problem—"

Then his beeper sounded. Dove reached down to his belt, turned the pager off, then took his ultralight cellular telephone from his jacket pocket.

Kate exhaled loudly.

Punching in the speed dialer, he tried to smile at her, but she averted her eyes.

His call was answered on the first ring. "Bomb Disposal Unit."

"Dove. Where?"

"MIT, Lieutenant . . ." Then the dispatcher gave him the building location and noted the urgency of the call.

"On my way." He stood, donned his jacket, and made sure the flap was covering his snub-nosed revolver and handcuffs. "Tell Lizzy I'll make it up to her."

"Don't worry about it," Kate said.

"Look, it's just over in Cambridge—"

"Don't they have their own people to handle it?"

"No, their city's too small. They use us on mutual aid." He ran his fingertips down the inside of her bare arm. "It's probably nothing."

"I know. Just a tease. Isn't that what you call a phony scare?"

"Right." He kissed her again. "And oh how I hate a tease."

At last, she offered him a fleeting smile. It was also seductive. "I'll save you a piece of cake."

Dove tried Massachusetts Avenue, but the midday weekend traffic soon had him resorting to shortcuts he'd learned as a patrolman and now couldn't forget even if he tried. Leaning his head over the handlebars, he sped along, hugging the center line when confronted with cars going both ways. A marked cruiser fell in behind him near the river, but then the patrolman recognized him and turned off with a parting yelp of his siren.

Nightmares.

Those were what had come between Kate and him, although the department shrink called them night terrors. Bolting up out of a sound sleep, screaming, flailing at God only knew what. Dove knew that he was suffering from a classic stress reaction, but he saw no point in seeking counseling, as Kate wanted him to. She had made up her mind that the job was doing it to him. But not so, at least not entirely. If that were the case, he was sure that he'd seek help in a blink. No shame in being a human being. But the thing he relived almost every night had nothing to do with Boston.

It was beginning to intrude on his waking hours.

That was the frightening part. It could demand his attention at any moment.

He sped over the Charles on the Harvard Bridge, took the first right onto the campus of the Massachusetts Institute of Technology. A few of the resident geeks, bearded and anemic, were laughing inanely at the police chopper that was circling over the building for which Dove was bound. MIT security tried to flag him to a halt, but he just waved his badge as he barreled through the cordon and parked beside a truck marked "Boston Police Department Bomb Disposal Unit." Two men from the squad, Maner and McNulty, were sitting on a picnic table, making a last-minute check of their gear.

"What gives?" Dove asked them.

"Well, Lieutenant," Dale " 'Bama" Maner drawled, scratching his Elvis-length sideburns, "some goddamn loser just figured a dandy new way to check out." To the former pride of the Mobile P.D., all known life was divided into two species. Losers and worms. Dove wasn't sure which was higher on the evolutionary scale. Moot point. Maner was from the Bible Belt and probably a Creationist. Maner lit up a Marlboro, then petted one of the bomb-sniffing Labradors that was chained to a table leg. "What's this lousy world comin' to?"

"To shit," answered Edward "Blanket" McNulty—black, introspective, and going prematurely gray. He'd gotten his nickname his first day on the squad. Somebody had said what a comfort it was to have a rookie as big as a bomb blanket to hide behind.

"Where's the captain?" Dove asked.

McNulty pointed at the rear door of the heavily armored truck. "On the screen, Lieut." McNulty divided all life into smokers and nonsmokers. He himself had managed to quit and now had a Born Again contempt for abusers. He wrinkled his nose as 'Bama deeply inhaled. "Will you put that fuckin' thing out? We are walkin' into a place with a *device*, man!"

Dove slipped the cigarette from 'Bama's fingers as he strode for the truck. "Waste not, want not," he said over the puttering of the gasoline generator that ran the air conditioner. Not that the chiller did much good. The cluttered interior of the truck still felt as stuffy as a locker room. Rita Durgin, the squad's token who'd turned out not to be anybody's token, just a tough person with a steady hand, grinned with her own cigarette going between her teeth as Dove came down the aisle between the storage lockers.

"Hey, Captain," she said, "you can relax now. We got some expertise on the scene."

"Don't stir it up, lady," Dove whispered as he squeezed past her and nodded hello to Captain Fred Roarke, his boss, who was seated at the command module. He offered Dove a cautious but relieved smile, which probably summed up his mixed feelings for his lieutenant. Dove tried to understand. It was probably hard to like the man who one day might replace you. Not that Dove wanted the squad. That was the irony of it. But the more he said this, the less Roarke seemed to believe him.

He glanced at the screen.

The picture was being beamed from the video camera in Manfred, the squad's remote-controlled robot. It showed a young woman, vaguely pretty, typing madly away at a computer keyboard. "Manfred in there on his own?"

"No," the captain murmured, rubbing his bulbous nose with his fingers. "Cortez is with him for the moment." The squad's technician. Cuban-American. Programmed by the streets of Miami's Little Havana with a lexicon of dirty Spanish that could scorch Fidel's beard. "Hang tight a minute, Jim—we're trying to invent something here."

Not figure out. Invent. Interesting.

Manfred's microphone was picking up the clack of the keys, then the young woman's voice. "I'm getting tired," she said in a desperately weary tone.

"Keep typing, goddammit," Cortez said to her. He wasn't visible.

She was filling her computer screen with "luv u luv u luv u luv u luv u ..." Dove felt exhausted just watching. He noticed the digital counter labeled "Bytes Free" ticking downward: 0340, 0339, 0338 ...

A half-distracted Roarke, fiddling with the joystick that manipulated Manfred's arms among other things, said quietly, "Sorry to call you on your day off, Jim."

"No problem, Fred," Dove lied. I'll just find another gorgeous violinist who can make me whimper with just a glance.

"Dogs sniffed out some C-four," the captain went on, meaning military plastique. "Half a pound of the shit buried in the girl's computer. She's hooked up to the thing ..." He gave the joystick a twist, and Manfred's right arm glided into view.

Dove asked, "Hooked up?"

"Yeah, her hacker boyfriend got jealous, rigged it up so she's gotta keep typing. She quits, the building lands somewhere in Concord."

"So she keeps typing till we get it figured."

"Not quite. Boyfriend put a counter on the thing. When the hard drive gets full . . ." Roarke didn't have to finish.

"Where is this asshole?" Dove said.

Using the joystick, Roarke had Manfred pan to the floor on one side of the woman. There a young man sprawled in a small pool of blood. The muzzle of a forty-five automatic was still lodged in his mouth. The camera zoomed in. The exit wound in the back of his head looked as big as a punchbowl.

"Lovely," Dove said under his breath.

"Now I'm trying to teach Manfred to type."

Roarke glanced up at the lieutenant, obviously for moral support.

Dove started to cock his head in doubt, but then stopped.

Roarke depressed his own microphone button, activating the speaker mounted in Manfred's head. "Okay, Mary—almost ready to go."

"It's Nancy," she said adamantly. Like someone who wanted to be remembered correctly.

"Right . . . Nancy."

Eyes glued to the monitor, Dave watched as one of Manfred's clawlike digits typed out "luv," then crisply slid over to the "U" key and struck it.

Roarke let out a thunderous breath. "Christ . . . great." Then he said into the microphone, "We're ready to go on autopilot, folks. Cortez, do it, then get yourself and Mary outta there."

The technician came into view, saucer-eyed behind his protective goggles. His body armor was wet around the openings for his arms and head. He flicked a toggle on the robot, then backed out of sight.

Manfred went on typing.

Dove could no longer see Nancy's face on the screen, but her hands hesitantly levitated off the keyboard and moved away.

"We're bookin', Cap," Cortez's voice said, followed by the rattle of Nancy rising from her swivel chair.

Dove was briefly distracted when Roarke's fist chucked him on the arm, knocking the long ash off the Marlboro he'd bummed from 'Bama. "This hunk of alloy might pay for itself yet—huh, Jimbo?"

But then Dove lunged over the startled captain and seized the joystick. "Get her back on the keyboard, Cortez!" he cried, depressing the mike button with both thumbs.

Manfred was frozen, the task too complex for his internal computer.

"What?" Nancy's voice wailed, apparently from completely across the room.

"Type, Nancy!"

"Wha . . . ?"

"Type! Cortez, hit the toggle, get it back on manual!"

Both pairs of human hands darted back in front of Manfred's lens. Nancy made a soft moaning sound, but her fingers flexed over the keyboard and fell again into "luv u luv u luv u . . ."

"What went wrong?" Roarke asked no one in particular.

"Got an hour?" Rita murmured from the passageway.

Cortez struggled to lower Manfred's arm. The metal phalange was quivering uselessly in midair. *"Se caga en mí!"* the technician hissed, giving Manfred's head a whack that jarred the picture.

Dove started for the rear door.

Rita plucked the cigarette butt from the corner of his mouth and handed him a saddlebag of tools. "Luck."

'Bama and Blanket, both suited up, were still waiting outside. The disposal team, they'd go in only after the device was disarmed. If there was time now to disarm it. Otherwise, they would search the rubble for evidence and body parts.

"What gives?" 'Bama asked.

Dove jerked his thumb back toward the command module. "Go see for yourselves, boys."

He ran for the building.

The evacuation was complete now. The deserted walkways and lanes of the campus gave it an air of postnuclear holocaust. A warm breeze rocked the branches of the old elms and oaks. Papers skittered

along the front of the nondescript building that might
go to concrete dust any second.

Luck.

Rita's word had been an observation as much as a
bit of encouragement. She knew as well as anyone
that risk could be managed but never eliminated.
How many bomb squaders all over the world had
died while simply approaching a device? Atomized
even before they could unpack their tools.

Dove had to wait in the lobby for the elevator car
to descend from the third floor. Actually, the pause
was good. From that point on, he would mentally
slow down. He would tell himself that he had time
enough for brisk action. Not hurried. Brisk.

He yawned.

The bell dinged, the doors parted, and he stepped
inside the car. He read the graffiti scratched into
brushed aluminum walls for omens. Nothing of significance. Except maybe: "I can't believe God plays
dice with the universe—A. Einstein." Then a number
for the Christian Students' Fellowship Society. "No,"
Dove whispered, "but blasters sure as hell do."

Ten seconds later, he went through the door of the
hot room, the location of a known device. Walking
up behind Nancy, he eyed the hard drive counter:
151, 150, 149 . . .

"Who the hell're you?" she asked without turning.

"Dove," he said sonorously. "James Dove."

A hint of a smile. But her voice was now reduced
to a dry croak, and she was hunched as she typed,
her thin cotton dress soaked with perspiration. "Who
was that supposed to be? Moore or Connery?"

"Doesn't matter if you have to ask." Dove caught
Cortez's eye. "Go down and get Manfred a drink,"
he said, patting the robot on its logo. "Looks like he
could use one."

The technician lost no time getting out. That was
only healthy. He'd stuck as long as he'd had some-

thing useful to do. Remaining after that was only ego.

Dove sealed the door after Cortez. The snick of the latch button rattled Nancy, for she demanded, "What're you doing?"

"Locking up."

"Why?"

"No distractions from now on. Just you and me to get out of this, Nancy." He knelt beside her, then listened.

"Are you the second string?" she asked, almost crying. "Am I down to second string?"

"Quiet, please." He shut down Manfred's computer, which left only its videocam and microphone operational. Then he focused on the whir that remained. It was coming from Nancy's disk drive. A warble pitched too low to be normal.

"What's wrong?" she asked.

"Your drive sounds funny. Something's slowing it down."

Dove gave the counter another glance: 115, 114 ... He took a worklight from the saddlebag and aimed it onto the drive. A thin red wire threaded from it up into the heart of the computer.

He was reaching from his small jigsaw when he realized that the woman was tottering in her chair. And she'd noticeably paled over the last several moments. "Sit up straight, Nancy."

"Huh?"

"Don't scrunch over like you are—you'll collapse your diaphragm and faint."

"How d'you know?"

"My lady's a violinist with the Pops. It's what the conductor always tells the wind players." Dove started up the jigsaw. "Got to get between your knees, Nance." She spread her skirted legs, and he went on his back to slide under the desk. He was on the verge of cutting the particleboard when his gaze fastened on the dead face leering at him.

He froze.

For a jolting second, he saw eyes and a gaping mouth showing from the slits of a black hood. Blood everywhere.

Dove bit the inside of his cheek hard, and the face became the hacker's again.

Quickly, squinting against the blizzard of sawdust, he sawed through the desktop and then, more carefully, into the bottom of the computer case.

Apparently, Nancy had caught him looking at her boyfriend. "He wasn't like this at the beginning," she said in a high, almost hysterical whine. "He started drinking heavily last semester. Then the accusations started. Said I was cheating on him. With his roomie . . ."

Dove shone his light up into the computer. Off-white putty was draped over the disk drive. C-4. Ordinarily, he would go for the blasting cap buried somewhere in it. But no time to root around now.

He fumbled inside his bag for some tongs.

"Nobody could talk him out of it," Nancy went on. "Especially me. I just made him madder when I tried to deny it. He kept this list in a ledger book. All the times he thought I'd done it with other guys. The dates and places. Like it'd really happened, you know? It was crazy. Then one night he just up and slapped me—"

"Us, Nancy!" Dove barked. "Keep your mind on us! Help me!" He probed a tangle of wires with his tongs, then lowered his voice. "How many bytes we got?"

"Twenty-four. I don't want to die."

"Nance!"

She'd stopped typing.

The keys began clicking again, but she was sobbing now. Grinding her heels into the linoleum.

"Don't give up on me," Dove said.

"Eleven," she said.

"Easy."

"Ten!"

He'd located a red wire thinner than the others and was getting ready to snip it when he suddenly noticed another of the same gauge. Except it was white. Either of them could connect to the device's power source. Either could set off a collapsing circuit, a triggering mechanism by which the cutting of one wire would automatically bring a secondary power source on line.

As he hesitated, the cutters slipped from his sweaty fingers and clattered against the floor.

"What was that?"

Dove picked them up. "You like red wine or white?"

"Who gives a shit! Do something!"

Fifty-fifty. Red or black. Odd or even. The lady or the tiger. Boom or no boom. Kate had a point. This was shit.

Dove severed red, then instinctively braced.

3

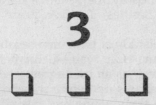

Dove got Nancy to the elevator on her own power, but once inside she leaned her back against the wall and slid down onto her buttocks as if she didn't have a bone in her body. There were runs in both her nylons and her mascara, but she was giggling. She wiped her eyes on the back of a trembling arm, made an effort to sober herself, but then went on laughing helplessly.

Dove hit the lobby button, then tried to help her to her feet. It was no good for the moment. She just flopped over on her side when he pulled her hand.

"How . . ." she said between the gales, "how'd you know I wear a diaphragm?"

"Oh Christ."

"Collapse my diaphragm!" she shrieked.

"Easy, love."

But then, abruptly, she clenched her underlip between her front teeth. "My God . . ." she moaned, burying her face in her hands. "My dear God . . ."

"It's all right," Dove said gently. "It'll be a roller-coaster ride for weeks to come. For both of us."

She looked up at him. "Did you ever think it was over?"

"Didn't consider it. No time." Not entirely true.

Little paroxysms of nerves had come and gone, which was probably the same as thinking about it. He smiled. "Besides, I never heard the Banshee croon."

She gaped blankly at him, then began snapping her fingers together. "Oh, wait—Celtic folklore, right? I had a course in it as an undergrad. The Banshee's an old hag who shows up before somebody dies."

"Sometimes she's young and beautiful."

"You Irish—James, wasn't it?"

"Distantly. And you can call me Jim."

The elevator reached the lobby, but Dove closed the doors as soon as they started to whisk open—to give her time to present herself with a little dignity to the media, who'd be lurking just outside.

"Come on." He took her under the arms and brought her to her feet.

Leaning against his chest, she said emphatically, "Thank you, Jim, thank you, thank you." Then she gave him a kiss that left him wondering if the poor loser lying on the floor upstairs had been entirely paranoid. After nine years on the squad, he'd never called in one of these debts of gratitude. But he'd been tempted a few times, particularly before he'd met Kate. Yet he also knew that within a week Nancy might be mad enough to sue the department over Manfred. She could no longer feel appropriate anger at her former beau, not with the back of his head missing. So the cops would have to do.

Still, he enjoyed the moment. He'd saved someone. Another inch closer to atonement.

Outside, the paramedics peeled her off him, and he continued alone to the picnic table near the truck. He sat unsteadily enough for 'Bama and Rita to deflect a blitz of reporters and cameramen off toward the ambulance. It was just pulling away with Nancy and a homicide detective from Cambridge P.D., who was already questioning her.

Dove felt a gaze on him. He turned his head. It was Blanket's.

"Got a smoke?" Dove asked. McNulty offered him a piece of nicotine gum instead. Better than nothing. "Thanks," he said, chewing.

"Thanks for shit," Blanket said angrily.

"What?"

"You partial to suicide, Lieut?"

Dove folded his hands together to keep them from shaking. "Wasn't like that."

"Fuck it wasn't. I heard every damn thing you said through that iron monkey's mike. You know the drill. Shit, you *taught* me the drill."

Dove spat out the gum. "Back off, Ed. I'm beat."

"Back off, my ass. We don't make no fifty-fifty choices. You said it yourself—guess fifty-fifty for a week workin' with Improvised Explosive Devices and you'll be lucky to see Tuesday noon. Your words, exact. That was the worst damn brain fart I seen in years."

"Sometimes you have to roll the dice." An unpleasant flutter passed through Dove's guts. "I was outta time."

"Then you shoulda turned on your heel and walked!"

"I couldn't walk, Blanket," Dove said, almost begging for understanding. "It was just a girl." Another face flickered in Dove's mind, then disappeared again into the blackness behind his eyes. "Just a kid."

"A civilian. Boston Police Department didn't plant that IED up there, so it can't take total, everlastin' responsibility for what happens if it blows. Save yourself, and then the innocent—*if you fuckin' reasonably can.* Jim Dove spoonfed me that happy horseshit too!"

"Okay, I'm horseshit."

"Man, you never done somethin' like this before. What's wrong with you lately, Jim?"

Dove bolted up and pushed past Blanket, looking for a hedge or anything to duck behind. Saliva was welling toward the front of his mouth.

Stumbling forward, he found an alley between two windowless brick buildings and doubled over with his hands on his knees. He vomited until he had nothing left to bring up.

In the dizzy, light-headed void that followed, he seemed to be peering down a passageway through time. A tunnel that opened on a market town. Open stalls. Fruits and vegetables. A lorry stopping in a square, figures jumping out of its bed with Sten guns and sawed-off shotguns, faces hidden under black hoods. An explosion rocked the ground. Fire. Smoke. Screaming—

"Lieut . . . ?" Blanket. Looking more worried than angry now. He eyed the vomit on the paving stones, then asked, "You gonna be okay?"

"Fuck your nicotine gum," Dove said, winking. "A good old-fashioned cigarette hasn't made me puke since I was eleven."

Leaving for rehearsal, Kate felt the usual reflexive guilt that made Lannie, the babysitter, seem far younger and less responsible than she truly was. The fourteen-year-old was sitting cross-legged in the middle of the sofa, biting at a hangnail as she gazed vacantly at the television.

"Lannie . . . ?" Kate waited for the eyes to finally shift toward her. Comprehension required the use of at least two senses with this ninth-grader. "Lannie, there's leftover cake in the kitchen. For you. Lizzy had enough at the party. Wake her soon from her nap or you'll never get her to sleep tonight."

Lannie gave a remote nod.

Kate was grabbing her violin case from the entryway closet when the girl asked indifferently, "Isn't that your boyfriend?"

Frowning, Kate parted a curtain for a look at the street. "Where?"

"No, on TV."

Kate turned in time to see Dove helping an unstrung young woman out the front doors of a building. He looked exhausted, but enormously pleased with himself. Victorious. ". . . at MIT this morning," the announcer was saying, "The military-style plastique was successfully disarmed in less than thirty minutes by members of the Boston bomb squad."

Then the news moved on to the weather. High pressure had settled in over New England, and it'd be miserably hot and humid for the next weeks, possibly right through the Fourth of July holiday. Perfect for a violin sliding against your sweaty neck like a freshly caught tuna.

"Good-bye, Lannie."

No response.

Kate fired up the Wrangler, then lolled her head against the warm vinyl of the backrest, waiting for the air conditioning to kick in. Add a freon recharge to the broken emergency brake for the next repair appointment. The odometer would turn 100,000 miles soon.

"Crap," she said.

It was a perverse thought, she realized, but she almost wished that things hadn't gone so swimmingly up in Cambridge that morning. Not that she wanted anyone dead. But last November, a disarming hadn't gone well, and Dove had come over afterward, shaken, outwardly fragile for the first time—and entirely hers. He'd said that he was fed up. There was no pleasure left in his work. Just pain.

But now another triumph would erase all that. He'd go on pretending that nothing was wrong, that he was invincible and could go on forever bottling things up inside himself.

Kate backed out of the driveway, started across

midtown for Hatch Memorial Shell on the Charles River.

Her first impression of him that morning they'd met at Symphony Hall was that James Dove was a man deeply within himself. Her ex-husband had been a man deeply within other women, several of them at any given time. Frank had been warm, funny, gregarious, and devious. James Dove was all of those things, except devious. She believed that of him even though she knew there was something he refused to share with anyone. Maybe even himself, for she'd lain in the dark with him when he would suddenly cry out in horror and fear. What worried her more than anything was the profound shame he felt afterward, his unwillingness to discuss any of it.

On the sly, she'd phoned the department's psychiatrist and described the episodes. No names, of course. And no mention of the bomb squad, even though she was sure that Dove's assignment was part of it.

"Night terrors are normal," the doctor said, "at least for most of the cops I treat."

"But what's *happening*?"

"See, to do his job day in and day out an officer has to have tight emotional control over himself. Suppression of what he truly feels. He can't afford the luxury of going off the deep end just because the rest of the world seems to be. With sleep, his defenses come down. No more denial. He experiences the truth that he can be killed or injured, not always somebody else—as he tells himself during waking hours. He can relive the past when he was almost killed, or when he lost a close friend."

"Well, if it's normal, what should I do? Nothing?"

"God no," the doctor said. "The normal work environment for cops would put most of general population on either lithium or Thorazine. He needs to talk to me. Right away. If not me, a therapist unconnected to the department."

"But what if he won't do that?"

"I don't want to speculate."

"Doctor, what am I facing here? What am I sleeping with . . . a bomb?" Bad choice of word, she immediately realized.

His outbreath sounded like the surf in the receiver. "Look, your husband is having a secondary reaction to a traumatic event. Or events. It's incredible what society puts its cops through. This reaction often comes months, even years after the blow. He develops a psychosomatic illness for no apparent reason. Right out of the blue. Fatigue. Sleep disorders. Changes in perception. Even what we might call altered states of consciousness. The list's as long as my arm—and I'm almost seven feet tall, okay?"

"Then he'll only have more problems," Kate said with a sinking feeling.

"I can almost guarantee it. This delayed reaction is being triggered by new pressures on an already fully loaded emotional system."

"Am I one of those pressures?"

"Nope," the shrink said decisively. "I can already tell that you're his support system. He needs you."

That night, Dove had come over after Lizzy went to sleep. After making love to Kate, he went to the window and watched a glittering snow fall through the light of the street lamp. She could tell that he was afraid to drop off, only to awaken her later with another night terror.

"Tell me about James Dove," she said from bed.

Still nude, he looked utterly defenseless, boyishly lean. But up went the same old walls as he came back with: "What's to tell?"

"Everything. What was it like growing up?"

"Bad."

"How, Jim?"

"Folks were on the . . ." He seemed to take a second to hunt for the right word. ". . . welfare. Alcoholic. So I took to the streets. And they were worse yet. Worse than home."

"Did you join a gang or something?"

"Yes, a gang." He turned toward her. "Katie, I went through every page of this once before—and swore to myself I'd never wade back into it again. No matter how much I loved somebody. No matter how frightfully curious they were. It's a closed book."

That stung a little, but she pressed, "Then just tell me, when was this? When did you have to talk about it?"

"When I joined the department. The dicks in personnel conduct what they call a background investigation. They go through your life like it's a pile of manure." Then he came back to bed and shushed her by tenderly holding his fingers over her lips.

They made love once again.

She felt slightly reassured. The P.D. had taken a good long look at James Dove's past and hired him anyway. So he'd had a rebellious youth. So had Kate O'Bradaigh, and there were things about it she would never tell her lover. They were none of his business. Was Dove out of line for standing on the same right?

The next morning, for Lizzy's sake, he insisted on sneaking out the back. He immediately came up the walkway to the front door, knocked, and pretended he had just arrived. For breakfast, which he intended to make. He cheerfully fried up a mess of potatoes, onions, and fresh parsley.

"What's this called, Jimmy?" Lizzy asked, standing on a chair at his elbow.

"Colcannon."

"What kind of word's that?"

"South Philly," he claimed. "Didn't you see *Rocky*? Colcannon's what made him so strong."

But later Kate had asked her aunt in Brookline,

who'd been born and raised in Cork, about colcannon. Was it Irish?

"Oh yes," the old woman had answered, "but we never used that word in the south, dearie. That's from way up north. Ulster, I'm sure. The kind of thing a Belfast man might say."

Kate saw that she'd arrived at the outdoor concert shell. Her fellow members of the Pops had already taken the few parking spaces in the staff lot. She sped up Embankment Road, praying for a bit of open curb.

Alarmingly, she realized that she couldn't recall a single block of the drive from home.

The Jacuzzi had been won in a police benefit raffle two years ago. And hadn't worked properly for a full month since. This time it was the pump, which made the bubbles. "It could rain whiskey," Max O'Bannon bellowed up into the late afternoon sky, brandishing a crescent wrench, "and I wouldn't have a glass in the house!"

That got the neighborhood dogs barking.

He tossed the wrench into his open toolbox, then grunted and pulled up his swim trunks. He felt them immediately slide down the curve of his belly again. Finally, he sat down in the slack waters. "Who needs the bloody mechanical effervescence anyways!"

"Not with all the cabbage you've eaten in your lifetime, Max," a voice said from the far side of the gate.

It swung open, and O'Bannon pointed at the small ice chest on the lip of the pool. "Harps. And I always count 'em before I get skuttered blind, so don't go home, Jimmy Dee, with two in your gut and three in your pockets."

"You can always tell an Armagh man by his generosity—with the sarcasm." Smiling, Dove got himself a beer and eased into a deck chair. He eyed the tools, then toasted. "Bless the work."

"Shut your gob. One more breakdown and you'll be out here with the squad tryin' to talk me outta blowin' it up." With a mild start, O'Bannon realized that Dove was no longer a kid, as he'd always seen him. He was now a tired-looking man in early middle age. That's what a lieutenancy did to you. And the bloody bomb squad. "Did you drop by for a dip, Jimmy?"

"Not without bubbles."

"Fuck the bubbles."

Dove asked, "How can you wear a Donegal tweed in a hot tub?"

"I hold me head real steady."

"And how can you parboil yourself on a day like this? It's already like a Turkish bath outside."

"Comparisons, me boy," O'Bannon said.

"How's that?"

"When I get out, the air will seem as cool as a Lough Neagh mist. It's how a wise fella tricks himself into an easy mind, Jimmy. He always trades hot for warm. Ulster for New England."

Dove nodded, then took a thoughtful sip.

"But if it gets any sweltier, I might go down to my place on the cape." O'Bannon paused to reach for a Harp—and inwardly saw his Emma sunning herself on the cottage's deck. He shut his eyes for a moment, then said, "Heard you had yourself a doozy in Cambridge this morning."

"Big wicked doozy."

"Shoulda taken my advice and stayed a beat cop like me." O'Bannon grabbed some ice along with the bottle, then ran the cubes over his forehead. "Easier dodgin' bullets than bombs."

"Then what's that on your shoulder?"

Briefly, O'Bannon glanced down at the starfishlike scar. "I was hung over, or it never woulda happened.

Besides, the fella apologized like a real gentleman later—" Then he saw that Dove wasn't listening. He'd turned sideways in the chair and was staring out across the harbor, absently watching a big freighter waiting off the channel between the Deer Island House of Correction and the Gallops Island for the pilot to come out to it. "Last time I saw that look," O'Bannon said in nearly a whisper, "you were sittin' on a pilin' along the Battery Street Wharf . . . wearin' clothes that stuck out like a sore thumb . . ."

Dove looked back at him, tried to smile but failed. "Max, how do you know when it's time to get out?"

"So that's it, then."

"That's it."

O'Bannon put an ice cube into his mouth, chewed, then washed it down with a swallow of beer. "Remember you comin' to me a couple months after the academy, askin' when you'd know it was the right time to shoot some poor soul?"

"Yeah." An embarrassed chuckle.

"Well, at least you had the brains and prior experience to ask. Remember what I told you, Jimmy?"

"One night I'd see a green light in my head. After months, even years of being stopped by a red light each time I got ready to pull the trigger, I'd suddenly see green."

"And did you when you finally had to bust a cap on human flesh and bone?" O'Bannon prodded.

"I did. I had no doubts about what I had to do."

"Then there you have it, boy."

"Have what?"

O'Bannon took a swig, then contemplated the coldly sweating bottle. "Never will understand how I got hooked on drinkin' this stuff chilled. Vile habit."

Dove was leaning forward. "There I have *what*?"

"Are you goin' to work each day with a red light behind your eyes? Ask yourself that real hard. And don't flinch from the answer. Accept it."

Dove apparently did, for he sat back and stared off again. "It doesn't start here in Boston," he finally said. "It goes back, Max."

"I know," O'Bannon said somberly. "But a red light's a red light, no matter the juice that feeds it."

A minute passed in silence.

"It's time, friend," O'Bannon said. "I think you've done your penance."

"Yeah?" Dove's eyes had filled, and O'Bannon looked away so as not to shame him. "Then how come I don't feel absolved?"

"I don't know, dear Jimmy Dee. How come?"

4

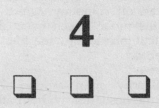

The Moroccan freighter had stopped out in Massachusetts Bay, engines idling. The captain was waiting for the harbor pilot to show up. No sign of any approaching small craft yet. Gaerity was standing on the ship's prow, hands braced on the lifelines. There wasn't a hint of a breeze. Under the declining sun, the sea was a sheet of copper, barely a swell on its surface. To the west lay Boston's skyline, jutting out of a sulfurous-looking mist. He rather liked that vaporous quality to the dusk—as if the entire Boston metropolitan area were smoldering on the verge of ignition.

It was hard for him to believe that Castle Gleigh was already almost fourteen months behind him. That it'd taken him this long to stand where he did now, no more than two hours away from setting foot in Boston. Yet the breakout, the rental of the fishing boat from Donegal, had exhausted the resources he'd set aside before imprisonment. Booty from robbing Ulster banks in the early seventies. This was an enterprise he couldn't fall back upon in the nineties, not with his face plastered all over the United Kingdom.

So Gaerity had looked up old friends for temporary employment. The Libyans. They indeed had a thing or two for him to do. The bombing of a moderate Egyptian politician in Cairo. A Lear jet belonging to an American oil company, which mysteriously vanished off the radar screen over Chad. Nothing more than a few jobs to provide him with a grubstake for Amerikay.

"Mr. Cawton—"

Instantly, Gaerity spun around. A trick he'd learned. Show no hesitation with an alias. "Yes?"

The captain, a Libyan national, was approaching. Lovely people, Libyans. Individually. "My dear Mr. Cawton . . ." He grinned, touching his fingers to the bill of his salt-stained cap. Brilliantly white teeth. Either that or it was the contrast with his dark sepia complexion. "Sir, I must beg you to stay off the weatherdecks as we dock."

"Of course, Captain," Gaerity said. "I was just enjoying the view. Do you mind if I take just a few moments more?"

"Please do. I didn't mean to order you about." Libyans made lousy disciplinarians: too naturally ingratiating. "Is this your first time to Boston?"

"No. Unfortunately, I've reached the unenviable time in life when one has done everything at least twice."

"I know precisely what you mean, Mr. Cawton."

No, he didn't. Not one bit. It was high time to smash the old world and create a new one from the debris, that's what he meant.

"You seem very eager to reach land," the captain went on.

Gaerity glanced up from the water. Filthy. Garlands of half-dissolved toilet paper floating past. "I am, Captain. I mean to get well here."

"The hospitals are excellent. I have heard that."

Gaerity just smiled. There was but one person in all the world he could open himself up to. One equally tortured soul who might understand. He hoped that there would be time for a meeting before he killed that man.

"I trust you're not feeling poorly, Mr. Cawton."

"Oh, no, I feel wonderful. And I mean to enjoy every minute of my therapy ..." Originally, it had been prescribed by a radical psychiatrist in Heidelberg to his patients, mostly members of the Red Army Faction, but also Gaerity, who'd been hiding out on the continent. They were all encouraged to cure their personal compulsions and obsessions by making therapeutic attacks on their tormentors. Don't learn to cope with the source of your disturbance. Attack it. Destroy it. On that thought, Gaerity inhaled deeply. "Freedom, Captain. I smell freedom in the air."

"I'm afraid I don't subscribe to the myth of American freedom, Mr. Cawton." Resolute but also afraid of giving offense. Bloody Libyans.

"Neither do I, sir."

"I thought not." The captain's grin was short-lived. "We must sail again on July fifth—with or without you, my dear Mr. Cawton."

The hot, still atmosphere seemed to amplify the roar of jet aircraft taking off from Logan International less than two miles away. The orchestra had just launched into *New England Triptych* when an especially loud one, a 747 maybe, rocketed up into the murk. The conductor flung his baton across the stage, and the music unraveled into a few squeaks and blats.

Kate lowered her violin, then used the score to fan herself. What would August be like? She didn't like the heat. Irish blood was too thick for it.

The conductor strode into the wings and retrieved his baton. He returned, grim-faced, and took the podium once more. "Shall we begin again?" he asked with a brittle smile.

"Why the fuck not?" Someone back in percussion muttered, trusting that his voice would carry no farther forward than the flutes.

Kate's mind was on the first several bars, but after that she wondered again where Dove had gone. She thought she could recall his saying that he'd come back to the house as soon as the Cambridge thing was over. Maybe he hadn't. Maybe all the promises were bleeding together into one big, hopeless muddle.

The conductor hurled his baton at the wings again.

Someday the bastard was going to put out an eye. Then the strings would launch all their bows at him. A shower of bows. Sherwood Forest.

This time, he didn't immediately go for the strings. Instead, he turned toward the first violins. "Ms. O'Bradaigh . . ."

She froze. After all these years, it still felt like being sent to the principal's office.

"You look as if you're here," he continued, "but you don't sound as if you are here."

"Sorry."

"Yes, you are indeed." Thankfully, he quickly included the others. "A little more than two weeks, people. That's all we have. Are we going to let down our Founding Fathers?"

A murmurous "no" followed.

The weak reply sent the conductor to the top of his lungs. *"Are we going to disappoint the Founding Fathers!"*

"No!"

Kate turned to the viola player behind her, a slight Jewish woman who appreciated her jokes. "Shit no—everybody from John Hancock to Paul Revere is six feet under up at the Granary Burial Ground. Where was this guy's last gig? The Marine Band?"

"Shut up, O'Bradaigh, before you give me the hiccups."

Another screeching jet lifted off from Logan.

"There are going to be fireworks overhead," the conductor ranted on as soon as the sound had faded. "I want to hear them popping out of you too! Now, everyone—from the top!"

They were midway through the piece when Kate had a new distraction to deal with.

James Dove. In the flesh.

He was lounging in the last row, his bare arms outstretched along the backs of the seats on both sides of him. He appeared to be more relaxed than she'd ever seen him. And for the first time in memory, he was in neither a coat nor a jacket. Like all plainclothesmen, he constantly wore one or the other to conceal his revolver and handcuffs, even if the temperature was hitting the century mark.

Dove wasn't packing a weapon this evening.

Kate gave herself a shake, trying to jar her mind back onto the rehearsal. Otherwise, they'd all be there until midnight.

But she couldn't keep her eyes off him.

He'd come to a decision. She just knew it by looking at him. Yet realizing this made her feel apprehensive. He was calling it quits. With something. If not with the bomb squad, with her.

But then it came over her again: surprise that he apparently wasn't carrying a weapon. He was making a statement with that. No more NRA paranoia, viewing each human being he met as a potential target.

Twenty minutes later, the conductor dismissed them with a defeatist shrug.

Kate took her time casing her violin, wondering what to say to Dove. He'd strolled down to the apron of the stage and was waiting there, smiling, hands bulging the pockets of his khaki trousers. Maybe he'd bought an ankle holster for his revolver. He'd once said something about buying one, so he could dress more casually.

Her heart was trip-hammering as she descended the steps at the side of the stage to him.

"Hi," he said, a clear, steady look in his eye.

"Hi." Then she couldn't help herself. "You packing heat, Dove?"

"Nope. Hungry?"

"Starving."

Dove sat alone in a darkened corner booth of Bernardo's Restaurant on Fleet Street. Tired, slightly deflated, feeling unsure now about the decision he'd made in Max O'Bannon's backyard. Earlier, when he'd joined Kate at Hatch Shell, he'd felt free, almost as if he were floating. But her mood had eaten away at his own. Despite four glasses of Chianti, she was still on tenterhooks. The only effect of the alcohol he could see had been a slight tipsiness as she rose for a trip to the restroom a few minutes ago.

She slid back into the booth. "How're the mussels?"

He crooked his right arm and flexed. It didn't feel very funny to him, but she laughed, saving the moment.

"Looked good on TV too." Then her gaze dropped to her plate of seafood pasta. "About that . . ."

"Uh-huh?"

"Was your captain there? What's his name?"

"Roarke. Yeah, he was on the scene."

"And all the rest of the squad? McNulty, Maner, everybody?"

"Yeah, the usual suspects."

She dipped her index finger in her wine and made kind of a moaning sound by running it around the lip of the glass. "Then why'd they call you in on your day off?"

"Kate . . ."

"Just asking."

He had no intention of going down this road again. But he found himself explaining, "Because it was an unusual call. Not just another pipe bomb in the dumpster behind K mart."

"Then it was a compliment that they called you in."

"I suppose."

Kate nodded, drank, then held the empty bottle up at the waitress. "More *vino*, please." Her face was rocking slightly. Maybe she was a little drunk. "Always gotta be you up on that white horse, doesn't it, Jimmy Dove?"

"Katie—"

"Why . . . just once will you tell me *why*?"

"Please," he begged. He saw his mistake. He'd wasted the inspiration that had sent him off to Hatch Shell. Should've said his spiel there. Instead, he'd beaten around the bush, and now her keen antennae were picking up the doubts he was feeling. He suddenly realized that it was now or never. Win her or lose her. "No more white horse, Kate. I've just dismounted."

That gave her pause. "When?"

"Today. I mean I made up my mind this afternoon."

"Bullshit, Dove."

Heads were turning, but he ignored them and said, "Monday morning, eight sharp—I'm putting in for a teaching job."

"Where's this?"

"Training Division. They've asked me before. I'll work out of the academy. Eight to five. No overtime. No beeper. Teach device recognition to cadets and advanced disarming to new squad members. Three years of this and I'm eligible for early retirement. Okay?"

She just stared at him, eyes narrow with suspicion.

"Blink," he said. "Do something, for chrissake."

She told him to go screw himself.

"Come on, Katie," he said, hushed. "What're you doing? Why force the issue like this? You win." Wrong thing to say—he knew it as soon as it escaped his mouth.

"I win?"

"Forget I said that. We both win."

She sat back. "You said a ton with that slip, James Dove."

"Kate—"

"Go-wan. You're good at what you do. We both know you want to do it. And you're going to keep doing it. Regardless of the cost to you and anybody who gives a crap about you." She bit sullenly into a breadstick. "Pass the cheese."

"Fuck the cheese." He backhanded the antipasto plate off the table. "Are you listening to me, lady? I said I'm putting in for a teaching job!"

"Really? And then what?"

"I'll teach!" Dove turned to the elderly couple seated in the booth behind him. "Excuse me, is English coming out of my mouth or what?" He faced Kate again before their shock wore off. "I will teach!"

"And be miserable for the rest of your life, James Dove. Guess who gets blamed?"

Dove dropped his voice. "Hey, I don't quite know how to break it to you—but I'm not doing this shit for you!"

That quieted her for a moment. "What're you talking about?"

He tossed his napkin onto his seafood pasta, then folded his hands and rested his forehead on them. Where to begin? But even more importantly, where to leave off? He lifted his head, forced a smile on her. "We're arguing over nothing, Kate. Fact is—I'm not fit for the work anymore ... all right?" She said nothing, just watched. "Can't sleep decently. Puke my guts out every time I shut a device down. You think I love it. Well, I don't. I never did. Maybe I just felt I had to. Some kind of moral obligation. Well, no more. My life's different now. I *want* it to be different . . . all right, lady?"

Her eyes were glistening.

"Say something, Kate."

"I guess I'm like you," she said, after giving him one last searching look.

"Pity the woman . . . how?"

"I wanted to wade into this only one time. And never have to go through it again. I want it settled now and forever."

He shook his head, laughing softly. "Well, Kate O'Bradaigh, I guess there are worse reasons for a row." Then he said to the busboy, who was picking chunks of antipasto off the floor, "go ahead and leave it, son. This is our engagement party, and more of the crockery's sure to take a beating before we're done."

Kate asked, "What're you saying, Dove?"

He slipped a plush-covered box from his back trouser pocket and flipped it open, revealing a diamond ring.

"Go-wan," he said. But she was crying.

Gaerity sat at the head of a long table of American paddies, singing as loudly as the drunkest of them. They'd been drawn to his accent from the first minute he'd bellied up to the bar, and he'd been drinking free ever since.

. . . feelings dark and passions vain or lowly . . .

He pounded his glass of porter on the tabletop, letting the foam fly.

A nation once again, a nation once again.
And Ireland long a province be, a nation once again.

The anthem ended with a boisterous cheer and much backslapping. It was amusing, the boozy innocence of these far-flung cousins.

"Mr. Barry," one of them asked Gaerity, "are you involved in the 'troubles' back home?"

Back home, he'd said. The drunk, a confessed cable television repairman, had probably been no closer to Old Erin than the tip of Cape Cod.

"Can't say that I am," Gaerity answered coyly. "I'm from County Kerry, which as you know is as far across the island from Belfast as you can get without getting your feet soaked." He paused, gave them a broad wink. "But I do have my sympathies in the matter."

"And those?" some simpleton pressed.

"Gentlemen, please—the Queen of England's had a rough go lately, what with Charles wishing on the phone that he was some royal tart's sanitary napkin.

They laughed uproariously, and Gaerity's glass was filled again from a pitcher.

He checked his wristwatch. "Now where the devil's Liam?"

"Your cousin?" the repairman asked.

"Yes, distant cousin. First he was to pick me up at Logan. When I phoned him from the airport, he changed it to here. Two hours ago. No, three. He's turning out to be more distant than I imagined."

One of them asked, "What's his last name?"

"McGivney. Liam McGivney. Have you heard of him maybe?"

Lips were pursed, heads shook. "Ain't a local."

"Sometimes he goes by a more English-sounding last name. For business reasons, he says. Now what the hell was it?"

"Sawford? A Liam Sawford comes in here now and again."

"How old's he?"

"Pushin' sixty."

"No, Liam's in his late thirties," Gaerity said. Then he sighed. "Well, it's a lot to ask of poor shirttail kin. Bed, breakfast, and the key to the liquor cabinet."

A hollow-cheeked man took a long pull off his cigarette, then said, "It's a small son of a bitch who turns his back on his family and his country."

"Ah boys," Gaerity said generously, "I'm sure Liam has his reasons. I'll get by somehow."

"How're you fixed, Mr. Barry?" the repairman asked, the clump of keys on his belt ring jingling as he leaned closer.

"Pardon?"

"How're you fixed for cash?"

"Oh," Gaerity said, briefly threading his arm around the man's waist, "thank God— for a moment I thought you were asking if the surgeon had had a go at me parsnip!" More drunken chortling. "I'll be fine. I heard there's a free lunch in this country."

"Not no more." The repairman tossed his Red Sox baseball cap onto the table, and quickly it was filled with ten- and twenty-dollar bills.

"Boys . . . boys," Gaerity protested, "I can't accept your charity."

The hollow-cheeked one said, "We'd be insulted if you didn't, Barry. No Irishman comes to Boston and sleeps on the streets."

"You're all too kind. And that porter's heavy on me poor bladder. If you'll excuse me a minute . . . ?" Gaerity took a few staggering steps toward the back of the pub, but then spun around on an apparent afterthought and returned for his glass. "It's a long, long way to Zipperary."

They howled.

But as he turned again, his face went taut. He had a faint hope that McGivney had kept his name. If not both of them, at least his first. Some novices found that easier than conditioning themselves to respond to a Bill or a Bob that didn't wear well.

Yet a check of the Boston white pages had left him with no leads.

Alone in the restroom, Gaerity dumped the full glass of porter down the urinal drain, then peed.

He knew for sure that McGivney had reached Boston in 1972. And two years ago an inmate who had come into Castle Gleigh was positive he'd seen Liam on the streets of Somerville, a suburb of Boston, in 1985. They hadn't spoken, and McGivney had swiftly vanished. But a man who'd spent more than a decade in the same city developed connections, private and professional, that might well keep him there as long as he lived.

Gaerity zipped up and went outside to the alley. The repairman's panel truck was parked in the small lot there.

Gaerity couldn't make use of the IRA's Boston liaison in his search for Liam McGivney. Personal endeavors were frowned upon, and the brotherhood had graphic ways of showing its displeasure, the least of which was kneecapping—crippling an errant fellow with a bullet to the knee. Or both knees. Or to the brain, if it was a second warning. And Gaerity already had been warned to lie low until his escape had faded in the memories of the various British law enforcement authorities.

He took the repairman's keys from his pocket and entered the truck through the double doors at its rear. Just as he'd expected. A saddlebag of fine tools.

These he tossed in a trash can down the alley for later retrieval, then went back inside.

"How was Zipperary?" the repairman asked, grinning stupidly.

"Warm and wet this time of year." Gaerity sat down beside him. A moment later, while chatting to another of the men, he casually let the keys drop to the floor. The tinkling sound made the repairman slap his belt, then grope for them in the dimness under the table. He hooked them on, tested the clip a few times with his thumb, and finally went back to his porter.

"Don't be forgettin' this." The hollow-cheeked man forced the wad of bills on Gaerity.

"Like I said, too kind . . . just too . . ." Gaerity's voice trailed off, his eyes on the screen of the television mounted to the ceiling over the bar. Any sound from it was drowned out by the noise of the patrons, but he rose as if in a trance.

"Mr. Barry?" someone asked from behind.

Using an empty stool as a step, he climbed up onto the countertop and stood there, raising hysterical laughter from the table he'd just left. He clasped the set in both palms as if holding the face that was flickering there. ". . . in Cambridge this morning. Lieutenant James Dove of the Boston bomb squad, seen here exiting the building with the twenty-two-year-old intended victim of a murder-suicide plot, is credited with . . ."

"My God, boys!" Gaerity roared down at the table. "You're damn well wrong—there is a free lunch!"

5

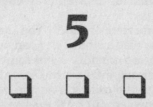

K ate figured that it'd been arranged to cause Dove and her maximum embarrassment.

The leader of Shamrock Ambitions, the semitraditional, semirock, semigood band Dove's best man, Max O'Bannon, had hired for the reception, suddenly called the bride and groom to the stage of the hall "to give us a tune." Kate resisted, but O'Bannon, blasted since midmorning on Bushmill's whiskey and Harp beer chasers, lifted her to her feet by the elbows. Dove took her by the hand. Giving up, she hiked the long skirt of her yellow gown and followed her husband of three hours off the dais and up into the hot lights. "But before we hear from the pride of the Pops," the bandleader said, falling into a Barry Fitzgerald brogue, "I've been asked by the best man to inquire into a matter of some delicacy."

"Oh Christ," Dove blurted, then his face flamed red when he realized that the priest was still there, sipping claret with Kate's maiden aunt, who was keeping an eye on Lizzy.

"When exactly, Mr. Dove, did you propose to your lovely wife?"

"Saturday," he mumbled.

"*Last* Saturday, you mean to say?"

"Yes."

Dove had insisted on a quick wedding. And she too hadn't wanted to wait.

"You waste no time then, do you, sir?"

The bomb squad hooted, clapped, and whistled. "Disarm and dispose before it goes up in your face!" the crude Alabaman, Maner, hollered. He was wearing a souvenir tie from the Virgin Islands, a red blazer, and Levi's. His wife, Connie, swatted him on the back of the head, making a strand of lank blond hair fall over his eyes.

"Honey," he whined, which got the squad hooting, clapping, and whistling all the louder.

"Let's get this over with," Kate said to the leader, grabbing a fiddle. "Do you all know 'The Rakes of Mallow'?"

The younger players rolled their eyes, but she tapped her foot twice and they fell in with tin whistles, piano, and bodhran, a primitive Irish drum with a hollow sound Dove had said could be duplicated only by beating on a mummy's chest with two wooden spoons. He himself was now plugging in his electric guitar, which meant that he'd put O'Bannon up to this. He fancied himself a rock musician. The less she assured him that he had talent, the less she lied.

Now, strumming, he segued from *The Rakes* into Chuck Berry. 'Bama Maner let go with a mindlessly joyous whoop, slopping beer over his white shoes.

The band joined the mutiny, and Kate soon found herself on her own to carry the traditional melody. "T'hell with the ham," she said, giving up, laughing. Dove was down on his knees, living the fantasy, eyes clenched as he fumbled for at least one decent chord.

The priest and auntie looked as if they'd eaten something bad, but the squad loved him. As did Lizzy.

Thankfully, O'Bannon unplugged him after a couple of minutes. "All right, all right," he said, slurred, "cut the shenanigans. Back to your chairs, everybody. It's time to toast the bride and groom."

"How'd I do?" Dove asked on their way back to the dais.

"We'll call you," Kate said.

"Raise your glasses," O'Bannon ordered, then apparently forgot his speech, for he just stood tottering at the podium, rubbing his heavy jowls with a hand. "Oh yes," he said at last. "Twenty or so years ago, a rookie patrolman, fresh out of the academy, arrived at me precinct for the night watch—"

"*Your* precinct?" Rita, the sloe-eyed female squader, interrupted. "What were you, a captain?"

O'Bannon retorted, "No, darlin'—I worked for a livin'."

The squad put down their glasses to applaud that, and Captain Roarke, Dove's former boss, pasted on a grin.

"Anyways," O'Bannon plunged ahead, "there at that distant roll call stood a young fella with sleeves so slick you could ski cockroaches on 'em. Never did I dream that one fine evenin' I'd be here at his behest . . ." The first time Dove had introduced O'Bannon to her, she'd assumed that he was an uncle, so visibly tight was the bond between the two men. It had taken her aback to learn that they'd worked together for only six months before Dove was reassigned to another precinct. ". . . and so here's to the wings of love, ladies and gents. May they never lose a feather while his big shoes and her little shoes are under the bed together."

Everyone drank.

Except O'Bannon. He had more to say. "And Jimmy, a kindly word of advice before I forget . . ."

Dove knocked his forehead against the table.

O'Bannon gestured toward the squad. "Get yourself a better class of friends now that you're free of this lot. It's a sick bunch what enjoys dealin' with bombs and such. I think the good father will back me up on this. If God wanted us defusin' bombs, he woulda hung our balls off our backsides. So part company with these cretins, Jimmy."

The squad hooted and raspberried him. Blanket shouted, "Get your fat mick ass down here and say that!"

Dove had once said that he was the quiet one.

Gaerity stared down the stick at the cue ball. Lifting his gaze slightly, he checked the angle one more time. Then smack. The white ball streaked for the opposite corner, banked off two velvet cushions, and came directly back at him.

He straightened, listening to the satisfying crack of the eight ball being rapped into the pocket nearest him. Then, yawning, he glanced through the front windows of the Cambridge bar. He could see the River Street Bridge. Beyond its towers, headlights were wending around the concrete convolutions that fed into the turnpike toll plazas on the Brighton side of the Charles.

"You set to go?" a voice asked him from one of chrome and Naugahyde chairs set against the far wall.

Gaerity ignored it as he fished the eight ball out of the pocket and set up precisely the same shot. Same angles. Same everything.

And same result. The black ball plopped out of sight.

He smiled to himself.

"You want to play or what?"

Gaerity did it one more time, then turned toward the voice. It belonged to a boy in his late teens. Washed-out denim from neck to toe, and a cigarette dangling from the corner of his mouth. Gold wire-rimmed glasses. A young Harvard intellectual on an evening sabbatical from the nearby campus, out among the unwashed proles, hoping a little color might rub off on him before he ultimately went ahead and joined daddy's law firm.

"What're you doing, mister? This joint has only one pool table, and you've been plunking that same fucking bank shot for thirty minutes now."

"That long?" Gaerity put down the stick, rubbed the back of his neck.

"You set to go?"

"Oh, hours ago," Gaerity said amiably.

Then he strolled out.

Dove tried to have a word and drink with each member of the squad before Kate and he left for the night. Blanket and he were talking over old times at the bar when O'Bannon cut a winding path through the dancers toward them. Grinning, red-eyed, he hung an arm around each of them. "Ah, you look like a thirsty pup, McNulty." Before Blanket could respond to that, Max turned to Dove. "You're gonna enjoy retirement, Jimmy. You can drink till the cows come home."

"I'm not retiring."

"Well, you're gonna teach. Same thing."

"You got a mouth, old man," Blanket said. Not entirely friendly.

"I do now—don't I though, McNulty?" O'Bannon lowered his head in mock shame, then raised it again, a sly look in his eye. "That's a fine Irish name you have. And a fine clan too. Means son of the Ulsterman ... did you know that, McNulty?"

Blanket didn't answer.

"Listen to me—there are five counties in Ulster. Antrim. Londonderry. Down. Armagh. Tyrone. No, six—Fermanagh. They say memory's the second thing to go. Now, McNulty, which one are your folks from?"

"Stow it, old man."

"You're black Irish, then. That's it. And a fine specimen too."

Dove felt O'Bannon's left hand drop off his shoulder and begin groping along the bar.

"You're a mean drunk, old man," Blanket said.

"No, a devious one," Dove said, pinning O'Bannon's hand to the bar. It'd come within inches of snatching Blanket's glass. "I think he's been cut off."

"Damn you, Jimmy. Damn you to hell."

"Who ordered it?" Dove asked.

O'Bannon's doleful look turned resentful. "That son of a bitch priest. And your lovely bride. And her biddy aunt. The whole goddamn place, now that I think of it. It's a conspiracy. *Please*, Jimmy, that music's gettin' on me nerves."

"Sounds pretty good to me." The band had given up on traditional Gaelic and gone on to straight American rock.

Blanket burst out laughing as it hit him. "You mean this old bastard was willin' to start a fight just so he could cop our drinks?"

Nodding, Dove said, "You have to understand the culture."

"Yes, you wouldn't understand, McNulty," O'Bannon said loftily. "It's an Irish thing." He slumped down onto a stool. "I'm a shameful man," he said, downing the last of Dove's whiskey before Dove could stop him. "Thanks, Jimmy."

Dove sighed, then caught the bartender's eye. Pointing at O'Bannon with one hand, he ran the forefinger of the other across his throat.

"Gotcha," the man said.

"You're doin' the right thing, Lieut," Blanket said so quietly Dove almost missed it. Clearly, he meant quitting the squad.

"Am I?"

"But I'm still gonna miss your crazy ass."

"Same here," Dove said as he surveyed the dancers. Rita was hanging all over one of Kate's fellow violinists from the Pops. She'd regret that soon enough. He was GBG, according to Kate. Georgeous But Gay. Let her have her illusions. 'Bama was cheek-to-cheek with his wife, his expression so rapturous Dove was sure that he'd forgotten in his bourbon fog who he was with. Katie was doing the two-step with the priest. And at the center of the dance floor was a light-skinned black man and his date, putting them all to shame with their moves.

"Who invited Michael Jackson?" Dove asked.

Blanket admitted, "Didn't think you'd mind."

"No, of course not. Friend of yours?"

"Not exactly. Name's Franklin. Sergeant from SWAT. I guess he's your replacement." Blanket shrugged.

Roarke, who'd been sitting alone at a table for some time, must have been eavesdropping, for he approached with glass in hand. Probably his first and last snort of the night. "Yeah, Jimbo," he said. "The brass balked at filling your spot with another lieutenant. Said the detail's too top-heavy as is." The captain paused as if realizing for the first time that he might've been insulted. But then he added, "Franklin's a good kid. Comes highly touted."

"Comes what?" Dove asked, making a face.

Roarke said, "I'll drag him over for an intro."

Kate joined Dove just as the captain and Franklin walked up. She threaded her arm through Dove's, smiled up at him.

The sergeant offered his hand. "Felicitations, Lieutenant. Mrs. Dove. Wonderful party." Certainly knew his social graces: felicitations for a wedding, congratulations for a promotion. Condolences for a demotion to Training Division. "I'm Anthony Franklin."

"So I heard." Everyone was watching for his next

move, so Dove shook Franklin's hand. "Glad you could make it, Tony."

"Uh . . . it's Anthony."

Dove inclined his head toward Franklin's date and asked, "Cleopatra?"

"Sir . . . ?"

Kate jabbed Dove in the ribs. "Nothing," he said. "Long day, bad joke."

But Franklin chuckled. A breezy, meaningless chuckle. "Oh, cute. I'll have to tell Cecily. She'll get a kick out of it. Hope you don't mind me crashing. McNulty told me it'd probably be all right."

"It's just a party."

Franklin's look turned serious. "I suppose I mean the squad and all too. Your team."

"Not mine. Don't see my name stenciled on the truck."

"That's right," Roarke said. "Something we should all remember. How's it go? Put your hand in a bucket of water, pull it out—and the hole's how much you'll be missed."

Franklin smiled at the captain as if he were an absolute moron, then said, "Well, don't want to keep my lady waiting. Lieutenant, Mrs. Dove."

"Who's that?" Kate whispered as soon as Franklin was out of earshot.

"A bona fide fast-tracker. Two years in SWAT. Two in Bomb Disposal. Then five as a captain in Internal Affairs. After that, chief."

Blanket said, "I mean to give him a chance."

After a moment, Dove dipped his head. "No, you're right. Give him his shot. Maybe I do see my name stenciled on that truck."

Kate took his hand, gave it a squeeze.

All at once, beepers were going off like a meadow full of crickets. Rita disentangled herself from Mr. GBG and ran for her purse. The male members of the squad, almost as one, flipped up their jackets and reached for their belt units to hit the off buttons.

Dove started to do the same, but then caught himself.

"Jaysus," O'Bannon said in a funk, "let it blow. Some bombs were just meant to blow. Some ships meant to sink."

The band had quit making music. The members just stared as most of their audience started for the red exit light. "Won't be a minute, folks," Roarke apologized for the squad. "Probably just a tease. Party forward."

"Back in no time," Blanket said, giving Kate a peck on the cheek before he jogged to catch up with the others. Franklin was in the middle of them as if he'd been on the squad for years.

"Hey, Dove," Kate warned, catching the look on his face.

"I was only wondering . . ."

"What?"

He leaned into her ear. "Who's going to have the bigger bang tonight . . . them or me?"

"Hush your mouth." But she laughed under her breath.

"Hey, boys," O'Bannon hollered at the band, "how 'bout a wee fox trot?" Then he found Lizzy, who was still hard at the cake, and pulled her onto the dance floor.

Dove watched the exit door glide shut.

Blanket stood on the Brighton approach to the River Street Bridge. Beside him was Franklin, smoking a Winston. It smelled utterly delicious. McNulty's old brand. How'd the jingle go, before the government stopped tobacco advertising on television and radio? *Winston tastes good, like a cig—*

"How come we don't see no lights where Roarke's working?" Franklin asked, checking his watch. The captain had been at the device for over an hour now. It'd been found by the paint rigging crew on a beam under the center of the span. A fifty-gallon drum showing wires.

Blanket doubted that the sergeant would've said "no lights" to anybody but a brother. Franklin was looking for allies. Blanket simply answered, "Thing might have an infrared trigger."

"Oh yeah, shine a flashlight on it—and boom," Franklin said. He'd already gone through the basic course. Unfortunately, Roarke had taught that session instead of Dove. "Man, this outfit deals with some bad folks, doesn't it?"

"Damn smart too, or they blow themselves up in their own kitchens before they can go public." Blanket shifted into Franklin's exhalations. It was only passive smoking, he told himself. "Ain't exactly like SWAT, is it, Sarge?"

"No," Franklin said. "That was usually taking down some dummy who'd had a robbery or a family argument go sour on him."

Blanket nodded. An honest answer. There was hope.

Franklin lit a fresh Winston off the old one.

Clasping his hands behind his band, Blanket strolled off a short way, propped one of his steel-toed boots on the bumper of the squad's truck. He hadn't had an urge this strong in months. He tried deep breaths. No good. Then he snapped the rubberband he'd looped around his wrist. Still no good. He simply wanted a fucking cigarette. A Winston.

"Damn," he said, standing back and kicking the bumper.

Horns were braying in the distance. Interstate 90 had been shut down between Boston University and the last Brighton exit. Cars were jamming up on the surface streets. Fireflies were twinkling below along the greenbelt of the Charles River Reservation. Looked like cigarette coals being sucked bright.

"Fuck it," Blanket said, striding back to Franklin. "Lemme bum a smoke there, Sarge . . . will you?"

"Sure, man." Franklin tossed him the whole pack. A book of matches was lodged under the cellophane wrapping.

Blanket hesitated, then did what would've been unthinkable only a few hours ago. He inhaled. Wonderful. A slight, dizzy-headed high followed his long deprivation. But it mystified him, frightened him even—what had led to this downfall? Whatever it was, the feeling was strong. Overpowering.

Then he saw Roarke coming toward them on foot. He chucked the smoke over the side of the bridge, watched the sparking coal go out in the black water.

"This is no tease," the captain said.

"How's that, sir?" Franklin asked.

All right, Blanket thought, *he isn't afraid to ask questions.* This was no business for putting on airs.

"There's a shitpot full of anti-handling triggers on our IED," Roarke said rather evasively. "I didn't even try to screw with it."

McNulty said nothing. But how'd the captain know about the triggers without having made an attempt to disarm the device? And what the hell had he been doing for the last hour—just squatting on the beam and scratching his ass?

"What d'you think, Blanket?" Roarke asked.

McNulty let his opinion be known by glancing all around. One of the busiest bridges in town. High-density development on the Cambridge shore, the Harvard business grad school on the south side. And just across the interstate a three-hundred-room motel. He knew that Dove would attempt to disarm it. But it wasn't his to suggest.

Roarke finally said, "Why don't you go get the Barrett, Blanket?"

"Fifty caliber?" Franklin asked.

"Yeah," McNulty said, starting for the gun locker inside the truck.

As soon as the bellboy withdrew with tip in hand, Dove and Kate flopped back-first onto the bed. They said nothing for a minute or two, then he asked tentatively, "You as shot as I am?"

"Uh-huh."

"Thank God."

They both laughed.

He brushed the side of her face with his fingers. "Now that that's settled, wife, where'd you say you're taking me on our honeymoon? Some Pacific paradise called Compost . . . ?"

"Quepos, pal. Costa Rica."

"Why Costa Rica?"

"I've never been there before. Except in song."

He rolled on his side to look at her. "Song?"

Her voice an exhausted rasp, she broke into some ridiculous ditty about getting your liquor down in Costa Rica, and it was nobody's business but your own.

"Why would somebody have to go all the way to Costa Rica for a drink?" he asked, stroking her hair. It was beautiful against the white satin bedspread. Billows of red fanning out from her face. "Not that I won't have a nip or two down there."

"Prohibition, you idiot." For a moment, her expression was quizzical. "Don't you know anything?"

"Less and less all the time."

She went on with the song, but he kissed her quiet.

Their faces separated by a few inches, and she fully caught his look. "Feeling perkier, Dove?"

"Remarkably. I think your singing did it."

"Go-wan, my being flat on my back did it."

"That too."

"You're very prone to suggestion."

"Yes, as long as you're prone," he said, huskily now.

She bussed him on the tip of the nose. "Give me a minute."

While she was in the bathroom, he gravitated toward the balcony, scooping up the telephone on the way. It was miserably hot outside, the kind of night you sweated bullets trying to disarm something tricky. You could lose ten pounds over a device on a summer night like this.

"Nobody's business but my own," he said, repeating part of the lyrics Kate had just sung. She was right, of course. The squad's business was no longer his.

He began to return the phone to the nightstand, but then swore under his breath and dialed the number he'd vowed to forget.

"Bomb Disposal, Cortez speaking," the technician answered on the third ring.

"It's Dove."

"Hey, Jimmy. Sorry I missed the wedding. Roarke wouldn't let me off. *Imaricon de mierda! Bastardo!*"

"Yes, I think he's quite the gentleman too. Don't worry, you weren't missed."

Another burst of Spanish maledicta.

"Listen," Dove interrupted, his eyes shifting toward the bathroom door, "what happened with the call?"

"They're still out on it."

Dove checked his wristwatch. Almost two hours now. Not a good sign. "Where is it?"

"River Street Bridge. Roarke called a while ago, telling me to bust my ass and get Manfred ready to shut this one down. And then Rita phoned, saying forget it. Typical, isn't it?"

"Do me a favor. Call me if you hear anything."

"You crazy? This is your wedding night. First marriage?"

"Yes."

"Then you need some coaching. Hang up and ravage her, man. She expects it."

"I'm serious, Cortez. Call."

"Shit. Where are you?"

"The Four Seasons."

Cortez whistled. "Classy."

"The whole nine yards. We even flew in a band from Miami for the reception."

"You're kidding. Tell me you're kidding, Jimmy. I'll kill Roarke. I'll have Manfred rip off his *pelotas*."

"Phone me."

"Yeah, yeah."

Kate caught him returning the phone to the nightstand. She shook her head.

"They're still not back," Dove said weakly.

Blanket bummed one last Winston from Franklin before setting off down the riverbank. He promised himself not to light up this cigarette. Instead, he tucked it behind an ear as a test of willpower. Whatever had come over him earlier was gone, replaced by shame.

"Okay, it's all yours, Blanket," Roarke said.

"Mind if I tag along, McNulty?" Franklin asked.

"No reason, Sarge," he replied, slinging the Barrett rifle over his shoulder. "Nothin' to this. Blast will dissipate over the middle of the river. Shouldn't break more'n a couple windows on Memorial Drive. Go back to the toll plaza in the truck."

"You sure?"

"He's sure," Roarke said. "We never send two people to do a job one can safely do. Get used to it."

Franklin gave up with a nod.

"Appreciate it though, Sarge," Blanket said, setting out. He wasn't a bad guy. Dove would never see it that way, and Blanket was disappointed that the changing of the guard hadn't gone off better. Dove could've been more supportive. The last thing this outfit needed was another supervisor lacking in confidence.

Carefully, he picked his way down the embankment. Above, he could hear the truck turning around. Bands of light were shimmering across the water from the Cambridge side. Whites and yellows and golds. A touch of red from a buoy.

He stopped on the river's edge downstream of the bridge and quickly saw that he'd be caught in the fan of shrapnel there. A lot more than a few windows on Memorial Drive were at risk, but it was best to let Franklin see that for himself. Nothing like experience.

He strolled under the south anchor of the bridge, gazed up at a catwalk that gave access to a door, some kind of maintenance room. The perfect place from which to shoot, if only he could see the device from there.

He climbed a metal ladder to the catwalk.

"All right," he said to himself. The fifty-gallon drum was clearly visible in the glow of the buoy lamp. The light-gathering scope on the rifle would help even more. He smoothly slid a .50-caliber shell into the chamber and used the catwalk railing for a bench rest.

Something brushed the hair on the side of his head. The Winston was slipping down.

Smiling, he flicked the cigarette away.

Then he took aim.

Dove braced. His hands were fisted, but he thrust them into his armpits to keep from flailing. He was near Kate. Something told him that he was only dreaming. He'd been chasing the lorry down the street. In black and white. Dream tones.

Kate was hollering something in the darkness of the hotel room, so he kept saying, "I'm all right. I'm awake. I'm all right, honey."

"Something blew up, Jim!"

"What?" Was *she* having a night terror?

"The hotel rocked!"

His eyes snapped open, and he stumbled out of bed for the glass doors of the balcony. A dark mushroom of smoke was just starting to flatten out over the Charles River two miles to the northwest. The butt of the pall was still tinged orange with flame. A long moment passed before he said, "It wasn't the hotel, Kate. We're safe."

"Where then?"

"River Street Bridge," he said, almost unable to speak.

She'd switched on a lamp and was clasping her legs in her arms. "My God—what happened?"

He rushed to the armchair and fumbled into his wedding clothes.

"Jim . . . ?"

6

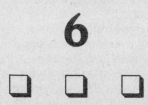

Dove ordered the bell desk to call him a taxi, then ran outside in the hope that one was already waiting on Boylston Street. Nothing. Just a champagne-colored glow of street lamps, then the darkness of Boston Common. A siren was approaching out of the southwest, emergency lights spangling off the faces of the buildings across Charles Street.

Seeing no taxi, he sprinted to the intersection.

The driver blatted the horn at him.

But Dove stood his ground, waving his arms, forcing the fire engine to slow to a crawl for the left turn. Then he jumped on the running board under the water pressure gauges.

"Hey, asshole!" a firefighter in the riding compartment bawled. "We aren't takin' applications tonight!" He reared back a rubber boot to kick him off.

Dove flashed his wallet badge just in time. "Bomb Disposal. You rolling to River Street Bridge?"

"Yeah."

"Any P.D. casualties?"

The fireman didn't want to say. But beyond him, the driver turned his head and said that there'd been at least one.

"Get inside the compartment here," the fireman said, holding out a gloved hand.

"What?"

"Get inside, dammit!"

Dove crouched on the floor, watched the Prudential Center slip past. The city lights were reflecting off a woolly overcast. It'd rain before morning. He felt something tickling his neck. His bow tie, unraveled but still clinging to his shirt collar. He tossed it out the hatch.

A voice crackled over the radio speaker above his head. It belonged to a paramedic, raising central dispatch. "Roll coroner on one."

"Sorry, guy," the fireman said quietly.

Dove leaned the back of his head against the steel bulkhead. He asked himself *who*, which loss would hurt the least. But all losses felt nearly the same at first. Only a few kept their edge after decades. *Ah, don't pout so,* she'd said, kissing him on the tip of the nose as Kate had done that evening. *I'll only be down in Crossmaglen for a wee bit. Some family business, and then I'm back to you . . .*

He was out on the running board as the engine slowed for the bridge. The center span was still standing, which told him that the force of the blast hadn't been directed against the road deck.

Fire units already on the scene were bouncing their spot-beams off the towers, giving the bomb squad some light in which to work among the twisted and blackened steel near what had been the seat of the explosion.

Roarke. Dove could see the captain. And 'Bama. Where were Rita and Blanket? Franklin?

The squad truck was parked beside an ambulance on the south anchor of the bridge. Dove badged his way through the line of patrolmen, then raced for Rita. She was dully smoking a cigarette, gazing downward into the space between the truck and the ambulance. There, a body bag came into view.

Dove grabbed her by the arm. "Who, babe?" But he no sooner asked than he saw Franklin sitting, dazed, on the parapet.

Rita's eyes were big and vacant. "Oh, Jimmy."

"What happened?"

"I don't know. Nobody knows."

"Where was he?"

"Under the bridge. Using the rifle to detonate. It was a simple gig, Jim. Why . . . ?"

Dove went to the bag, knelt, and started to unzip it.

"Don't do that, honey," Rita begged. "He don't wanna be remembered this way."

"Let him," 'Bama's voice said from behind. Angrily. "He's gotta see to know. Just like we all had to." But then a ringing smack made Dove turn. Maner had struck a steel brace with his fist and was shaking his bloody knuckles in the air. "Worms and losers!" He did it again. "Worms and fuckin' losers!"

Rita went over to him, and they embraced, stood motionlessly in the glare of the fire engine lights.

Dove opened the bag down to the chest.

Stark, glassy eyes stared back at him from the openings in a black hood. Suddenly, Dove felt as if he were tumbling back from the eyes, falling through empty space. Yet he could see his own hands rolling up the mask, revealing the burned, misshapen face of a girl. *I'll only be down in Crossmaglen for a wee bit . . . and then I'm back to you.*

Quickly, he zipped up the bag and stood.

Gaerity strolled past a small greengrocery whose owner was shutting it down for the night. Smoke was still lingering in the heavy air, although the store was two blocks off Memorial Drive. Gaerity halted and turned. "Lovely apples."

"T'ank you." Italian accent.

"You mind if I choose one?"

"If you be quick."

Gaerity stepped up into the bin, began gently squeezing apples. "They're all so firm. How can they be so fresh this time of year?"

"New Zealand."

"What's this beauty?" Red stripes over a rich yellow tone.

"Gravenstein." The owner paused in the midst of cranking down the canvas awning. "Some blow, eh? I betcha gas leak."

"And this oddly shaped fellow?"

"Uh . . . Red Astrachan."

"Good eating?"

"What you like? Tart or sweet?"

"Oh, the tarter the better."

"You like."

Gaerity started to reach inside his pocket, but the man waved him off.

"Why—thank you, sir. Good evening."

Gaerity bit into the apple. Delightful. Must remember the name. Red Astrachan. He made his way at a leisurely clip down to Memorial Drive, where a large crowd was pressing against a yellow streamer strung out by the police. Hordes of police. And more firefighting equipment than Gaerity had ever seen at one time. Different from Belfast or Londonderry. The British Army would still be running the show at this point, the Royal ordnancemen searching frantically for the inevitable second device.

He slipped into the noisy throng.

A bare-chested youth was jumping up and down on the balls of his feet, carrying on about what a great boom it had been. *Oh, the primal joy I give.* Long ago, seeing the same reaction from the children of Belfast, Gaerity had been foolish enough to believe that the reason was political. But it ran much deeper than politics. Fire and brimstone were what the world wanted. Not two hundred channels of cable television. Not video arcades and amusement parks as big as Luxembourg. They wanted to see it all come tumbling down—knowing that they'd feel released after the collapse.

A matron in a sequined gown was peering enraptured at the destruction through a pair of opera glasses. The wife of a Harvard professor on her way home from Symphony Hall, Gaerity supposed.

"Excuse me, madam," he said.

"Yes?" Still smiling. Recognized a gentleman when she saw one. Even at a bombing.

"Would you be so kind as to let me have a gander through your glasses? I'd be eternally grateful."

"Certainly."

Gaerity focused on the bomb squad, which was now sifting through the wreckage for clues. "Oh yes," he abruptly said.

"Something wrong?" the woman asked.

Gaerity wasn't sure. He felt a curious mixture of relief and disappointment. James Dove was alive. He was in civilian dress, a standout among the blue-suited members of his squad.

"No, madam," he finally said, "probably not." He returned her opera glasses to her and strolled on, chewing pensively on the apple.

It was difficult to have absolute control over a situation like this. Too many variables. Too many accidents, both tragic and fortuitous. Yet Gaerity knew what he most wanted. If possible. He wanted Liam McGivney eventually to beg for death. He wanted the final act to be a mercy killing, an unexpected kindness that would bring their torn friendship full circle. Only then would Gaerity himself be released.

And how to do that?

Torture Liam by killing and maiming those closest

to him. Make his life so horrible that death would look like a holiday.

Plainclothesmen were sifting through the crowd, notebooks out, asking the inane, listening to the useless. "You there," one of them said, snatching Gaerity by the sleeve. Same engaging personality type the world over. "See anything?"

"Nothin', officer," he said in an American accent, then broke free and moved on. "Nothing except the path before me."

Exhausted, Dove gazed up through a light rainfall at the scorched tower of the bridge. His hair and the shoulders of his tuxedo jacket were soaked, his hands black with char. He tried to concentrate on the bombing, deciphering how the explosion had played itself out among the girders. But everywhere he looked he saw Blanket McNulty. Saw him casting a clump of salmon eggs into that lake up in Maine, the time half the squad had gone fishing together. They'd all gotten toasted on margaritas and Dos Equis beer, and that night Blanket—who'd already lost one set of dental work on another drunken adventure—tossed his partial plate into the ice chest. He figured that he'd visit it before anything else at first light, even the camp toilet. But in the morning 'Bama had beaten him to the chest, groped in the icy water with eyes shut, and come out screaming with human teeth in his clutches. "Who'd we kill!" he cried.

Dove smiled to himself, remembering Blanket tearfully laughing with half his front teeth missing, calling Maner an ignorant cracker.

The smile quickly went out.

The sniffer dog gave an impatient tug on his lead. Dove had almost forgotten that he was holding it. "What you got, boy?"

The lab had thrust its nose into a tangle of debris. Dove reached inside for a seared piece of concrete.

He ran a light finger over it. A slightly oily feel. He sniffed, making the same sounds the dog had only moments before. Hard to tell anything about the residue that way. His nose was stuffed up from the rain. He touched the tip of his tongue to the concrete. A familiar taste . . . but from where? His experience file, which documented his expertise for court testimony, now included over four hundred separate IED calls.

He pocketed the piece just as 'Bama came back for the dog. His face, like all the others, looked pinched, drawn. "Find anythin', Lieut?"

'Bama had never called him that before. It'd always been Blanket's moniker for him.

"Maybe a bit of residue. You remember the color of the flash?"

'Bama shook his head. "Sorry, I was inside the truck. It came quicker'n I thought."

Rita half-recalled a yellow-orange flame. Black powder, possibly. Roarke thought the flash had tended toward a greenish orange. C-4. But, seeing the dying seconds of the blast through the balcony doors at the Four Seasons, Dove thought he'd seen an orange-red. ANFO. Ammonia nitrate and fuel oil. The oily feel of the residue he'd just found reinforced that. But too soon to tell for sure.

"Here's your pooch," Dove said, handing over the dog, giving it a parting scratch behind the ears. Standing awkwardly with his fists in his pockets, he exhaled and said, "I was just thinking about that time we went fishing up in Maine . . . and all you caught were Blanket's teeth."

"That fuckin' bastard," 'Bama growled, but then he looked away.

"Yeah, that fuckin' bastard." Dove didn't know what more to say. "Listen, I've gotta make a call. Oh, make sure for me—nobody uses a cellular on the bridge till we're absolutely sure it's clean. I don't want us cooking off a second device with one of our own transmissions."

"I'll pass it along, Lieut."

"I'll be over at that booth if you need me." Dove ambled wearily toward the intersection of Memorial Drive and River Street. 'Bama would be all right. It was Roarke who was in rough shape. He was grabbing anyone who'd listen, trying to justify why he hadn't tried to disarm the drum. He was coming up with more possible triggers every minute. Dove had tried to tell him that sometimes luck was luck, and nobody would have agreed more than McNulty. But the captain had just slapped his hands together and invented one more reason for having gone with the Barrett gun.

Dove stepped inside the booth, stared a moment through the rain-speckled glass at the bridge. The taste of the residue was hauntingly familiar, like stolen altar wine. Fuel, fertilizer—but something else too.

He dialed the hotel. His forehead pressed against the cool glass, he waited for the room to be rung.

"Yes?" Kate said.

"Blanket's dead."

Her voice softened. A little. "What happened?"

"I don't know. Still being sorted out . . ." Then for the first time, it hit him. McNulty was gone. Forever. He swiftly clamped his hand over the mouthpiece.

"Jim?"

He bit the sore place on the inside of his cheek, then dropped his hand. "Uh, I'm going to be tied up here awhile longer," he said. "Too dark last night to find much."

Silence.

"Can you check out for us?" he asked.

"I guess."

"I mean, this wasn't supposed to be our honeymoon. Costa Rica, right?"

More silence, then she said, "What're your plans, Dove?"

"Finish here as soon as I can. Get home and soak in a hot bath."

"I mean—about the squad."

He paused, trying to think of some way to make her see why he had to stick with the squad today. But he didn't know how to begin. Maybe you began with the first morning you showed at the Bomb Disposal building, and the people you'd grow to love were treating you like crap. You earned their love a call at a time. "Nothing has changed, Kate," he said at last. "Tomorrow morning I report to Training."

"Sure."

"Don't do this. I'm so beat I can barely stand up."

He could hear her sigh. "Okay. If I'm not home when you get there ..." His heart skipped a beat until she finished the sentence. "... I'll be at Saint Sebastian's with Lizzy. Rummage and bake sale followed by a potluck. Auntie was going to cover for me, but I might as well go now."

"Maybe I could join you for the supper."

"Maybe." But then she added, "I'm sorry about Blanket."

"Me too." Then he realized why Blanket's face had appeared so different last night. His partial had been missing. "Later, Katie," was all he could manage before hanging up.

7

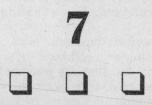

Gaerity nearly laughed when he rounded the corner and saw the statue.

The bloody irony of it.

There at the gates to the schoolyard—the Catholic school Liam McGivney's stepdaughter attended—stood Saint Sebastian. In eternal bronze. He was tied to a tree trunk, his eyes beseeching heaven, his body stitched with arrows. And for what had the Roman archers had a go at him? Why, he'd enlisted in the army under false pretenses, concealing within his manly bosom a tender Christian heart. Liam had done no differently to the IRA. He'd let his heart supersede the oath he'd taken. As legend had it, Sebastian hadn't died of those ghastly wounds. A Christian woman—Irene, wasn't it?—found him slumping unconscious against his bindings and nursed him back to health. Sebastian again declared his faith. Screw the imperial archers—the second time Emperor Diocletian had him clubbed to death.

And now, walking up to the gates, Gaerity fixed his amused eyes on Liam's Irene.

Kate O'Bradaigh-Dove.

At least that's what she probably thought her married name was.

She was offering clothing, an old waffle iron, and plastic-wrapped loaves from the tailgate of a station wagon. A Jeep Wrangler, a squiggle of rusted chrome advertised.

Gaerity memorized the license plate, noted the nice thick skidplate under the chassis.

The parents of the students were putting on some sort of flea market. On the Sabbath, yet. What was the Church coming to? Gaerity had read about the event in the newspaper. The Doves were certainly at the center of local life. Only Tuesday Gaerity had come across a wedding announcement and photograph of the bride on the society page. He'd thought the photo overly flattering.

But no.

She was all the more fetching in the flesh. Violinist for the Boston Pops. An interesting possibility there.

Gaerity stood across the crowded sidewalk from the Wrangler, feigning interest in some junk piled atop a card table. He could hear Liam's stepdaughter, Lizzy, say to her mother, "Eighteen dollars and thirty-five cents, Mama. Enough for a new dress."

And Kate answered affectionately but firmly, "It's not for new duds, bug. We're doing this to get computers for the school."

Yes, that was the kind of temperament that'd attract Liam McGivney. His own mother had prefaced every remark with a slap to his ear. And Old Man McGivney hadn't exactly been a role model. No, he'd been living proof of how British rule can warp the Irish spirit. A drunkard on the dole until the day both he and the missus burned together in a fire-bombing. At least they were spared the fate of Gaerity's own father, who went shitting his pants in the corner booth of a pub, and the fate of his mother ten years before that. She'd been cut down at tea by a stray bullet. It'd been fired by a rattled Orangeman cop banging away at some rock-throwers.

Examining Kate's loaves, Gaerity smiled at her. She smiled back, somewhat uneasily.

He moved on, glanced around for Liam. No sign of him. At work, no doubt.

"How much for the garden hose?" Gaerity asked a fat woman with jolly eyes.

"How 'bout a buck, sweetheart?"

"Here's two. One for Sebastian there. He looks like he could use a drop. For medicinal purposes, I'm sure."

She laughed, slapped her widespread knees with her palms. "Oh, you're a howl."

"Guilty as charged." Gaerity strolled on with the hose coiled over his left shoulder. He found an outdoor thermometer and a Krups coffeepot. All at bargain prices. Still no James Dove. *Well,* he told himself, *I've accomplished everything I came for today.*

He was almost to the last table in a long row of them when he noticed a homely boy sitting cross-legged in the rain-damp dirt. He was playing with a most amazing device.

"You hit the jackpot today, mister?" a woman asked, apparently just to let him know that the boy was hers.

The child was of no interest to Gaerity. It was the toy that fascinated him. He went to his knees, never minding the patches of mud, and watched intently as the boy released a black marble down a ramp. It ran a circular lap, dropped through a hole, careened around two more laps, and then came to a brisk halt. A gravity roller coaster for marbles.

"How much for this thing?" Gaerity asked.

"That's Justin's," the woman said. "It's not for sale."

"Pity." Gaerity frowned. "I was hoping to get it for my nephew. He lives in Dublin. Can't find such a fine toy there." He winked at the boy. "Know where Dublin is?"

"New Jersey?"

"Yes, precisely. Poor little Kevin. It'd mean so much to the lad. He's been laid up for months now."

Suspicion came into the boy's eyes. In Gaerity's day, the good sisters would've had a field day with this one. "Why's he laid up?"

"Car accident. Lost a leg, he did."

"He shouldn't been drivin'."

Gaerity chuckled. "No, he shouldn't. But this toy would mean so very much to him."

The boy raised his voice. "He ain't gettin' it!" Then he launched another marble on its way.

Gaerity glanced to the woman, looking gravely disappointed.

After a moment, she said, "Well, I guess I could find Justin another one."

"Mom!"

Gaerity took the wad of bills from a front trouser pocket. He peeled off a fiver and offered it to the boy.

"Ten."

"Very well."

The boy grabbed the two fives, and Gaerity took possession of the toy. Ingenious. He gave back the marbles. "I have no need of these."

The woman held up an audio cassette, beckoned with it like a bawd waiting at the top of the stairs. "Interest you in a U2 tape?"

"The spy plane, you mean?" Gaerity asked. "What's there to listen to?"

"No, the Irish band, silly. Come on, everybody knows U2. You're Irish, aren't you?"

"You'll have to forgive my ignorance. Been out of the mainstream for a while." Gaerity inspected the cassette cover, feeling very much like a visitor from outer space. Some Irish toughs backdropped by an eroded desert slope. "But I'll have a listen, if you recommend them so. Hear what the lads are doing these days. How much?"

"Twelve bucks."

She'd smelled a sucker. But Gaerity cheerfully paid up.

Just before rounding the corner again, he turned and glanced back, walking on his heels.

He could still see Kate O'Bradaigh's red hair. It was shining beneath Saint Sebastian's agony like a flame.

"Good night, Irene," he said.

Clutching a Styrofoam cup of coffee in one hand, Dove unlocked and pushed in the reinforced steel door. As always, the interior of the explosives storage hut smelled musty. Like a tomb, he imagined. But the air was also sharply acrid from all the substances containing nitric acid.

He fumbled for the light switch on the concrete wall.

A naked, dusty bulb came on, illuminating row after row of shelved devices and bomb fragments. Some were evidence, awaiting trial. Others were tagged for destruction, as soon as the squad found the time.

Dove made sure to lock the door behind him.

The magazine was designed so that, in the event of an accidental explosion, the roof would give before the walls—as long as the door was secured. The blast would then rocket harmlessly up into the air instead of flattening the vehicle impound yard that surrounded the structure.

Taking a gulp of lukewarm coffee, Dove glanced at his wristwatch. A quarter after five. *Forget trying to make the potluck supper at Saint Sebastian's.*

He tossed the coffee cup in a trash can and began walking slowly down the main corridor. His footfalls echoed around him. He flipped up evidence tags as he went, read them. Old cases. A flood of memories with each. One tag gave him a pang. Signed by Offi-

cer E. McNulty. October 9, 1988. Six more years to
live when Blanket's pen had jotted that down. Peculiar thought.

The day had been filled with them.

He found one of the cases he was looking for. Pipe
bomb explosion, convenience store. He took a curled
fragment out of its box and inhaled with his nostrils
held close to the residue. Black powder. Biting. Almost stinging.

He was here to refresh his olfactory memory.

"No," he said after a second test. The River Street
Bridge blast hadn't been black powder.

Next, he located some plastique residue, C-4 that
a disgruntled motorman had used to blow up a Mas-
sachusets Bay Transportation Authority car. Dove
sniffed deeply again, closed his eyes to fully capture
the scent.

"No way," he decided.

Finally, he unpackaged some evidence from an
old ANFO case. Ammonium nitrate and fuel oil.
Fertilizer and diesel, most commonly. In this in-
stance, a mob extortionist had made good on his
threats. He'd blown a trucking company owner to
vapor with this device, of which only shards remained. Dove smelled one of them, then stepped
away and checked the piece of concrete the dog
had found on the bridge.

"Yes," he said. "ANFO."

Lab analysis would confirm it in a couple of days,
but Dove had needed to know sooner than that. A
talented, maybe even world-class, blaster had the
jump on him. He was out there at this instant, putting together his next device.

Once more, Dove compared the two ANFO residues.

There was a difference, slight, but he could discern
it. The stuff off the bridge had more of a bite. It gave
him a headache for a few seconds.

*   *   *

Garage sales.

That's what the Americans called them. Marvelous custom, Gaerity thought as he pedaled into the warehouse district along the Inner Harbor. He had no sooner left Saint Sebastian's than he stumbled upon the solution to his transportation problem: a single-speed bicycle on a lawn cluttered with merchandise. It had sound tires and a wire basket, so a deal was promptly struck for fifteen dollars.

"You don't have a stout bag of some sort, do you?" Gaerity asked the proprietor of the garage sale, who hunted around for a minute before dumping some plastic egglike things out of a burlap sack.

"What're those?" Gaerity said.

"Silly Putty. I used to own a toy store in Roxbury. The niggers ran me out. Ain't you never heard of Silly Putty?"

The woman in the schoolyard had called him silly. And now here was Silly Putty. Words always seemed to come in bunches.

The man cracked open one of the eggs and showed Gaerity the substance inside. Looked like the more pinkish grades of plastique. He pulled it apart like taffy, then remolded it into a lump.

"How much?" Gaerity asked.

"Oh, I don't know . . . two bucks apiece?"

"Fine." Fascinating, all the odd and unexpectedly useful things in this country. Gaerity felt as if he'd suddenly come upon iron tools after having only stone ones at his disposal.

He now pedaled down an alleyway between two abandoned warehouses. It was so narrow that only a man afoot or a bicycle could pass through. No vehicles, which made Gaerity feel slightly more secure that the police wouldn't steal up on him from this approach. He turned onto a long wharf and went past the Moroccan freighter that had brought him to Boston.

The low clouds hovering over the harbor were obscuring Logan International, but he could hear the jets winding up and taking off.

It had started to drizzle again. Good night to be holed up with a bottle and some interesting work to do.

He dismounted at the bottom of the gangway and gazed smiling up at the *Dolphin Runner*. She had an alarming-looking list to starboard, which only pleased Gaerity. It made the old girl appear less inhabitable than she actually was. He walked his bicycle up the ramp, the weathered boards creaking ominously underfoot, and onto the badly rusted quarterdeck. Here, many years before, the crew had stood in their crisp whites, welcoming blue-haired matrons and their pot-bellied, cigar-champing husbands aboard. Gaerity could still feel the presence of these rather mundane ghosts, hear their ill-tempered calls for the steward echoing down the shadowy passageways.

He hid his bicycle behind a lifeboat, took his burlap sack full of treasures from the basket, and carried them through a hatch. Beyond it lay the main salon, red velvet hanging in tatters from the walls. Stagnant rainwater had pooled all along the starboard bulkhead. He passed along the tilting deck, in between the bolted-down gaming tables. Blackjack, roulette, craps. Everything necessary to ease the chief affliction of the well-to-do: boredom. Yet these were paltry forms of gambling compared to staking your life on a bomb.

Gaerity ascended a staircase to the bridge.

The chart table was covered with the tools he'd nicked from the cable TV repairman, plus some additional specialty items he'd managed to find at garage sales. Screwed to an overhead beam were the lids of Kerr jars, the glasses filled with a dozen different substances. The contrasting hues of red and yellow and green gave his workplace the ambience of a medieval apothecary, which he rather liked.

He sank into the captain's chair, sighed contentedly from the day's exertions, then emptied the sack onto the table. He'd propped up two of its legs to compensate for the *Dolphin Runner*'s list. Still, the Silly Putty egg rolled off onto the deck and stopped against the old Sylvania television he'd found in the purser's cabin.

Out of kilter, he thought, scooping up the plastic egg. A good reminder of how badly out of kilter the world was.

Swiveling, Gaerity faced the controls console where he'd placed a pewter figurine of Justice. From a judge's garage sale—apparently even the wealthy indulged. He tipped the scales with the Silly Putty, sat back, and smiled.

Then his eyes rested on the photograph he'd clipped to the console. Two boys clinging to a shuggey shoe rope in that distant Belfast schoolyard.

"Oh, dear Liam," he said sadly, "hard to believe that it's come to this between us." Gaerity leaned forward as if listening to that boyishly grinning mouth speak. "What's that you ask? Why am I taking my time to kill you? I'll explain with this fine whigmuleery. Say—do you slip now and again and use old words like whigmuleery? No?" Gaerity took the marble toy from the table and set it before the photograph. "Liam, do you see all the loops, whirls, and sudden drops built into this contraption? That's the way experience should be. Full of every possible sensation. Every possible thrill. Then, when's it all over and you're staring into your grave, you'll know that you've had your farthing's worth. So that's it then, boy-o—I want my farthing's worth with Liam McGivney."

Gaerity's wistful smile turned into a grimace as he picked up the cellular telephone one of the drunks at O'Dowell's Pub had loaned him. He dialed information. "In Boston, please," he said, "for the police department. Yes, the bomb squad. I need the address as well."

8

Dove paced back and forth at the front of the classroom. Not much of a class. Just Sergeant Franklin, plus three patrolmen who'd just been bumped up to special operations units, like SWAT and narcotics, that were likely to encounter explosive devices. Franklin seemed glum but attentive. No doubt it had finally occurred to him Saturday night that there were a few slick curves on the fast track to cop stardom.

"All right," Dove said, "let's review anti-handling mechanisms—and Bolinski, if you look at your fucking Timex one more time I'll jam it up your ass."

"Yes, Lieutenant." The patrolman sat back, crossed his arms over his burly chest. They all lifted weights these days.

Dove took a moment. *Slow down*, an inner voice told him. *You're driving them too hard. This is the first day of the basic course.* But every time he shut his eyes he saw Blanket's face framed by that body bag. "Pressure release, Franklin. It's you instead of Captain Roarke diddy-bopping up to that device on the River Street Bridge two nights ago. What might you look for in terms of a pressure release?"

The sergeant stirred, took a breath. "Micro-switch connected to the drum. Maybe a pull wire."

"That's a different category of trigger. But all right, look for a wire too. Look for everything under the sun. What's a trembler switch do, Bolinski?"

"Just how it sounds. Sets off the device if it's jarred."

Dove nodded. "What about a thermal mechanism, Hutchinson?"

A blank stare.

"Christ, man—you think this is fingerprint school?" Dove tried to hold down his temper, but once again he was unzipping that body bag. "You think you fuck up here and the damage is limited to a misfiled card!"

"No, sir."

Dove took a moment to calm himself. "Explain thermal to me, Franklin."

"Uhm . . ."

"Famous last words in bomb disposal, gentlemen. *Uhm.* It'll go on your tombstone, right along with *Oh shit.*"

Franklin glared, but then said, "This is a mechanism used to thwart disarming by means of freezing or heating. Freezing discharges the battery, rendering the device's power supply inoperative—"

"Maybe," Dove interrupted. "I always consider freezing a half-ass measure. Ever have trouble starting your car on a cold morning only to have the engine turn over on the first crank an hour later?" He met Franklin's angry eyes. "Sergeant?"

"I keep a good battery in my Mustang, *Lieutenant.*"

Dove paused again. *They think I'm a nutcase. Maybe that can work in my favor this morning.* "Anti-probe mechanism, Anderson."

Bolinski whispered, "Chastity belt."

What infuriated Dove even more than the cutup was that Franklin chuckled too. He was a supervisor.

He was going to have to lead out there, not make friends.

Dove said nothing for several seconds, just stared at the table shoved against the side wall. On it were bombs of all kinds, mines, rocket-propelled grenade launchers—enough diabolical inventions to sober a comedian.

Yet they were all laughing.

"Tomorrow," Dove began quietly, "we bury a member of this squad. He was a skilled cop. And a friend. Yet he or someone else on the team did something wrong. Overlooked something or forgot a basic rule. How do I know?" He stared at each of the four-some. "He's laid out on an autopsy table right now. That's how I know. Officer Edward McNulty does not pass go. He does not collect his retirement. He's dead!"

All but Franklin refused to meet his eyes.

"In other units, you can gloss over an occasional fuckup. It's probably good for morale to do so. But not here. Our fuckups are just too spectacular to be swept under the rug ..." Dove then realized from their somber faces that he'd made his point. "So this morning, we start with rule number one—always look for a second device. If you find one, plan on its cousin being in the neighborhood. Always expect the unexpected to get you—"

"Excuse me, Lieutenant ..."

"What, Franklin?"

"Isn't that more of an IRA trick? I think I read that somewhere in the materials the captain gave me."

Dove said nothing for a moment. "What're you saying?"

"Well, how often can we really expect to find that situation in this country?" Then Franklin gave him a serene smile, which Dove understood perfectly.

He'd prevailed upon Roarke to have the sergeant repeat the basic course—if only to make sure that there would be no gaps in his body of knowledge. Franklin, quite clearly, resented it.

Let him.

"Please go to the altar, Anthony," Dove said.

"Altar?"

Dove pointed at the table of devices. "Do you recognize the nifty little chick we call Bouncing Betty?"

"I do," Franklin said, approaching the table.

"Good. Treat her with respect. She's live."

Franklin stopped dead in his tracks but smiled. "Say what, Lieutenant?"

"Fresh out of the sand dunes of Kuwait, thanks to the generosity of the U.S. Army. Take it down."

Franklin didn't budge.

"Gentlemen," Dove said, "did you think we're stupid enough here to let you face live ordnance for the first time out in the field?"

Gingerly now, Franklin closed the rest of the distance to the table. Bolinski was half-smirking, yet he was also tapping the air with a nervous shoe.

"First tell us how Betty works, Anthony. The captain says you have a remarkable memory."

Franklin licked his lips. "Uh, the ejection-charge firing pin-spring drives the ejection-charge firing pin into the primer, which initiates the propelling charge . . ." He shifted slightly to the left, never hearing the faint click from the floor beneath him.

"Stand still," Dove ordered.

Franklin rubbernecked all around, then asked, "Why?"

"Just do what I say. I'm God in this classroom. The City of Boston has foolishly entrusted me with your lives, and I mean to abuse that trust. Proceed."

"The . . . the propelling charge ejects the fragmentation canister from the mortar projector sleeve, and uncoils the firing cable. When the, uh, canister reaches the end of the firing cable, the detonator firing pin carrier is pulled . . ."

"You're doing great," Dove said. "Music to my ears. How does the detonator firing pin carrier rotate?"

"By means of the spiral cam in the canister. The fuse then aligns with the detonator. The pull on the firing pin carrier forces the detonator firing pin into the detonator, initiating the explosive train. That's about it." Franklin couldn't help but smile in self-congratulation. "In short, the thing shoots crotch-high and blows your balls off."

Dove applauded slowly, derisively. "Well, you certainly talk the talk, Anthony. But you sure as shit don't walk the walk."

"Lieutenant?"

"The Betty before you on the table isn't live."

Franklin let out a long breath. "Then you lied."

"Yes. Just like the son of a bitch who murdered McNulty lied." Then, as Franklin began to move, Dove snapped, "Freeze!"

"Why, man? It isn't live."

"The one on the table isn't. The one you're stepping on is."

Slowly, Franklin leaned over and saw the linoleum tile with a more pronounced seam than the others. He was standing squarely on it. "Shit."

"Didn't you hear Betty click, Anthony?"

"No." Incensed now.

"Too bad. This business calls for the constant use of all five senses, plus a sixth one. In any event, how does the book say we take down Betty?"

Franklin looked up. His breathing had turned shallow again. "Have to find a way under it. Get a clean look at the bitch's detonator firing pin."

"Then you certainly have a challenge, *Tony*." Striding for the door, Dove said to the others, "Give him all the support you can, boys. I wash anybody who bolts for safety. The only safety you have from now on comes with teamwork." He expected at least one of them to balk. But nobody did. "Oh, by the way," he added as he turned the knob, "all my Bettys come equipped with a timer. Maybe you gentlemen have thirty seconds. Maybe thirty hours. This is what makes the business so interesting."

Dove had seen Rita's image through the pebbled glass of the door. He stepped halfway out into the hall, and she peeked past him. "See school's going well," she whispered. "Three of them have pissed their shorts and Franklin's on the verge of full cardiac arrest."

"I can't believe how dumb they are," Dove whispered.

"Remember how dumb I was?"

"Not this dumb."

"You're sweet." Rita took a manila envelope from inside her Ike jacket. "Keep it to yourself, will you?"

Dove checked to make sure the foursome were still engrossed in the practical exercise, then undid the twine fastener and pulled out the autopsy report. He scanned the first few pages. Hard to imagine that the weights, measurements, and pathologist's anatomical observations were describing a man Dove had gotten drunk with a hundred times, gone fishing with in Maine, seen alive and well less than forty-eight hours before.

"You okay, Jim?"

Recovering, he winked at her. "Fine."

"I bet Kate's hot at you for Saturday night."

"Why?"

"Why, he asks. Honey, being stood up at the church is one thing. Stood up in the bridal suite's another."

"Didn't quite go down that way."

"I know."

"She understands, Rita."

"You hope she understands." Rita pushed past him a little and said loud enough for the class to hear, "Oh, they're into Bettys. Worst part of the whole goddamn course, if you ask me." The three others had now decided to gather around Franklin to give him what was no doubt useless advice. "You know, I came into the program Mr. Rich Durgin," she droned on, "and walked away from Bettys day Ms. Rita Durgin."

The foursome just gaped at her.

She drew back into the hallway and growled at Dove, "None of the bastards laughed. They didn't know I was kidding, for chrissake!"

"They don't know anything right now. Except that I'm a complete lunatic."

She was slightly mollified. "You sure?"

"Positive."

She twirled around once as if to show off her hips.

"Get outta here," Dove said. "What is this—a sting operation to get me on sexual harassment?"

Rita continued down the hall, her nicotine-laugh echoing off the walls.

Dove went back inside the classroom. "Where are we?"

"Fucked," Franklin admitted.

"Bingo—right from the instant you focused on the first device without even remotely thinking there might be a second one lurking underfoot."

Bolinski asked, "Okay, Lieutenant—what would you do in the sergeant's situation?"

"Die."

"Oh bullshit, sir," Hutchinson said.

"I'm serious. Nobody's exempt. Stumble too deeply into the bomber's trap and there's no way out. No matter how much experience you have. McNulty had nine years on the squad." Dove went to the Kevlar bomb suit hanging on the wall.

"What're you doing?" Franklin asked.

"Call it safe sex. Taking precautions before I fuck the four of you."

Bolinski finally laughed. "He's not gonna blow up the whole building."

"I'm not. Betty would make a mess of this room, but not the whole building."

"He's just messin' with our minds," Anderson said conspiratorially.

"You positive?" Dove asked.

"Shit yes, Lieutenant," he said. "You're no crackpot."

"How well do you know me?"

Silence.

"That's right." Dove finished zipping up the suit and reached for the helmet. "I'll tell you a true story. Years ago, I went to the Army's Hazardous Device School at Redstone Arsenal down in Alabama. That's where I met Officer Maner, who's now part of this squad. You can ask him to verify what I'm about to tell you. We thought the instructor was messing with our minds during a practical just like this. Except he wasn't. He blew himself to pieces all over the range. Injured two students in the process. Turned out his wife of twenty years had just run off. He was badly in debt and drinking too much. And he hated dumb-ass students, especially those with curly hair like the son of a bitch who stole his old lady." Dove grinned as he flipped down the face shield. "Proceed. I can hear Betty ticking like a cheap alarm clock."

Anderson started to offer a suggestion just as the tile flew up, forcing Franklin's foot aside. The Vietnam-era Betty hovered for a split second three feet above the floor before detonating with a flash.

The foursome recoiled, instinctively shielding their faces with their hands. Franklin sank to his knees, and Bolinski toppled like a tree. One of them shrieked. Hutchinson, Dove believed.

The smoke cleared, and they frantically examined themselves. Anderson moaned when he saw the glistening dabs of red around his groin. "Oh Jesus!"

"Paint," Dove said.

"*What?*"

"I said it's just paint. This time." Dove took off the helmet, shed the bulky suit. "Trust no one to look out for your life," he said. "Everyone—even your best friend—will fail you now and again. Double-check everything. Triple-check if you have time. Trust nothing except your own skill and knowledge." He smiled at Franklin. "Class dismissed."

9

Boston Police Department had obviously learned from its Irish how to stage a funeral procession. A side street off the dingy old building that housed the bomb squad was crowded with official mourners waiting for the slow drive to the church. First in line were the motorcyclists, tall, straight-backed fellows in knee-high boots and helmets. After that came the department's black-and-whites, at least a hundred of them, drawn up three abreast. And then scores of cruisers from other agencies, including the military, which did much of the IED disarming in America.

And what was this now?

Gaerity shifted his binoculars—another garage sale acquisition—to the building entrance. Down the steps trooped six figures in dress blues and white gloves. Their polished shoes gleamed like raven wings. Leading them was their captain, Roarke, who was quick to press the panic button when confronted with a few simple anti-handling devices. Liam McGivney, of course, followed him, his face sad and careworn. This was by no means an unfamiliar ritual to McGivney, although it was the first time Gaerity had ever seen him take part in a procession without wearing a black hood. Maner was next. He handled the sniffer dog. Rita Durgin, a tough-looking lump of a woman, tossed a cigarette butt to pavement and crushed it under a low heel. A lithe young black fellow with sergeant's chevrons on his sleeves walked beside her. Gaerity had yet to find out anything about him. New to the squad, he believed. A Latin man in a civilian suit brought up the rear. Cortez, the technician.

"A fine-looking constabulary," Gaerity said, lowering the glasses as the squad piled into two cruisers. He rested his elbows on the lip of the roof parapet behind which he crouched, and smiled. "Sorry I can't go out to the cemetery with you, Liam. But I'd wear out the tires on my poor bicycle."

The two cruisers crept onto the street, and the rest of the procession fell in behind them, light bars flashing dimly under the bright noon sun.

"But I'll do this much, Liam."

Gaerity stood and raised a clenched fist in salute.

Blanket's mother had only a window-mounted air conditioner, so the men and Rita shed their uniform jackets in the entry hall. Dove envied the kids he'd passed on the way inside. They were frolicking in the spray of a fire hydrant they'd uncapped. Twilight, and the air was still stifling.

Everyone mumbled a few words to Mrs. McNulty and Blanket's grown sisters, then stood stiffly around the small living room. Roarke, who had less to say than anyone, turned on the television to the Red Sox game. Thankfully, he kept the volume low. O'Bannon, who'd insisted on coming although he'd known Blanket only through Dove, seemed to be more at ease with the wake than anyone else. He promptly threw on an apron and helped a handful of elderly black ladies pass out drinks and set up the buffet table.

Dove and Kate shuffled through the food line together, then separated. She paired off with Connie

Maner in a corner of the dining room, where they chatted quietly under a framed portrait of Martin Luther King. Dove gravitated toward the TV, although he had no great affection for baseball. He hadn't grown up with it.

O'Bannon brought him his second bottle of beer. "Will you look at this now, Jimmy? Why is it a man always gets thrown the best party of his life after he's gone?"

Dove just smiled.

O'Bannon patted his shoulder, then went back to the kitchen.

Roarke was filling his mouth with potato salad, eyes glued to the screen.

Dove saw that the bases were loaded. Mo Vaughn was up. "That's the guy you want at the plate with ducks on the pond," Dove noted. Just to break the ice.

"He's hitless in his last ten at bats."

But then Vaughn bounced a double off the Green Monster, the high wall in left field.

"Yes!" Roarke cried, trying to restrain himself as best he could. "Yes!"

O'Bannon's head ducked around the corner. "What happened?"

"Vaughnie just drove in three," Roarke answered without looking at Max.

"There is a God," O'Bannon said.

Oakland's manager, Tony LaRussa, decided that it was time to change pitchers, and the screen went to a men's cologne commercial. Charles Barkley pretending to be on a fox hunt. Old salts in the department had commented before that the basketball star resembled a younger Blanket McNulty.

Roarke stopped chewing as he stared at Barkley. His eyes glazed over.

"Captain . . . ?"

For the first time, he looked full-on at Dove. At

anyone since Blanket's rosewood casket had been cranked down into the ground. "Yeah, Jim?"

"I just wanted to say I'm sorry about leaving you in the lurch like this."

"How's that?"

"You know, skedaddling off to Training with two vets out of the squad's lineup." Dove meant Blanket and himself.

"We'll manage." Then Roarke jabbed with his fork at the TV. "Look, LaRussa's bringing in Eckersley early. Goddamn A's are falling apart this year. I love it."

Dove glanced toward Kate, then dropped his voice. "I want to come back for a while."

He thought that Roarke hadn't heard him, but then the captain said, *"How?"*

"On detached service."

"Christ, Jim—you mean detached from Training back to the unit you just left?"

"Something like that. I don't care how it's written up." Dove then made sure his eyes remained clear and his voice steady as he added, "I just care about getting the son of a bitch who got Blanket."

Roarke winced. Eckersley had just fanned the next Boston batter. "I dunno, Jim."

Dove checked on Kate again. And frowned. She was talking to Franklin, who was leaning insouciantly against the dining room wall. Dove turned back to Roarke. "It'd just be till we get this blaster. Not a minute more."

"We'll get him," the captain said. "FBI and I are working a lead on the theft of some C-four from Fort Devens."

"You're barking up the wrong tree, Fred."

"Oh really . . . ?"

Dove realized that he'd sounded accusatory. "I just mean this blaster built the bomb from scratch. He distilled the ANFO himself."

"How do you know?"

"I sniffed the crap. Tasted it."

Roarke took a swig of Budweiser, then said, "Well, that's certainly more conclusive than lab analysis." He stared at the screen, but failed to react to another Boston double. "We'll do fine with Franklin. He's a quick study."

Quick study, quick fatality. But Dove knew better than to say it. It had already occurred to him that Roarke might not want an arrest. That way, there'd be no blaster to admit that his anti-handling measures had been rudimentary—and the bomb should have been disarmed instead of detonated.

But then the captain said, "I'll see what I can do. Just temporary, mind you. Did you check in your pager?"

"No, still have it at home," Dove admitted.

Roarke nodded. "You know, Jimbo," he went on as the eighth inning drew to a close on a pop foul, "you're going to make a superb teacher."

"Thanks."

"But don't you think you oughta lighten up a little in the classroom?"

Dove didn't respond.

He said next to nothing for the next few hours. Then, as soon as he felt he gracefully could, he grabbed Kate, said good-bye to Blanket's family, and left.

He was so steamed on the drive to pick up Lizzy at Kate's aunt's in Brookline he scarcely noticed that she was locked in her own silence. Yet, as they skirted Roxbury's black neighborhoods on the drive home, he asked, "What's with you?"

"Nothing."

"Something's with you."

"I said nothing, Jim."

Carrying a sleeping Lizzy from the Wrangler up to the front door, he heard Boomer barking madly from his perch on the back of the loveseat below the bay window.

"Shut up!" he snapped.

"Don't you tell that animal to shut up," Kate warned.

"He's my dog, dammit."

"Don't tell anybody in this house to shut up, James Dove."

He was on the verge of telling *her* to shut up when he thought better of it. "Get the goddamn door for me, will you?"

"Goddamn door," she said, keys jingling furiously. "Right away, Lieutenant Dove."

It coasted open on the darkened living room.

He hesitated a moment, but Lizzy seemed to be growing heavier in his arms. He headed for her bedroom, Boomer barking in tight circles around his legs. "Trip me, dog, and you go to the meat rendering plant first thing in the morning." Then he stepped on the dog's rubber squeaky toy, half-scaring himself to death. "Shit!"

Lizzy was awake by the time Dove rested her on her feet. "Want your mama to help you undress?"

"No," she murmured, rubbing her eyes, "I can."

"Good night, sweetie." He gave her a kiss on the forehead, then went out to the kitchen. The microwave was whirring. Kate was watching a bag of popcorn billow up through the glass door.

"Didn't get enough to eat at the wake?" he asked, realizing at once that his voice was still too strident. He'd thought that he had simmered down.

"Didn't have an appetite at the wake." The bell dinged, and she removed the bag, ripped it open, scattering popcorn all over the floor. She ignored the spill and ate, glaring at him.

Suddenly, he felt too exhausted to hold his own against her. "Think I'll turn in."

"You going to make me ask, Jim?"

"Ask what?"

"Oh, I don't know," she said blithely. "Maybe why you're so chatty with Captain Roarke all of a sudden?"

"What d'you mean? We worked together, for crapsake."

"Of course. Never mind that I've seen you not say two words to him over an entire evening, James Dove." Then she nearly shouted, "Come clean, dammit!"

He broke off gazes with her and took a milk carton from the refrigerator with the hope of easing his churning stomach. "I just want to help out the squad till my replacement gets up to speed."

"Bullshit, you do." She hurled the popcorn bag into the sink. "Besides, Franklin seems competent enough."

"Oh, I'm sure he's smooth. Competence is another matter entirely."

"What kind of racist, shanty Irish shit is that!"

Suddenly, he'd had enough. "It isn't—bombs are color-blind. They give no affirmative action points when they test you. And don't call me shanty Irish, you foulmouthed Southie bohemian!"

She took a step back from him, tears welling in her eyes.

"Oh Jesus." He tried to touch her, but she pressed up against the sink like a cornered animal. "Look, Katie—we've lost Blanket."

"They've lost Blanket. You're not one of them anymore."

"But if I'd been there, maybe we would've gone to a show tonight instead of a wake."

"Oh, I see." Now she was really crying. "You're saying if you hadn't gone off your nut and gotten married McNulty would be alive."

"No, no." He groaned. "I'm saying Blanket's gone. There's nobody else who can find his killer!"

"That's just ego, Dove!"

"Fine, you're right. I'm all ego." With that, he gave up. He went to the cabinet over the refrigerator and took down a shoebox. In it were his revolver, handcuffs, and pager. He then headed for the front door, stringing his gear on his belt along the way. "Don't wait up."

A house across the street from the O'Bradaigh-Doves' showed no lights. No car in the driveway. And newspapers were littered on the veranda behind a lilac bush, where a neighbor had no doubt tried to hide them until the owners returned from vacation.

Gaerity leaned his bicycle against a porch pillar and eased down onto the steps. He sat quietly in the darkness, peering at the house across the street. Both the Wrangler and Dove's motorcycle were parked in the driveway. Light was spilling from the kitchen window onto the sunbrowned side lawn. He could see the shape of Kate's head through the thin curtains. And hear the row going on between the newlyweds.

"Ah, love can be a torment," Gaerity whispered.

A firefly winked on a few inches in front of his eyes.

Reacting instantly, he captured it in his cupped hands, then peeked through a tiny hole he created by slightly relaxing his curled thumb and forefinger. Suddenly the cramped blackness inside his hand flashed brilliantly. A miniature explosion.

He freed the little beetle into the night.

The front door across the street slammed shut, and Liam came hurtling down the walkway. Gaerity leaned back into the mottled shadow of the lilac bush.

Liam straddled his motorcycle, started the engine, and sped down the street. Quite recklessly, Gaerity believed.

* * *

Three hours after leaving the house, Dove felt cooled down enough to sleep, maybe. He cut the Harley's engine well down the block and coasted into the driveway. He was glad to see that the Wrangler was still there. While downing several Harps in a Somerville pub, he'd had visions of Kate packing up and leaving for a few days. Or weeks.

She was only human. And he'd been inhuman.

In passing, Dove felt the Jeep's hood. It was only faintly warm. No lights were visible through the windows. Kate had gone to bed, then. Thank God for sleep, or quarrels would last forever.

The front door was unlocked.

Dove frowned. Had he forgotten? Probably. Anger made a fool of man. Made him neglect his family, as his own father had. Sent him off into the dark to get buzzed. Brought him home dissipated and staggering.

Boomer yipped twice from his bed in the bathroom, then shut up. He knew a mean drunk when he smelled one.

Dove made sure he locked the door from the inside. Twice. There was danger on the other side of that door. A cop knew it better than anyone. Kate, ever trusting, generous to a fault, knew it less than anyone he'd ever met. She strolled through the worst sections of Boston as if angels were clearing the way for her. Maybe that was one of the things that had attracted him to her. But old Mrs. McNulty knew. It showed in how she'd calmly gone about the business of grieving her son today. She had no doubt whatsoever that it was a shitty, perilous world with mercy for no one.

He stopped in the darkened kitchen, flipped on a switch.

Popcorn still all over the linoleum. The milk carton

was overturned, resting on its own white pool on the sinkboard. He couldn't recall having done that either.

Not like Kate to leave a mess.

He hurried to the master bedroom door, started to turn on the overhead fixture, but then stopped himself. He could hear her breathing. A reassuring sound like waves breaking on a sandy shore.

He shut her door, then went back to the kitchen for the pack of Camel filters he'd squirreled away before he'd made a half-assed declaration to quit smoking on Saint Valentine's Day. Five fingers of O'Bannon's Christmas gift of Bushmill's Irish had survived a few previous nights as rough as this one.

Dove carried the smokes and whiskey out into the living room, set them on Kate's old upright piano. Making do with the light filtering in from the kitchen, he idly plinked out a few notes, then lit the cigarette. Lovely habit, smoking. Calmed the nerves, provided companionship on a lonely night. But bad in the long term.

"Ah, there's the rub," he said softly.

The squad had conditioned him to think only in the short term. Two days of wine, women, and song before the next disarming—and the possibility of sudden oblivion. Now here was pretty Kate all at once, tugging on the other end of the rope, making him think long term at every turn.

Dove repeated the same notes.

"What song's that?" a small voice asked from the hallway.

" 'The Ministrel Boy,' sweetheart." He habitually fell into it every time he sat down at a keyboard. It'd been the first tune to catch his fancy. A band had played it while the Republican flag was raised at a Sinn Fein picnic down in County Armagh. Sinn Fein, the political arm of the IRA. Different world. He couldn't have been much older than Lizzy that day, and the tears had flowed while he listened. Never before had he felt so proud, so wronged.

Lizzy crossed the room to him, sat beside him on the bench. Dove had played a few more measures when she interrupted, "No, I mean the words, Jimmy."

"Oh, they're too sad for a night like this."

"Please."

He had a sip of whiskey, then sang quietly:

> *"The minstrel boy to the war has gone.*
> *In the ranks of death you will find him.*
> *His father's sword he has girded on . . ."*

That was enough. He took a long drag off his Camel.

"You smell like beer," Lizzy noted.

"I'm drinking whiskey."

"But you *been* drinking beer too."

"You might consider a career with the Traffic Bureau."

Dove was laboring to tinkle out some spare blues, a la Duke Ellington, but Lizzy interrupted again. "Did it hurt when Blanket died?"

Then it hit Dove. This was her first death. Kate's parents had both passed away years before Lizzy was born. Nobody had given a second thought to what she was feeling, least of all James Dove. "Do you mean did it hurt me, darling?" he asked without giving her time to answer. "Yes, very much. He was my friend, and it made me feel . . . I don't know . . . *safe* just to be around him. Sometimes we like people just because they make us feel safe."

Lizzy was quiet for several seconds. "Not what I meant, Jimmy. Did it hurt Blanket?"

Holy God. Dove snubbed out his cigarette in the potted fern. It had fallen on him to explain death. But telling her to ask Kate would feel like a cop-out. "Some people think dying's like going up into a beautiful light."

"Do you?"

"Sometimes. And maybe Blanket just went faster into the light than most."

He could see her take it in. Then doubt burgeoned in her eyes, the doubt that would now last a lifetime.

"I really don't know, love," he finally admitted.

10

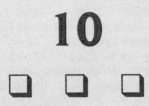

Dove stared down into the river.

He'd once believed that the human mind was only a tool for gauging dangers and opportunities. But he'd been wrong. It was a knot that fastened distant things together. The Charles here and the Lagan River in Belfast became one behind his eyes. The same industrial-spawned haze dimmed the shores. The same faces of the dead appeared out of the murk and then vanished back into it. He didn't know how long he'd been peering down into the flow, seeing the present and past in one nauseating jumble, when a voice said from behind, "What're the currents telling you, Lieutenant?"

Dove spun around.

Franklin offered a guarded smile. He was wearing a fawn-colored sports coat and a shirt without a tie.

"They're telling me we're missing what happened here," Dove said.

"Like what?"

Dove shook his head. One lane of bumper-to-bumper traffic was being allowed over the River Street Bridge by traffic cops at both approaches. Welders were mending the girders near the seat of the blast, their sparks dripping off into the water. "What're you doing here?" he asked.

Franklin shrugged. "Dispatch told me you phoned out here. I was in the neighborhood. Thought I might pick up a couple pointers." He paused. "Right answer?"

"It'll do." Dove gazed up at the blasted tower of the bridge. The riggers were already getting ready for the painters. Soon the only evidence of what had happened here would be buried in the P.D.'s Records Bureau. Amazing how life went on after something like this. A sudden thought made him frown. "Were you with the captain when he tried to disarm the drum?"

"No, I was standing with McNulty on the south anchor. But Roarke walked down to us right after he decided to give up."

Careful here, Dove reminded himself. The captain was still his boss now that he was apparently attached to the squad again, although Roarke hadn't gotten back to him with a firm decision on the matter from the brass.

Dove began walking toward the south shore. "Did he say what types of anti-handling triggers he'd seen?"

"No," Franklin said, catching up, the tail of his coat folding back over his holstered automatic. "Roarke just said there was a shitpot full of them."

"He saw these with his light?"

"Didn't use a light. McNulty said something about the possibility of an infrared trigger."

Dove vaulted over the parapet railing and started down the embankment. Franklin slipped on the slick soles of his patent-leather shoes but saved his dignity by planting an arm against the slope.

"So Roarke told McNulty to get the Barrett and set up for a shot."

"That's right, Lieutenant."

"Did the captain tell him where to shoot from?"

"Not that I heard. I got the feeling that was left up to McNulty."

Dove pointed at a catwalk. It'd been bent inward as if by a gigantic thumb. "Is that where he was found?"

"Yeah," Franklin said quietly.

A corpse sprawled on the square in Crossmaglen. A lorry spinning through the flames. Dove shook off the images. "Who found him first?"

"Me, I guess. Everybody came running down here as soon as the smoke cleared."

Lucky a second device, radio-controlled, hadn't taken them all out, Dove thought. But he knew that he'd already made this point to Franklin. Maybe Roarke was right: he was leaning on them too hard. But, then again, maybe Roarke was wrong. "Was McNulty still against the door?"

Franklin nodded, obviously reliving the moment.

"And the rifle—did you have to pry it out of him?"

"No." Franklin paused, looking a little ill. "Why would that matter?"

"It tells me that the air pressure of the blast hit Blanket straight-on. Right back toward the muzzle of the Barrett. Had the overpressure come at him from the side, you might've had to dislodge the rifle to get him in the body bag."

"Jesus. No offense, Lieutenant—but how can you talk about your friend that way?"

"Because, wherever he is," Dove said evenly, "Blanket's relying on me to get the son of a bitch who killed him."

Pulling himself together, Franklin nodded, then gestured at the catwalk. "Why'd he decide to shoot from there?"

Dove climbed up, careful not to open his palms on any torn metal edges. Franklin clambered after him, his gold academy ring chiming on the rungs. Dove checked the line of sight to the cross-beam on which the drum had been perched. "It was the safest place," he finally explained. "Almost zero likelihood of shrapnel. See that brace in the way?"

"It *seemed* the safest place," Franklin said.

"That's right. You're getting the picture."

Turning, Dove examined the steel door to a maintenance area in a recess under the south anchor. It had been buckled as if a sack of cement had been dropped on it from a thousand feet—the force with which Blanket had been driven back. Yet that kind of blast overpressure at just one point wasn't consistent with the general pattern of damage. The center of the span hadn't been collapsed, and there might've been enough explosive to accomplish that packed in the fifty-gallon drum Roarke had described in his report.

An iron-hard fist of compressed air had found the very man who'd dared to confront the device.

"Can I ask what you're thinking, Lieutenant?"

"If there's a clock, you assume there's a clockmaker."

"Pardon?"

"Just what I said."

"Sorry, I must've been sick the day they covered metaphysics at the academy."

Dove gave the buckled door a kick. "Somebody designed this effect. This is no more an accident of nature than a clock is."

"How'd the blaster do it?"

Then Dove saw. The counterweight to the lift bridge. Most of the huge chunk of steel had rusted to a vermilion color, but one area had been scuffed down to bright metal.

Again, he glanced at the dented door. Then he said, "Son of a bitch."

"What?"

Dove pointed. "Most of the bomb's force was

aimed up at that tower ..." Its base was mangled—
even the squad rookie had to see what he was talking
about. "But that drum was like a bazooka. There was
a recoil. Where'd it go?"

"Down."

"Angling toward the Cambridge shore."

"Then where?"

Franklin's eyes went blank. Finally, he hiked his
shoulders. "Sorry—"

"Autopsy report said McNulty died from concussion. Don't you see?"

"Well—"

"Watch this, dammit." With his right fist, Dove
traced the path of the residual force as it had
slammed into and then off the counterweight Saturday night. "The bastard bounced it."

"Bounced? Wait, you're saying he shaped the
residual?"

"Yeah—and then played it for a bank shot. Look
at all the angles. That's skill at work. Not chance.
Awesome skill on an order we haven't seen around
here ... until now."

Franklin was massaging his forehead with a hand.
"He was *aiming* for Blanket?"

"Bingo, Sister Mary. I think we have a winner."

"But ... how'd he know where to—"

"You said it yourself. This seemed the safest place.
He knew our shooter would set up here. What's the
second most predictable thing next to the sun coming up?"

Franklin slowly shook his head.

"And Roarke said you were a fast study," Dove
said. "Cops and how they respond to incidents. We
are so goddamn predictable it hurts!"

The sergeant looked shell-shocked. He glanced
over the web of intricate angles one more time, then
said, "He wasn't trying to really fuck with the bridge.

Damage wasn't what he wanted. He was trying to kill one of us."

Maybe he was a quick study, after all.

Both their beepers started chirping. They climbed down from the catwalk and jogged up the embankment.

"You on your Harley?" Franklin asked.

"Yeah."

"Want a lift?"

"No, I'll make better time on the hog." Dove whipped his cellular from his jacket pocket and speed-dialed dispatch. The traffic noise and hiss of the welding torches forced him to ask the dispatcher to repeat herself. "IED at Copley Square," he finally told Franklin, and they parted company.

Actually, Dove had hoped that the motorcycle ride would calm him down before he reached the square. His chest felt tight, and his mouth was dry. Boston no longer felt like Boston. It felt like Belfast, a war zone. He almost expected to see troops in full battle dress, window-shopping when not clearing the kids off the corners if more than two of them gathered together.

He threaded through the cars, ignoring the horns that brayed at him.

It was early rush hour, and Commonwealth Avenue came to a halt in both directions east of the Back Bay Fens. The stench of this long, meandering swampland was especially sour today. Like peat bogs. Standing at a train door, watching County Armagh roll past greenly through an open window. The smell of bogs and reed-choked ponds filled his nostrils. *I'll only be down in Crossmaglen for a wee bit . . . and then I'm back to you.* He had decided that her business down in that border town had nothing to do with family. Her kin were from Tandragee, at least twenty miles from Crossmaglen. And three other members of the cell had left Belfast at first light with Gaerity. He had begun to fear the power Ryan had over her. Over himself.

Dove took to the center divider and went on full throttle, his necktie fluttering over his shoulder.

Kate was right. He'd had enough. Every sign was against what he was doing. Roarke didn't want him back.

If only Blanket hadn't been killed. This afternoon, Dove would be wrapping up another day of teaching. Getting ready to go home. Beers and a barbecue, lounging in the backyard with Kate and Lizzy. That was what he truly wanted. What he needed to make Boston feel like good old Beantown again. Normalcy. How precious it was. The thing for which he'd come to the New World. Not adventure. He'd had more than enough excitement by the time he'd turned sixteen.

He sped up Dartmouth Street, past Old South Church, and to the edge of the cordon there. The patrolmen waved him through. A line of fire engines and ambulances were waiting in the shade of the public library. He parked on the west side of Copley Square and walked toward the bomb squad truck. Bad place for a blast to thunder around in. The square was enclosed by tall structures, especially on the east with the Romanesque spires of Trinity Church and the John Hancock Tower.

Striding in and out of shadow, Dove shivered a little.

A department chopper was doing figure-eights overhead, mostly to drive off the news aircraft. Its rotor was beating loudly against the heavy air.

He met Rita and Cortez beside the truck. They were just returning with Manfred. "Just a tease, Jimmy," Rita said, her relief evident in her smile. "Some moron's idea of a joke."

"Where is it?" Dove asked.

"In the trolley over there." One of the tourist buses made to look like an old municipal car.

Cortez said, patting the robot, "Our boy did good today. Give me a hand, Lieutenant?"

"Sure." Dove helped him hoist Manfred up into the back of the truck. "This son of a bitch putting on weight?"

"That he is. And it's all in *cojones*. Shoulda seen him take down that tease."

"Where's Roarke?" Dove asked, looking around, counting the vehicles that remained parked in the area after the evacuation. Lots of them. Had they been searched?

"Captain's still in the trolley." Rita lit up, coughed. "He's waiting for the reporter-photographer from the *Globe*. Wants to assure the public after the River Street fiasco that all's well."

"Right." Dove cut across the square, checking the trash receptacles along the way. The lighting fixtures in the planters. The perfect location for the blaster to use an improvised claymore mine, a shrapnel bomb. Reaching the trolley, he went around it twice, ducking repeatedly to inspect the undercarriage.

Franklin came up from behind. "Durgin says it's just a dummy."

"So are you if you don't search for a second device. Check under the engine cowling. Carefully. Remember pressure releases?"

"Wouldn't the team have already done this?"

Dove looked out from under the chassis and glared at him.

"Sorry," Franklin said as he moved for the engine.

At last, Dove entered the trolley. Another device was here in the square somewhere. He was sure of it, particularly since the first was a tease.

Roarke was holding on to a handstrap, his hair plastered to his scalp with sweat. He watched Dove come up the aisle and smiled only at the last second. "Jimbo."

"Cap."

An empty shoebox lay on the seat nearest Roarke. Neatly stacked next to it were a wad of crepe paper, an egg timer, a length of what looked to be speaker wire, and a pancake of flesh-colored putty, on which Dove scraped a fingernail and sniffed. He was sure but wanted to be more than sure. Franklin had just stepped into the bus, so Dove snapped, "Find me a newspaper."

The sergeant searched the seats, came up with a sports section. "Good enough?"

"Fine." Dove picked up the pancake and pressed the newsprint against it. The putty accepted the text. Genuine plastique wouldn't do that.

"I could've told you it was Silly Putty and not the real stuff, Jimbo," Roarke said drolly.

Dove made no comment.

The captain caught Franklin's eye. "Anthony, see if you can't hunt up that reporter from the *Globe*. We can't wait here all day."

"Sure thing."

Franklin drummed down the back steps, and Roarke let go of the handstrap. He sat down. "It's not gonna fly, Jim."

"What's not?"

"Bringing you back to the squad on temporary duty."

Dove paused. "That's the decision?"

Roarke began chewing on a nail, then made himself stop. "Oh, you know how the brass is. It's a decision and it's not a decision. They *suggested* now that you're paid through the Training budget it's best for all concerned if you train. I mean, they didn't come right out and say no. They never do."

"Then they left it up to you," Dove said.

"What?"

"Sounds like they gave you some latitude to call the shot on this one."

Roarke shifted uncomfortably in the worn trolley seat, then checked his watch. "Jim, I'd need some kind of crisis to take this on my own shoulders. Don't you see?"

Yes, Dove thought to himself, all too perfectly. A vacancy was coming up in the next few months. Commander of Special Ops. "You've got that crisis, Captain."

"I do?"

"The River Street Bridge blaster is targeting us."

"Us?"

"The squad. Maybe just one member."

"Why?"

"I don't know, sir. He hasn't written his autobiography, that I know of."

"Oh Jimbo." Roarke smiled vacantly. "I can hear 'em now if I take that argument upstairs. You're just blowing steam, Fred. And then what happens when the day comes I honestly need additional support from another division?"

"You need it now."

Roarke sat back. "What's that supposed to mean?"

Dove picked up the Silly Putty and examined it if only to keep himself from answering. He flopped it over into his other palm. On the back, something was incised into the surface of the material. He angled it to get a better view from the sunlight streaming in through the windows. Backward letters in relief:

ᗡ Ǝ Я ꟻ И A

There was a seventh letter, but it was distorted. Maybe N. No, Dove decided after a few moments, M.

He quickly asked Roarke, "Did this stuff come in contact with Manfred's logo during the takedown?"

"What?"

"The logo on his head."

"Uh . . . no. He just handled it with his claws."

"Nobody was screwing around, slapping this stuff on the robot?"

"Of course not."

Dove grabbed Roarke's radio handset off the seat and bolted through the back door. "Cortez! Rita!" he cried, running for the truck. But the chopper was in the middle of the leg that took it directly over the square, and he doubted that either of them could hear him over the echoing rotor wash. Still, he kept trying. "Get away from Manfred! Away from the truck!" Nothing but squelch noise came back at him. He flung the radio aside and sprinted. Yet it was like running a race in a nightmare. His legs moved, his breath came out in little explosions, but he seemed to cover no ground.

The facades of the library and Trinity Church bleared into another time, another square. He was running through an outdoor market. Brightly colored fruits. Green vegetables. Mounds of cabbages. Women, their faces framed by kerchiefs, startled as he ran past. Children shrieked as he called for them to move aside. Ahead, Dove saw the lorry pulling away from him. Four teenagers, including Gaerity, sat in the bed, squeezed between bushel baskets of produce. The fifth member of the cell drove.

Ryan grinned and waved.

"Gaerity!" Dove cried out to him, begging him to stop, for he had glimpsed the bulky thing sprouting wires attached to the lorry's undercarriage. "Ryan, please!"

Dove crashed into a vendor's stall, tomatoes bouncing all around, and scrambled up again. "Shiofra, stop him!"

Just when he thought he'd lost the lorry for good, the driver slowed. Dove closed the distance, but

Gaerity bounded from the bed and dropped him with a crack on the head from the butt of his pistol.

Dove's vision went to white, and he could taste blood where the blow had made him bite his tongue. When he could see again, two British soldiers were hurrying toward the lorry, fingers on the triggers of their assault rifles.

He half-turned, his ears still ringing, and watched helplessly as Shiofra and the three others, faces hidden under black hoods now, reached down among the baskets for their own weapons, Sten guns and sawed-off twelve-gauges. They were trapped in and around the lorry, forced to make their stand there, for two more Royal grenadiers were charging across the square to reinforce the first pair.

Where was Gaerity?

Dove rolled over and saw Ryan across the square. In his hands was his latest fascination, the remote control for a flying model airplane. The plane had been discarded and the device altered to ignite explosives from a safe distance.

Crying out, Dove lunged forward at a frantic crawl, quickly staggered to his feet, and raced for Gaerity, who looked terribly disappointed. Betrayed. Astonished that his most loyal comrade would turn against him. Dove slammed into him just as Ryan poised both thumbs over the frequency transmission button. The two boys went down to the pavement with Dove thinking that he'd caught Gaerity in time. But then, sickeningly, he felt a hot, blinding wind pass over him. A sound like the Banshee's howl. Mixed in it, faintly, were the screams of women and children.

Dove could see the lorry tumbling through the air. Then he covered his head with his sweater as the fireball reached out to him, sucked the air out of his lungs, and passed on. Chunks of hot metal and asphalt danced around him. Flinching, he crept forward on his knees and elbows to a body. Hand trembling, he reached out and rolled up the black hood to reveal the scorched and misshapen face beneath.

"Help me, Liam," she said, her eyes fixed dully on his. "Help me."

"Shiofra."

"Help me."

He grasped her hand, which squeezed back, weakly. "He said he'd never use you like this. He promised."

Help me, Liam.

Someone pounded on Dove's back with an open hand. He ignored it as he begged Shiofra to hang on. He'd get her to a hospital. The hand roughly took hold of his neck and shook him."

"Lieutenant!"

Dove looked behind. It was Franklin. His fawn-colored sports coat was dark with soot.

"Lieutenant, let go of her! She's gone!"

"Gone?" He faced Shiofra again. Yet it was no longer the girl in the black hood before him. It was no longer her hand he clasped. It was Rita Durgin's. She was sprawled atop the rear door to the squad's truck, her back bent at an unnatural angle, her uniform smoldering.

Beyond her, the truck itself lay on its side, crackling with flame.

"Where's Cortez?" Dove finally asked.

"I don't know," Franklin said. "Still in the truck, I guess. Gone. Let's get you up on your feet, man."

With the sergeant's help, Dove stood, but then almost fell from dizziness.

"You hit anywhere?" a paramedic asked him.

Dove stared blankly at the white uniform. "See to Rita."

"She's dead. I'm asking you if you're hurt."

Dove seized a handful of white cloth and twisted. "Rita, you son of a bitch!"

"He's in shock," the paramedic said to Franklin. "Get him over to the ambulance. I'll be there in a minute."

Franklin supported him over to a bench, sat him down. "I may as well come out and say it, Dove. When you're right, you're really right."

"Yeah," he said bleakly, "it's grand to be right." Then he grabbed Franklin by the lapels. "Here's what you do. Work the perimeter. He's probably still here. Looking down from a window. Standing right in the middle of the crowd. This was probably too big for him to miss."

"How will I know him?"

Dove hesitated. "You'll just know him. Gut instinct. Listen to your instincts. He'll be smug. Too cool. He won't break off eye contact. Maybe foreign. Clothes of a different cut."

"All right," Franklin said. "Anything you say."

The sergeant had no sooner gone than Dove's cellular phone rang. He took it from his jacket pocket. The case was cracked, but it still worked. It was a moment before he could hold it steady against his ear. "Yes."

11

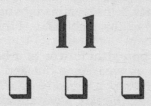

"**Y**es," said the older but still familiar voice at the other end. Sirens were wailing in the background.

Gaerity sat in a deep easy chair with his feet propped up on an ottoman. He was holding his wristwatch in his right hand. His eyes were on its face as he said, "Hello, Liam. It's been a very long time . . . hasn't it?" Then, grinning, he timed the silence.

Exactly thirty-four seconds elapsed before McGivney said, "Ryan."

"You don't sound awfully surprised, Liam."

"I might've been this morning. Not now. Not after you left your calling card in the trolley."

"Damn sporting of me, wouldn't you say?" Gaerity strapped his watch back on his wrist. "At least I gave you a running start. More than you gave me." He went on leafing through the family photograph album he'd rested on his lap. "I had the Royal Special Air Service on my heels all the way into County Monaghan that night. Nothing like a crack British anti-terrorist squad to keep a fella on his toes. Well, at least I had six years of relative freedom before Interpol nabbed me in West Berlin."

"How'd you get to the robot?" McGivney asked.

"Listen, I don't mean to lecture Boston's finest—but you could learn a thing or two from the old country. Always best to include a barracks as part of your headquarters complex. All I had to do was by-pass the foil strip sensor on a window last night and I had the run of the place till seven this morning, when . . . Who's the good old boy who farts like a foghorn—Maner? Yes, I believe it's Maner. He showed to open the shop."

Another troubled silence.

"Oh, I know exactly what you're thinking, Liam," Gaerity said. "Now we've got to sweep the whole bloody building. One thing after another."

"Is this a sanctioned hit?"

Gaerity asked coyly, "Sanctioned?"

"The leadership collective of the old group. Did they send you here? If they did, come after me, you son of a bitch. Not my friends."

"Calm down, Liam. I can tell you're having a difficult time with your temper. You must learn to manage it. God knows I did in Castle Gleigh. A stone cell is a very tight space in which to be left alone with your anger." Gaerity yawned and stretched. He heard a slight wheeze beneath him. Reaching down between the seat cushion and the arm of the chair, he found a rubber toy in the shape of a dog bone. It wheezed like an asthmatic when he gave it a squeeze. "No, Liam. I'm not here for the old gang. I've outgrown that. The IRA and all its misguided splinters. They're nothing more than territorial terrorists." He paused, examining the fang-chewed toy. "Dogs are territorial."

"Then *why?*"

"To give you pain and ease my own. I'd love to give you my pain. But that's not humanly possible. I can't put you in a stone cell for seventeen years, can I? So my options are few." Gaerity glanced at a photograph of McGivney with Lizzy and Kate wrapped around him. "Interesting, but few."

"I didn't kill those kids. Neither did the Brits. You did. You're the reason they died. Not me."

"I could care less about that. You talked, Liam."

"Like hell I did. I ran. All the way to Boston."

"On your lonesome?"

"No, I had help. Both sides of the Atlantic."

"From whom?"

"Sinn Fein."

A new wrinkle, but it changed nothing for Gaerity. "You betrayed the cause, boy-o."

"Shit," McGivney hissed, losing his enforced calm entirely now, "you never gave a damn about the cause. You just got your rocks off by—"

"*Rocks?*"

"—your puny little balls off by using people and then destroying them. And you really creamed in your jeans if you could do both at the same time. Say it, you're enraged because I had the guts to cross you!"

"Yes!" Gaerity roared. "I took you, a waif born of rummies, befriended you, lifted you out of the gutter, and made you a Titan! A leveler of cities, a destroyer of worlds!"

"I wasn't a Titan, Ryan. I was a soldier in an ugly little war. And I drew the line at killing civilians."

"The line, boy-o?" Gaerity asked contemptuously, recovering his calm. "Do you think a smattering of Latin and a headful of catechism prepared you to see an inch further than your ginhead of a father did? I hate to tell you, but there is no line. And if you make on, it's as artificial as the Greenwich meridian. There is no division between right and wrong. They are one, hopelessly intertwined like a ball of snakes. Kali and Vishnu are one. Out of death came life." He flung the dog toy across the living room, and it bounced off an upright piano. "Ever hear of the Big

Bang? They think the universe was created by blast. Imagine that—an explosion was the seat of creation!"

"Oh Christ."

"I taught you how to pay true homage to that, McGivney." Gaerity dropped the photo album to the floor and rose from the chair. He could hear a car pulling into the driveway. "And how did you repay me? You cast me into a hole for seventeen years."

"I can't believe I ever bought your shit."

"You still do—and I'll prove it, Liam. I now present you with a moral dilemma. A riddle, if you like. Let's see if you have the imagination to deal with it. River Street Bridge and Copley Square were just the beginning. You can save your dear ones or your hard-won incognito of James Dove. Can't have it both ways . . . or can you? See, here's the nasty bit— I *did* talk when they finally got hold of me. I told them you helped that day in the market. Have you checked yourself out lately on the Interpol network?"

McGivney was finally shouting. "I'll find you, you son of a bitch!"

"Oh, I'm sure you will. Must run now. Kate and Lizzy just got home."

Franklin had no clear idea what he was looking for. There was no personality profile for the average blaster, as there was for the typical arsonist. But he did as Dove had said, worked the crowd behind the cordon, scanned the windows of the surrounding buildings even though all of them had been evacuated.

Three casualties in five days.

The bomb squad was not SWAT. In all his months with the team no one had been hurt.

Secretly, he wanted out. He wasn't sleeping well, and twice he'd caught himself snapping at Cecily, his girl, over nothing. But he couldn't bring himself to ask for a reassignment. Naturally, there would be career repercussions. He'd be sent back to Patrol supervision, graveyard shift, and might wind up being marooned there for years. But that wasn't it. He wanted to leave the bomb squad on his own terms. He wanted to be as good as Dove when he finally pulled the plug.

The lieutenant was an emotional basket case—Franklin could now see him screaming at somebody on his cellular phone—and maybe even a closet bigot. But he was the key to surviving this detail. It amazed Franklin that Roarke had lasted as long as he had, let alone kept all his fingers. No, Dove was the one who had the knowledge, and that is what drew Franklin to him.

Finally, he came across someone with a foreign cut to his clothes. Long sleeves on a summer day and baggy trousers. He wore a dark, brooding expression and refused to glance away when Franklin stared directly at him. "May I please see some identification, sir?" he demanded, flashing his wallet badge.

"Fuck you, pal."

"*What?*"

"I'm the assistant coroner." He flashed his own badge. "Is it safe to drive my station wagon in there yet? They'll be sending somebody out to pick up my fucking body if I have to wait any longer."

"I'll check with my lieutenant."

"Do it."

Smoldering, Franklin crossed the square back to Dove. He immediately realized that he should never have left the man alone. He was ghastly pale, his phone dangling from his limp right hand.

"Lieutenant?"

Dove continued to stare off into space.

"Sir, I think maybe you ought to lie down on the bench. You know, elevate your feet."

But Dove suddenly stirred and began dialing. Franklin saw him press two buttons, then stop and disconnect. The buttons had been the nine and the one. Then he was up and running. It happened with the suddenness of a good wide receiver bursting from the line.

"Lieutenant!"

But Dove had mounted his Harley and was turning around in the middle of Dartmouth Street, sparks shooting from one of the foot pegs as it scraped the asphalt.

Kate went through the front door but paused in the middle of the living room. Dove was home early. The ottoman wasn't pushed flush against the easy chair, as he always left it, and one of the photo albums lay open on the carpet. Good, she thought. He had taken time off to think about things. His bike was probably in the side yard. "Jim?"

Lizzy came in from the front porch, having dawdled there a few moments to talk across the street to Sandra, her friend, who'd just returned from vacation. "Put Boomer's toy in his bed for me, bug," Kate said. "James Dove?"

There wasn't an answer from the house or the backyard, so she assumed that there was no truce in the war of silence that had begun the evening of McNulty's wake. "Screw it," she whispered to herself. She wouldn't be the first to go to the negotiating table. He was the one with the testosterone time bomb slowly ticking away in his groin.

She went to the kitchen and opened the refrigerator.

There was a flash and a faint popping noise.

She crouched for a better look inside. "Shit." The bulb had finally blown. She heard Lizzy's steps behind her. "You thirsty, bug?"

"I'd like red juice, please."

Kate poured her a glass, then, on a sudden curiosity, went through the back screen door and out onto the stairs overlooking the yard. "Boomer?"

Lizzy came to her side, a cherry-red mustache on her upper lip. "He musta dug under the fence again."

"We'll find him." Back inside the kitchen, Kate asked, "You want to cook dinner tonight?"

"Yeah! Can I invite Sandra over?"

"I'll call her mom and ask. What're you going to make?"

"Garlic toast."

"First let's see how we're set for the fixings." Kate tugged on the pantry door. It finally gave with a click. Dove had installed magnetic closers to keep Boomer from prying it open with a paw. The dog was a natural-born burglar.

She fumbled for the pull-chain, yanked gently, and the neon light inside the pantry came on with a hum. "Yeah, you can make garlic toast."

"Will you call, Mom?"

In the living room, Kate found more evidence of Dove's brief stay. The telephone was disconnected from the wall jack. Another good sign? He hadn't wanted to be disturbed. He was taking stock of things. Didn't want the department to interrupt.

She got down on her knees and plugged in the phone cord.

"Mom," Lizzy asked from the kitchen, "can I start the oven?"

"Hang on a minute. And use the broiler." Dialing, she heard the tick-tick-tick of a burner being ignited. "Stop it, Lizzy. Besides, that's not the broiler!" Sandra's mother answered, and a shorthand conversation followed. Kate hung up and caught Lizzy starting her second burner. "No, it's the one on the right. Sandra can come."

Yet another ring of blue flame erupted.

"That's your left, dumb," Kate said, smiling as she

turned the burners off. "Which hand do you pledge allegiance with?"

"Oh yeah." Lizzy's small hand touched over her heart, then finally reached for the correct knob.

Dove used the walkway of the Broadway Bridge to speed into South Boston. Rush hour had arrived in full, and nothing was moving within ten miles of downtown. But he found the narrow corridors between the cars, even if it meant scraping paint.

Damn Gaerity. He built an anti-handling device into everything he did.

Yet Dove told himself that he wouldn't have relied on the department in any event. He was now no more than two minutes from the house. Had he stayed with the phone, the call could still be tied up in dispatch as the communications sergeant lit up a Havatampa and pondered which patrol unit he most wanted to pull out of dinner.

"Fuck you, Gaerity!" Dove cried, the sole of his left shoe chittering as he made a sharp turn. His anger kept overpowering his fear for Kate and Lizzy. He was already thinking of revenge, and he knew that was only a symptom of his helplessness.

Several blocks ahead, an engine company, running with lights and siren, flashed past on the cross street Dove himself meant to use. A ladder truck followed close behind, and finally an ambulance.

"No!" He weaved in and out of the traffic, standing on the pegs every few hundred yards to look for a plume of smoke rising out of the southeast. He had brought this to Kate's door. He knew already he would never forgive himself for that. Killing Gaerity would never be enough to erase it.

He motored down their street, afraid to see the house.

But it was still standing. The windows were still intact to reflect the late afternoon sun. He dumped the Harley on the lawn and sprinted around to the side of the house. Vaulting over the fence, he glanced at the gate. It was clean. Next he hurried to the underside of the exterior wooden stairs. A quick check, then he climbed to the kitchen screen door and halted without touching it.

Through the mesh, he could dimly see Kate and Lizzy. They were standing at the stove. "Either of you already come through this door?"

"Yes," Kate said. "Why?"

He entered. "Get Lizzy out of the house. Where's Boomer?"

"Gone. Under the fence again. Jim, what's wrong?"

"Get out, Kate," he said as insistently as he could without shouting. "Now." He held the screen door open for them. Lizzy looked scared to death as she went past, but there was nothing he could do about that for the moment. He grabbed a flashlight from a drawer. "Go through the side gate. Get to a neighbor's."

"It's all right, bug," Kate said to Lizzy, avoiding Dove's gaze as she scurried the girl before her down the stairs.

He started with the living room.

Gaerity hadn't detonated his device upon Kate's arrival home. That was no cause for immediate celebration. It might mean that he'd rigged it with a delay mechanism. God only knew that he wouldn't go with something as simple as an alarm clock. A thermal delay maybe, set to blow with the cooling of the night air. Or a battery with a short lifespan. A water drip system. The list went on and on.

Dove left everything as he'd found it. If an appliance was on, it stayed on. If off, it remained off. Kneeling, he scanned the carpet for bulges, pressure-reactive switches. Then he ran his hands behind the stereo, unscrewed the smoke alarm, and disassembled the thermostat. He climbed through the crawl-space into the torrid attic, dumped out the contents of Kate's mother's old steamer trunks, riffled frantically through a century of family memorabilia. His clothes sopping wet with perspiration, he went down to the basement next, taking the service panels off the washer and dryer, the furnace, and the water heater.

He grew light-headed from fatigue and dehydration.

He returned to the kitchen on his last sweep of the house, drank from the tap, soaked his head. He figured that, had Gaerity planted anything in this room, Kate and Lizzy most likely would have already tripped it off.

Hall closet.

He couldn't recall if he'd already been through it.

Drying his hair with one of Kate's tea towels, he shuffled down the hall and opened the door. He looked inside for a long moment, then spun away, covering his mouth with the towel.

Boomer was inside, dead, dangling on his leash from the hanger bar.

From the sidewalk, Kate heard a shovel striking the earth in the backyard. She hesitated, turned for the neighbor's, but then strode for the gate. "Jim?"

No answer but the thunk of the spade biting into the earth.

Angry now that he refused to speak, she cracked the gate and peeked into the twilit yard. Dove was digging a hole. He paused briefly, his face glistening with sweat, then went on digging.

Boomer was lying on his side near it, obviously dead.

"Oh Jimmy," she said.

"My name is Liam." He added nothing more, just went on digging.

She went the rest of the way into the yard, sank into a lawn chair. She had known for months now that this was coming, that one day the revelation would break free and nothing would be the same from then on. She felt a strange buzzing inside her head, just as she had when hearing that her father had died in a boating accident, her mother two years later of cancer. This was like learning of a death.

"Liam what?" she finally asked. Her tone was flat.

"McGivney." He jiggled the handle to penetrate the tough mat of grass, then stopped. He looked up. The evening star had risen over the sumac tree in the rear of the yard. "I've never even been to Philadelphia. I was born and raised in Belfast."

Somehow, she knew all this. None of it was unexpected. He was too careful in how he talked. Like someone masking an accent to blend in. "And Belfast has finally made it here."

"No use keeping anything from you."

"I wish you'd seen that sooner . . . Liam."

"Rather like how you say it." He began digging again. "So, you see, it wasn't the job. Not completely. I'd accumulated more than enough of the stuff of nightmares before I ever got to Boston. I didn't have a childhood like you or Lizzy. Grew up with troops on the corners. Armored vehicles at the crossroads. Sting of tear gas, and so-and-so from the neighborhood gunned down by the Ulster Defense Association." At last, he looked at her. "Know how black children sometimes look up to pimps and drug dealers? Works the same the world over. My idol was an adolescent terrorist who knew how to turn bleach into bombs. A bright, funny, charismatic sociopath who made me feel important for the first time in my life. Made me feel as if I had prospects. A destiny."

"What happened over there? What d'you keep dreaming about, Jimmy?"

"Come to think of it, I like the way you say that better." He thought a moment, his hands twisting over the haft of the shovel. "A bombing attack on market day. He sacrificed four of my young friends to take out four British soldiers. A draw in my book. But a victory in his, I suppose. There was a bit of self-serving cunning in what he did, I later figured out. The foursome had delivered a lot of bombs for him. Sooner or later, one of them was bound to get caught. And talk. Better to recruit a whole new batch off the schoolyard, as he did all of us."

"But what do you *see* at night when you cry out?"

"There was a girl among them . . ." Then he couldn't go on. At least not about the vision that snapped him awake, screaming. "I was young, but I suppose I was in love with her."

"What was her name?"

He just shook his head. Then he tossed aside the shovel and gently lowered Boomer into the ground.

"If you won't talk about that," she pressed, "then at least tell me this—how safe is your identity here?"

"Reasonably safe, Kate."

"What about the checking the department does on new hires?"

"Mine was whitewashed by a captain in personnel. See, his brother was a Sinn Fein man in Belfast, and it was held to be in the best interests of the cause for Liam McGivney to vanish. But I have to tell you, there could be problems now."

"How?"

"He's over here."

"Who?"

"My schoolyard recruiter, Ryan Gaerity. He killed Blanket. And today he got Rita and Cortez at Copley Square."

She leaned over with her elbows on her knees, took several deep breaths.

"But it's me he wants. He came to the house this afternoon for me."

"*Why?*"

"I tried to stop him back then. And that's the one

thing he won't tolerate." He stepped over to her. The nightfall was almost complete, and she couldn't catch his expression. But she thought he was going to touch her. Instead, he deposited a key in her hand. "You've got to leave, Kate."

"This is my home. What about Lizzy?"

"Listen, go to Max's place out on the cape. We've stayed there in better times, so Lizzy doesn't have to be wise to why you're going now. Tell her I'll be out for a weekend as soon as I can get away from work. Make it sound like a vacation." Then he went back to the grave, began covering Boomer with earth.

"Is that it?" she asked.

He said nothing.

"I leave just because you say I should leave? I don't even know who you are."

"Yes, you do, Katie," he said quietly.

12

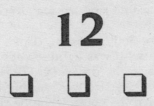

Keeping well back from the Wrangler, Dove tailed Kate and Lizzy down Highway Three as far as the outskirts of Plymouth. It scared him how oblivious Kate was even to his presence on the Harley. She had no instincts for danger.

He weaved in and out of the Cape Cod–bound vehicles, checking faces caught in the glow of the dashlights. Difficult not to be looking for Gaerity's adolescent face. It'd be fuller now, crueler perhaps.

When the time came, Dove found it almost impossible to turn back for Boston. This was all too foreign to Kate. She didn't know what precautions to take. Not like someone born and raised in Ulster. He watched the Wrangler's taillights get small, blend into the line of others. Kate had shrunk from him as he'd tried to kiss her good-bye at the house. It had hurt him, even though he reminded himself that this had to be a horrible shock to her. To learn that her married name was a fiction.

He'd wanted to take her in his arms and reassure her that the man himself was no fabrication. *A rose by any other name.* And that he loved her and Lizzy deeply. He would have rather died than bring this upon them.

Yet there'd been no time to explain.

Gaerity had located them. This afternoon had been a tease, but he would stop teasing as soon as it failed to amuse him.

Returning to South Boston, Dove dropped by O'Bannon's house. It was lightless, but Max's ragtop Bonneville was in the driveway. "Shit," Dove said, his stomach lurching. He was starting to shut down the bike to search the house when he recalled one of Max's favorite nocturnal habits.

He motored down half a block to a parking lot filled with imported cars on the Inner Harbor. He left the Harley a hundred yards back from the jumble of boulders marking the water's edge. No use scaring the fish with the vibration.

Walking through the ranks of new Volkswagens, Audis, and Fiats, he glimpsed O'Bannon sitting in a beach chair. The tip of the old man's fishing rod was twitching down toward the water. "Great behemoth," he grunted with satisfaction as he adjusted the drag.

Dove checked the lot behind him.

More than anything now, he feared leading Gaerity to his friends. Not that this tough old bastard wouldn't give Ryan a time of it. Inwardly, Dove saw Blanket's face for an instant. Then Rita's and Cortez's. His stomach started to seize again, but he made himself think only of Gaerity's face. Must put everything on the back burner except finding him before the next attack on the squad.

"Poacher," Dove called down to O'Bannon, "put up your hands."

"Why?"

"It's the county gamekeeper."

"Which county?"

"Armagh. Let me see your fishing permit."

"To hell with your English permit," O'Bannon

said, still reeling. He leaned back, and his Donegal tweed cap fell off.

Dove approached and squared Max's cap back on his head. "What've you got?"

"Mackerel, I'm sure."

"Fine night for them."

"Aye." The moon had risen. "A fighter."

Dove said, "Most anything will fight when it's hooked in the gob."

"You're soundin' particularly Irish tonight."

Dove kept silent about that for the moment. But yes, he felt easier about it now. Kate knew.

O'Bannon landed his fish, a portly mackerel. "Pregnant," he said after inspecting her with his flashlight. "Will you look at that? Almost burstin' with her spawn." He gently released her. "Go forth and multiply."

"How late do you usually stay out here?"

"As late as it takes to get sleepy," O'Bannon said, easing back with a sigh. "Grow old and your head gets too thunderin' full for sleep." He dug two Harps out of his ice chest, offered one to Dove.

"Not tonight."

O'Bannon nodded as if he understood. "Heard what happened at Copley Square. What's this city comin' to? As bad as bloody Ulster."

"More than you know."

O'Bannon's moonlit face turned toward him.

"It's Gaerity," Dove went on.

"Oh Jimmy, that can't be. They caught up with him several years after . . ." A hesitation came into O'Bannon's voice, perhaps unconscious. ". . . Crossmaglen. They sent him up to Castle Gleigh and threw away the key."

"I talked to him on the phone today."

"Go on. Are you sure?"

Dove touched his hand to his eyes for a second, then lowered his voice. "He murdered McNulty with a concussion bounce. Blew Rita out of the truck today. Cortez ..." He saw the truck on its side in the square, flames shooting out of the broken windows. "Gaerity's using them to get back at me. Using and destroying them. Just as he did Shiofra and the others back then. He blames me for what happened."

"The devil can take that bastard," O'Bannon said, his voice suddenly raw with bitterness. "If you hadn't tossed the monkey wrench in, that lorry would've blown smack dab in the middle of the square, not on the fringe like it did. Dozens killed. Maybe hundreds. And not just my niece and those other poor kids." Max fell silent, and Dove knew that he was seeing Shiofra O'Bannon's face. He hoped that Max's recollection was more pleasant than his own last memory of it.

Dove then said, "I told Kate this evening."

"Everything?"

"Yes. Except I kept your name out of it. Shiofra's too."

"Ah, Jimmy—she's your wife, not your priest. How do you step back from it now?"

"I don't know if I will."

"You better—or it's off to Castle Gleigh with you too."

"I mean I'm not going to lie to Kate anymore. I can't, not after what's happened." Dove paused. "Max, Gaerity was at the house this afternoon. He was sitting in my chair when Katie drove up with Lizzy. I spent an hour tearing the place apart for a device."

"Holy Mary." O'Bannon took a fierce pull off his bottle. "Well, you've got to get her and the child out of town. There's no doubt about that."

"Already done. Hope you don't mind, but I gave Kate my key to the cottage. They should be there by now."

"Mind? I'd belt you in the head if you'd thought

twice about it." O'Bannon rebaited and cast again. "I'll find out what I can about Gaerity through the network. If he's here like you say, he's using the community. A bastard like him can't get by without milkin' some poor mindless paddies."

"I don't want you getting involved."

O'Bannon gave a soft harrumph as he stared out across the harbor. "You tried to save my brother's only child. I wish there'd been a way to humanly pull it off. For her sake as well as yours, for I know how you've suffered from the thing all these years, Liam McGivney. Now you've thanked me a thousand times for bringin' you over, greasin' your way past personnel. But the greater debt is still mine. And so it'll be till I take my last breath."

Dove couldn't speak for a long moment. He watched the landing lights of a jet glimmer down over the harbor. "Then pay me back this way, Max. Stay out of it." He started back for the bike.

"Where you headed, Jimmy?" O'Bannon called after him.

"Squad building. Gotta sweep it. Gaerity was inside it too."

"Just like the devil," O'Bannon said angrily. "Everyplace at once, and nowhere up to any good."

Franklin was late for work.

He'd gotten up early enough, his usual five o'clock. A moment of temptation came when the bathroom light fell across the curvature of Cecily's back and buttocks. But he resolved to stick to his routine. He drove through a gray dawn to the exercise trail, parked, locked his Mustang, and started running from station to station. The morning felt cool, but not enough to hold back a quick sweat that ran into his eyes, despite the headband that clasped the headphones of his Walkman to his ears. He was slowing down for the push-up area when a bicyclist almost clipped him from the side. The rider immediately slowed and said something Franklin couldn't hear over the music. "What's that?" he asked, hitting the off button.

"Sorry," the man said. Accent maybe Canadian. Clothes just a cut above Salvation Army. Yet he looked bright enough. Possible MIT burnout case. "Thought you'd hear me coming up on you."

Franklin shrugged and pointed at his headset. He went to the ground, began pumping out push-ups.

"Careful then, friend," the rider said, slowly circling Franklin. "Those contraptions'll be the death of you."

Franklin peered up at the man. He was gently smiling, yet something in his eyes made the sergeant wish that he'd brought the small .25 automatic he usually carried in the pocket of his running shorts when he used the trail later in the day. He'd never had any trouble this early.

He stood and faced the rider, who had finally chuckled and pedaled off.

Franklin now sped into the squad building's lot, remembered once again to lock up—which hadn't been his habit until now. He ran up the stairs to the briefing room and burst through the door just as Captain Roarke was saying, "Where the hell is—?"

"Present," Franklin said in apology. He took the seat next to Dove's. The lieutenant looked as if he'd been on a bender: two days' growth and eyes badly in need of a Visine wash. He ignored Franklin—as if he had no intention of explaining why he'd torn off from Copley Square yesterday afternoon.

Glancing around, Franklin felt slightly better that he wasn't the only late show. Only Roarke, Dove, and 'Bama were in the room.

Then it hit him. This was it.

Roarke said, "One word about the funerals, and then no more on that . . ." Curiously, Franklin felt as if he were an actor in a war movie. One of those flicks about some World War I squadron in which combat attrition was gradually paring it down to extinction. "This unit will not participate in the services for Durgin and Cortez. Repeat: we will *not* go. I have explained to the families that the squad is being targeted, and it's unwise for all of us to congregate in public. They understood."

"Doesn't matter," Dove said fatalistically.

"What's that, Jim?"

"I'm sure the blaster has us all pegged by now. Our homes. Where we eat out. The dry cleaners we all take our uniforms to." Dove lit a Camel. "Don't know about you, but I'd like to say good-bye to Rita and Cortez."

"Negatory," Roarke said, his eyes flaring a little. "I believe I've made myself clear about this."

Dove said nothing more, just exhaled smoke out of his nostrils and returned a book of matches to 'Bama.

"All right," Roarke went on, "here's what we do over the coming days. We are the mark. Us, personally . . ."

From the corner of his eye, Franklin watched Dove squirm a little in his chair.

"That means property doesn't matter worth a shit. Let it blow. We disarm only when lives are at stake. We don't try to play hero. We keep ourselves alive." Roarke picked up a sheaf of computer paper. "I ran a survey on every blaster this squad has put behind bars in the last thirty years. Only one is still alive and out of the joint. Name's Wesley . . . anybody remember his gig?"

Silence.

"Well, he's down in Florida, dying of emphysema in ICU. Dade County confirmed for me that Wesley hasn't set foot out of his hospital bed in nine months. He can't make it to the john, let alone Boston."

Maner asked, "How 'bout Kozolski? He's junkyard-dog mean enough for this."

"William Kozolski," Roarke said, glancing at Franklin, "blew up the judge in Worcester who sent him away for five years on an explosives possession charge. No, 'Bama—he's doing life without possibility of parole."

"That mean we're left completely in the dark, Cap?" Maner asked.

"No," Dove said.

Roarke asked, "Pardon, Jim?"

"His name is Ryan Gaerity. He blasted out of prison in Northern Ireland fourteen months ago. Used ANFO he made from cricket field fertilizer and hydraulic fluid. Has a trademark of adding a dash of nitroglycerin to his mix. I got a slight nitro-headache off the River Street Bridge residue—"

"What?" The captain seemed on the verge of laughing. "You go to Mass or something with him?"

"Sir?"

"You mind telling me how you put this together, Lieutenant?"

Dove snubbed out his smoke on the bottom of his boot, then began shredding the filter apart. "This thing has smelled foreign from the get-go. I punched up every crime Interpol had on computer involving an IED. Gaerity's file jumped right out at me. Back in the seventies, he took out a British soldier standing sentry duty on a drawbridge over the River Bann. By bouncing the concussion off the counterweight."

Franklin liked the way Dove paused to let it sink in.

"Last fall," the lieutenant continued, "he's suspected of doing a contract for the Libyans. Killed an Egyptian minister. Planted a dummy bomb in his armored limousine, which was promptly discovered by security. The minister was being whisked out of his vehicle into another when a second shrapnel device was detonated in the street by remote."

Roarke looked mesmerized. Finally, he said, "Why's he after us?"

Dove was just staring back at the captain when the phone rang. Everyone braced. 'Bama had explained that a blaster this talented invariably called the squad to gloat. The lieutenant grabbed the receiver while Roarke clicked on the recorder.

"Boston Bomb Disposal . . ." Dove began blinking again, let out a breath. "He's right here, Connie. Hang on." He passed the phone to Maner.

"Hey, sugar." 'Bama immediately dropped his voice.

Dove came to his feet and began passing out photocopies of a mug shot. Roarke accepted his, grimly studied it.

Franklin could overhear 'Bama almost whining as he said with his hand cupped around the receiver, "How many times I gotta tell you, girl? I don't believe in that astrology crap. Baby, please, this is my regular scheduled day. I can't take off . . . what?" He paused, listening. "Sugar, that could mean damn near anythin'. I stay home in bed the day it reads: Maner, keep your ass home in bed, boy."

Dove gave Franklin his copy, and the sergeant froze. Once again, the eyes sent a chill through him. He'd seen them in person less than three hours before. Along the exercise trail. "Lieutenant . . . ?"

Kate preferred the deck over the interior of O'Bannon's cottage, even if the wind kept fluttering the pages of the Toni Morrison novel she was trying to read. The living room, especially, was filled with reminders of Max's dead wife. Photographs of her. Decidedly feminine bric-a-brac. A stack of *Ladies' Home Journal*s in the corner. It was like vacationing in a mausoleum. No wonder O'Bannon seldom used it.

Cover it with sand and leave it for the archaeologists as an example of twentieth-century grieving rituals.

Thinking of sand—Lizzy was sitting out on it, busy dredging it over her legs. Her nose and bony shoulders were pinking up. Time for more sunscreen. Yet now the most recent study said that some ingredient in it was suspected of being a carcinogen.

Was anything safe anymore?

Shading her eyes, Kate tracked the progress of the ferry to the Vineyard. It'd be so wonderful to just sail away from everything now and again. This enforced stay on Cape Cod wasn't an escape. It was a sentence. And how long would it drag on? She couldn't miss more than a few rehearsals, not with the Fourth of July performance just days away.

The phone rang.

Kate ducked inside, carried it to the open door, trailing the cord behind her. So she could keep an eye on Lizzy. "Yes?"

"Kate O'Bradaigh?"

"Who is this please?"

"Sister Beatrice."

"Oh, I'm sorry, Sister . . ." The vice principal at Kate's school. "I didn't recognize your voice."

"Sorry to disturb your vacation. But something unexpected has come up."

Kate felt her heart beat faster. "Nothing bad, I hope."

"I don't think so. But better safe than sorry, my dear. I received a call from the city health department. It seems that several months after the fact there have been a few problems—well, reactions, I suppose one would call them—with the DPT vaccine our nurse gave last September to our seven-year-olds."

"DPT?"

"Oh, forgive me, dear . . . diphtheria, pertussis, and tetanus."

"Are these reactions dangerous?" Kate asked, looking at Lizzy, who'd now half-buried herself with sand.

"So far, no. But the physician-in-charge would like to be able to contact the parents of all the affected children." Then the nun added a bit ominously, "Immediately if it becomes necessary. May I give the doctor your number out there?"

As Kate hesitated, something occurred to her. "Sister, how'd *you* get this number?"

"From Mrs. Monahan." Sandra's mother. "She mentioned that she was watching your home while you're on vacation. I got no answer at your regular number. I do hope you don't mind the intrusion."

"No, not at all. Please do give this number to the health department. I appreciate your taking the time to do this. Good-bye."

Kate hung up and returned to the deck. *What next?*

Gaerity patiently bored a tiny hole into each holder of the contact lens case that lay before him on the chart table. One through the L and one through the R. Only while working did he feel close to being at peace. He was inching toward a goal, which seemed to ease his otherwise constant anxiety. He hadn't known he suffered from chronic anxiety until his German psychiatrist brought it to his attention. "You are under enormous stress, Ryan," he had said in that somber Heidelberg office paneled with dark wood. "But it gives me hope that you feel no guilt. That is the most common response. Guilt followed by the lassitude of depression. You alone of all my patients seem to sense that the fault lies outside yourself. With this utterly sick capitalist society. Still, despite your insight, you face many dangers. I believe you will either liberate or destroy yourself. The choice must be obvious to you. Either you must have revolution or you shall implode."

"Quite," Gaerity said fervently to himself, then un-

screwed one of the Kerr jars and meticulously sprinkled some powder into both holders of the case. He
was snapping them shut when his cellular rang.

He took a moment to remember himself. "Oh yes."
Then he answered, "Doctor Stackpole."

"Doctor, this is Sister Beatrice from Saint
Sebastian's."

"Oh, how very nice to hear from you again,
Sister."

"I have those last three numbers for you."

Gaerity reached for a pencil. "I am prepared to
copy." The first two were local. South Boston and
Brookline. Too close to town to suit McGivney's
mounting paranoia. But the third made him raise his
eyebrows. "Very good. Have the O'Bradaighs moved
or something?"

"Vacation residence on the cape. That's a Falmouth
prefix, I believe."

"Excellent, Sister. I'm sure this will come to nothing and the lab will prove that those two children
ate some bad shellfish or whatever. But one can't be
too careful. Not when it comes to children."

"I agree wholeheartedly, Doctor. Will we hear
from you on this again?"

"Most assuredly. One way or the other. Good day,
Sister Beatrice." Hanging up, Gaerity glanced over
the table. "Where was I?"

Then he recalled. "Oh yes."

He picked up a single-edged razor blade and
skinned the plastic off a length of copper wire, from
which he then unraveled a solitary strand. This he
slid through one of the holes he had just bored in
the two lens holders.

He listened to the sound of his own respiration as
he worked. Calm. Rhythmic. As sure of its purpose
as the sea.

13

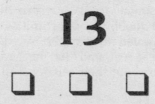

The next morning, Franklin carried his .25 automatic in his running shorts as he ran the exercise course. But the bicyclist didn't appear a second time. Reaching the parking lot, the sergeant checked his car for every device he could possibly imagine—and still held his breath as he turned the key.

He abruptly changed lanes several times on the drive home, made a few unnecessary right turns to see if anybody was following him, and finally parked on the street instead of using his numbered space in the underground garage.

"Good morning, Mr. Franklin," Drago, the Croatian maintenance man, said.

"Morning." Franklin slipped Gaerity's mugshot from his sweatshirt pocket. "Haven't seen this joker around the building, have you?"

Drago shook his head. "A friend?"

"No. Please phone me or the department if you see him."

"Sure will."

Last night, Franklin had slept alone for the first time in months.

It'd been hard to explain to Cecily that he wanted her to keep her distance for a while. He needed his space. Exactly enough space to blow up without her getting injured—although he hadn't told her that some genius maniac from Northern Ireland was creating upward mobility opportunities for any blue-suiter who wanted to transfer into Bomb Disposal right now. He'd just said that he had some serious thinking to do about their relationship. Needed a little time alone.

Maybe he did.

What right did he have to drag an innocent woman into this kind of shit? Dove had said that the son of a bitch knew where everyone in the squad lived, what cleaners they used. How many times had Cecily taken his uniforms in for him?

Franklin examined his front door, then slowly went through it and swept his apartment twice before he felt secure enough to take a shower. He hoped that if he had to go it wasn't in the tub. The thought of watching his own blood trickle down the drain made him half-sick.

But the warm needles of water soon began to relax him. He lathered his face, held it up to the stream.

Yesterday, the squad—what remained of it—had stayed inside the building all shift. Captain's orders. Lunch came from the pizza joint around the corner, and the box was sniffed and searched before being taken inside. No IED calls came in, although Franklin jerked upright in his chair each time the phone rang. Dove used some of the long wait by going through known IRA setups with 'Bama and Franklin. Amazing, his encyclopedic knowledge of Irish devices. But instead of reassuring Franklin, Dove's lecture only left him more uneasy. The best way to deal with some of this intricate stuff seemed to be to drive to New Hampshire and flop down behind a big rock. Dove had put up a brave front, but Franklin could tell that, deep down, he was pessimistic about the coming days. A call would eventually come in, and the squad would have to leave its fortress.

But all that was forty-eight hours away, Franklin reminded himself. He was on scheduled days off. Towel wrapped around his waist, he went into the living room.

He fired up his stereo for the first time in a few days, slipped on his headphones, and sank into his chair. A resounding click drowned out Aretha Franklin's voice.

Franklin sat perfectly still.

For five minutes.

Finally, he inched his left leg over, threaded the phone cord between his toes, and pulled the instrument closer. With his big toe, he hit the speed dialer and then the speaker button.

He was afraid his headphones would slide off, he was perspiring so heavily.

No one answered.

"Fuck," he whispered. His head was starting to tremble from the effort to keep it perfectly still. He wanted to bolt out of the chair and run. But he knew that he would be wrapped in a fireball by the time he reached the door—or would sail right through it like a cruise missile.

Franklin's telephone call was just being electronically diverted to the dispatch center when someone interrupted the transfer and answered, "Bomb Disposal. Dove."

"Man," Franklin rasped, "I never thought I'd be so glad to hear somebody's voice." The only man who might be able to shut down Gaerity's device.

Dove picked up on his tone at once. "You're in a hot room, right?"

"Can't get much hotter."

"Where's the demon?"

"Wrapped around my fucking ears."

"How can you hear me then?"

"Left stereo headphone's slipping down. I think it's from the sweat pouring off me."

"Okay," Dove said. "If it's moved that far and you're still running up a phone bill, pull it down a bit more . . . but *carefully*."

"The left headphone?"

"Yeah. Just enough so you can see inside."

Franklin did so, gingerly, then had to close his eyes and catch his breath.

"Still with me, Anthony?"

"I guess." Franklin gave a dry chuckle. "How d'you know if you're gone?"

"You'll see your butt flaming past your nose. Look into the audio hole. What's there?"

Without turning his head, Franklin strained for a glimpse. "I see . . . something."

"Another successful graduate of Dove's basic course. Any wires, you stupid son of a bitch?"

"Don't call me that," Franklin said sharply. "Like shit I want that to be the last thing I ever hear."

"You're right," Dove said. "Sorry."

"I see a thin strand of copper wire leading into something small. Gray plastic. Has an L on it."

"Contact lens case. Don't unplug the headphones. That'd only set off a collapsing circuit."

"What about a timer?"

"Probably."

"How . . . ?"

"The motion of putting on the headphones no doubt activated a micro-switch, kicking off both an electronic timer and an anti-trembler getup. So don't move while you're wondering when the timer goes. Got it?"

"Got it."

"All right, guy—we're on the way. You sitting down?"

"Yeah. But it feels like I'm ten feet off the floor and still rising like a balloon."

"Well, sit straight so you don't collapse your diaphragm."

"My fucking *what?*"

"I'll explain later. Patrol will probably arrive first to clear the building. Keep this line open . . . I'm going to divert it to communications now."

"Dove—" Then Franklin didn't know how to go on.

"I know. Life's a bloody bitch."

"Yeah."

Franklin inched back slightly, breathed deeply through his mouth. A thought saddened him. He'd probably made love for the last time. The intensity of those couplings over the last few days now made sense to him. Something within him had known that this was coming. He'd wanted some part of himself to survive.

"Franklin?" A new voice came through the telephone speaker.

"Yeah. Who are—?"

"Webster. Communications sergeant. You doing okay?"

"Just ducky."

"We're all with you, guy."

Franklin came within a breath of laughing. It was the most absurdly insincere thing he'd ever heard. He was the most alone man on the face of the earth.

"Franklin?"

"Shoot."

"Dove told me to tell you something."

"What?"

"He said it's no big thing if your head blows off. You'll just make captain that much sooner."

'Bama drove forty miles an hour over the speed limit while Dove reached across the front seat and lifted the pack of cigarettes from his uniform pocket. "Use one too?" he asked over the yelp of the siren.

"Hell yes."

Dove lit one for Maner, then another for himself. A comforting pall of smoke soon filled the interior of the sedan.

'Bama inhaled like a teenager trying to get a tobacco high. "What kind of worm is this son of a bitch?"

"World class," Dove said. "Watch the Ford up here. Old lady's creeping into the intersection." Maner deftly jinked the wheel and cut behind the car. "Where'd you learn to drive like that? Running moonshine?"

"Matter of fact . . ." 'Bama took the microphone from the dashboard clip and radioed, "We're there. Gimme an ETA on fire and ambulance."

After a few seconds, the dispatcher said, "Less than a minute."

Several Patrol units had already arrived, and the blue-suiters were herding tenants out of the complex, women with their hair in curlers and old men in bathrobes. As Dove and 'Bama started up the walkway, a duffer could be heard giving a patrolman the devil: "Listen, Gestapo—I'm not going anywhere till I find my Siamese. So you can go screw yourself."

"Arrest him," Dove said in passing. Then, pointing at the entrance to the garage beneath Franklin's building, he said to 'Bama, "Check down there for a second device."

Maner peeled off.

Dove could tell that he was shaken. Maybe he and the rest of the squad deserved the truth: that Gaerity was a better known quantity than Dove had let on. Yet what more of use would they know if he admitted that he was Liam McGivney?

He put down his saddlebag of tools and inspected the front door light fixture. Clear. Then, once again, he steeled himself for the worst moment—coming into the hot room, not knowing if the device was timed to go at that precise moment. Yet he felt less anxious than he'd expected. Maybe confession was good for the soul, at least when it came to wives.

Franklin sat like a statue in an upholstered chair. He looked as if he'd been basted in honey.

"Good," Dove said, "I was afraid you'd left, Anthony." He could hear a whine of music through the headphones that lay skewed atop Franklin's head. "What're you listening to?"

"Sister Aretha."

"Kin?"

"Sure." Franklin visibly swallowed around the obvious lump in his throat, but then smiled faintly as he said, "Still, may not prove to be a bad choice for this morning. She's doing 'Jesus Hears Every Prayer' right now."

Dove donned a visor light and traced the spiral cord back into the stereo jack. " 'Packing Up, Getting Ready to Go' on that album?"

"You're a prick, Dove."

"Tell me something I don't know." He drew close to Franklin's face, shone the light through the audio hole. Behind him, someone entered the apartment. He could tell from the plodding tread that it was Maner. "Kill the volume for me, 'Bama."

"You sure?" Franklin asked.

"It's okay. Different circuit."

Maner turned down the music. "Garage is clear, Jim."

"Thanks."

"Do me a favor," Franklin said.

"Name it," Dove answered.

"Take something and wipe that fucking sweatball off the end of my nose."

Chuckling, Dove gently dabbed Franklin's face with his handkerchief, then turned to Maner. "Bedroom, bathroom, and kitchen, friend."

"Right away."

As 'Bama went down the hallway, Franklin said, "There's another one somewhere in here . . . isn't there?"

"I'd take it to Vegas." Dove paused, thinking. Contact lens cases came with two compartments. So far, he'd seen only the left one. "You're slumping over, Anthony. Sit back. Try to relax. I've got some delicate work to do in a minute, and I don't want you suddenly twitching on me." He lightly wiped the sergeant's face again. "Tell me—why'd you ever leave SWAT?"

"Missions stopped scaring me."

Dove gave him a skeptical glance as he readied his drill. "Then why'd you come to Bomb Disposal?"

"Just the thought of getting blown up scares the holy shit out of me."

Dove nodded. So he wasn't as shallow as he'd seemed the night of the reception. "And what happens when you stop being afraid of bombs?"

"I get out. Wouldn't you? Wouldn't anybody in his right mind?"

Dove tested the drill. It was no time for weak batteries. "All right . . . so what happens when you're not afraid of anything anymore?"

"I move back to Roxbury, where I grew up in the projects."

Smiling, Dove mulled that over. Yes, that would take courage. He thought of going back to Belfast, and it almost gave him a shudder. "Roxbury, huh? I pictured your father a doctor or a lawyer."

"Picture him *gone* when I was six months old."

'Bama returned once more and said, "Can't find shit." He was hyperventilating slightly.

Dove closely studied him a moment. Maner grinned, but he'd lost color. "All right, gentlemen—let's do it." Dove shook his left hand a few times, then grasped the left headphone and ground a hole into the earpad. "Small prongs," he said, holding his palm over his shoulder.

Maner slapped them firmly into Dove's grasp, and he eased the prongs into a tangle of wires. He saw the L on the contact case. The detonator. It was crammed next to a micro-circuit. "Damn," he whispered.

"What . . . what?"

Dove told Franklin to shut up, then reached for his visor and flipped the magnifying lens down over his right eye. He saw two miniscule posts set a hairbreadth apart. A red wire was connected to each before threading off into invisibility.

"'Bama," Dove said, "you ever seen one of these?"

Maner peered through his own lens. Dove noticed that the man's fingers were trembling. "No, Lieut . . . but there's just two wires goin' in."

Franklin piped up, "One of them's got to be the ground . . . right?"

Dove nudged up the lens, then rubbed his eyes and exhaled. Dilemma. Gaerity's favorite weapon. Moral. Mechanical. It was always the same—he gave you two equally unpleasant choices, then sat back and chortled. Yet he could be defeated. He was human. If men could make bombs, other men could undo them. An article of faith. Maybe the only one Dove truly believed in.

"Dove?" Franklin asked, his eyes beseeching.

"Two triggers," he said decisively.

"Say what, boss?" 'Bama asked.

"We're looking at two triggers on this son of a bitch."

Franklin asked, "But where?"

Dove turned and looked at the big Bose 901 speaker on the stereo rack. He approached it, inspected the cone. It was intact but the center was missing. He aimed his light inside, and there waited the other half of the contact case, an R embossed on the gray plastic. Molded around the inside of the cone was at least a half-pound of RDX. Plastic-bonded explosive.

"What you got?"

Dove leaned aside for 'Bama, who shone his own light into the cone. "Shee-it," he said.

Franklin was gazing at the second, bigger charge that was only four feet away from his head. He tried to lick his lips, but his tongue was too parched. "Just tell me," he said, the corners of his mouth crackling.

Dove explained, "They're slated for simultaneous detonation."

"Meaning?"

"We shut 'em both down at the same instant or . . ." Dove decided to let it go at that.

But Franklin said, "We don't work on Captain Roarke's plantation no mo'."

Dove smiled approvingly at him. Usually, humor was the first casualty of fear. Franklin would do all right. If he survived the next few minutes. "Ready?"

"Where *is* Roarke?" the sergeant asked.

"Went up to Lowell. Said he had a lead on something."

"Sure," Franklin muttered sarcastically.

"Careful, guy," Dove said, "you're not dead yet." He took two pairs of precision snips from his saddle-bag, handed one to Maner, who had to wipe his palm on his trouser leg before accepting it. "You take the woofer, 'Bama. Just the red wire. And don't touch the other post."

Maner was staring right through him.

" 'Bama?"

The man tried to steady his grasp by using both hands. But it was no good. He lowered the snips between his legs and laughed weakly. "Goddamn woofer."

"What about it?" Dove asked.

"Connie read me my horoscope for the week. Said

I oughta be wary of big dogs." Maner's grin faltered, then disappeared. "You get it, Lieut? Woofer . . . dog. Y'all believe that shit?"

Dove said nothing.

Here, in the space of a single morning, it might be over for Dale Maner and Bomb Disposal. Dove had once heard courage described as a bank account. A man could only make so many withdrawals before he was operating on insufficient funds. There was no shame in that. A week ago, Dove had wondered if he himself was finally bankrupt. Strangely, he no longer felt that way—maybe only because, thanks to Gaerity, he had to stick this out.

"I've got to be here," Franklin said evenly. " 'Bama doesn't."

Maner looked away.

Dove said, "He's right, 'Bama. I need just two sets of hands."

"Sorry, boys," Maner said pathetically.

"Don't be." Dove took the snips from him, deposited them into Franklin's right hand. "Wasn't in the stars."

Nothing more was said as Maner left the apartment.

Then Dove caught Franklin's eye. "You still scared?"

At that moment, the play button clicked off. The cassette was done. Franklin had started at the sound, but he then said, smiling, "Scared shitless, Dove."

"Good. Can you see the wire?"

"Barely."

"No, dammit—can you get the snips on it?"

"Yeah."

"Positive?"

"Yes, for godsake!"

"One last thing . . ."

"Don't put it that way," Franklin said, snips poised to cut his stretch of tiny wire.

"Where do you see yourself five years from now? Internal Affairs?"

"No, I was already offered a spot there. Turned it down."

"Really?" Dove asked, eyes widening. "Why?"

"That's the scariest assignment of all. Going around getting dirt on other people—and learning to enjoy it."

"Good for you, Anthony. If we don't die right now, I may wind up almost liking you. On it?"

"Waiting for you, Lieutenant."

"On three." Dove began counting. "One . . ."

Franklin blinked away some sweat that had rolled out of his brows into his eyes.

"Two . . . still with me?"

The sergeant nodded. Almost imperceptibly.

"Go."

The two soft snicks were nearly simultaneous. But there was enough of a lapse for Dove to cringe slightly, waiting.

"We all right?" Franklin asked frantically. "Did we get it, man?"

Five seconds had elapsed, but Dove went on theatrically plugging his ears with his two index fingers.

"You motherfucker," Franklin gasped, taking off the headphones and slumping exhausted in the chair. "Answer your goddamn phone."

"What?" Dove dropped his fingers from his ears and heard his cellular telephone ringing.

14

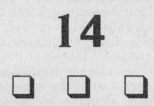

Kate had begun to hate O'Bannon's hideaway.
The wooden floor creaked in the middle of the
night for no apparent reason. The furniture stank of
mold. And the window glass had been indelibly
blurred by salt spray, making her feel as if she were
trapped inside a dirty fish tank. Even Lizzy was starting to get bored. The water was really too cold for
swimming, and she had no playmates.

Early that morning, they had disobeyed Dove's orders and gone out. They drove to the wildlife sanctu-
ary in East Falmouth and hiked a narrow, twisting
trail through the scrub and marshland. Barn swal-
lows darted overhead like bats, and Lizzy swore that
she saw a rabbit—or something—hopping over a
dune. On the way back to the cottage, Kate had
stopped at a mom-and-pop grocery in Teaticket for
a few things, including a paper kite, which she hoped
would keep Lizzy occupied for a few days.

Now, standing vigil on the windswept deck, Kate
watched her daughter run back and forth across the
beach, trying to get the kite airborne.

"No, bug!" Kate shouted. Then she licked the tips
of two fingers to remind Lizzy how to determine
wind direction.

The girl finally realized that the breeze was coming out of the southwest, and turned into it. The kite wobbled aloft, but then plunged into the beach.

"Broke?" Kate called down to her.

Lizzy shook her head, but her hands were on her hips.

Everything was ending in frustration.

Kate went back inside the cottage. "How long, Dove?" she asked aloud. A few more days of this and she'd blow up the place herself. She thought about calling him, then dismissed the idea when she imagined his reaction—irritation with her that she'd felt the need. Yet he'd failed to phone her. He hadn't promised, but why the hell hadn't he?

She dialed.

"Dove." He sounded breathless.

"It's me," she said.

Pause. More labored breathing. "What's wrong, Kate? You okay?"

"Great. Never been better. How about you?"

"Uh, better than I was about three minutes ago."

"Where are you?"

"Franklin's pad."

"The new guy?"

"Yeah," Dove said.

"What're you doing there?"

"Oh, you know rookies. Always losing their heads over something."

"You two getting along better?"

"Somewhat." Then his voice jiggled. He was walking with the cellular to someplace more private, she surmised. "You sure everything's okay?"

She started to give another insincere answer when he cupped his hand over the mouthpiece. His muffled voice said to someone else, "No, keep the goddamn tenants out. We're only half-done here. Got the disposal to go." He came back to her. "So how's Lizzy?"

His question didn't register for a few seconds. It had just hit her that a bomb had been found in Franklin's place. Then she hurriedly said, "Sunburned but fine. She's having a big time. Listen, you sound busy. I don't know why I even called. Bye for now."

She hung up, strolled back out onto the deck.

At last, the kite was up. Kate applauded, and a pleased-looking Lizzy gave a wave with her free hand.

There was a museum in Falmouth on the village green. Maybe she and Lizzy could go there tomorrow morning. She'd picked up a flyer at the market. Two restored houses of the whaling era. Period paintings, glass, and china. Scrimshaw. Farm equipment in the barn.

Suddenly, her eyes were wet with anger. "Fuck the museum," she said, going back inside for the phone.

"Dove."

"You know what pisses me off, you son of a bitch!"

"You mind holding on for just one minute?"

"Not at all," she said primly. She folded her arms over her haltertop and waited.

Twenty seconds later, he came on the line again. "Okay, Kate O'Bradaigh, what pisses you off?" His voice was echoing. Bathroom. He sounded infuriatingly reasonable.

"How stupid you made me feel. Jesus Christ, Dove—did you think I wasn't a big enough girl to handle it?"

Silence.

"Talk, Dove, or I'm coming back to Boston for this little chat."

"Listen," he said, sounding completely frazzled, "I'm not sure if *I'm* big enough to handle it."

"What's that supposed to mean?"

"I don't know. Any chance of putting this off for a couple days?"

"None."

"Didn't think so." She could hear him inhale, then slowly let the breath out. "I was afraid," he said.

"*Why?*"

"It's all something outside your experience. I was afraid the truth wouldn't add up to you."

"Were you *ever* going to tell me?"

"I'm not sure, Katie. It's a fair question, but I just don't know. I didn't want to lose you. I still don't."

"Did it ever even cross your mind to tell me?"

"Of course. Especially when the night terrors started. But if you want me to say I was just procrastinating, I won't do that."

She pressed a finger to her lips to keep them from trembling, then let go and said, "Did you honestly believe I have so little imagination I couldn't understand?"

Another long silence.

"Oh, Dove," she said, her disappointment so deep she began to cry.

"It's an alien world, Katie—that Ireland. It's not the quaint little isle of shamrocks and leprechauns you American paddies celebrate on March seventeenth. It's a bloody ride you've never taken. A person rides the devil in Belfast, whether or not he wants to. Choice is something you have when you run off to America. It'd take me the whole day to tell you all the shitty things I did. And all the shitty things that were done to me."

"Forget that—why'd you lie to me?" she demanded, struggling to keep her voice strong.

"Did I? I believe I did the Belfast thing. The game I learned just to survive. I tiptoed between truth and deceit. I gave you the content without the context."

"What kind of answer is—?"

"No, listen. Yes, I grew up hard. Got in plenty of

trouble with the authorities. They happened to be the enemies of my own people. Your people. That's how I was brought up to see them. Foreign enemies. I was a soldier. Nothing more or less than that. I made bombs and then planted them to get back at an army of occupation." His words were coming rapid-fire now. "Yes, my parents died in a fire. But it was no accident from smoking in bed. My father, drunk as always, spoke out in public for the IRA. The next night a Molotov cocktail came through the front window. It caught the two of them watching 'Gunsmoke' on the tele—"

"Stop," she begged. He was right. It was too much. The gulf he was talking about was real. "I . . . I've got to check on Lizzy."

"Kate—I'll get down there as soon as I can. Next day or two. I've got a photo of Gaerity. I want you to take a good look at it. In the meantime, I want you to—"

"No," she snapped. "I don't want to see it. I don't want any of this, Dove." Then she hung up on him.

She stood for several minutes gripping the edge of the kitchen table, crying. She felt bruised and empty, almost violated for having slept with a man who'd made bombs. Not just defused them. Actually manufactured them. Then, once again, she remembered Lizzy and went outside.

The kite was no longer in sight. Neither was the girl.

Gaerity found the cottage thanks to the Jeep Wrangler. It was openly parked beside the weathered little structure. All the footprints in the sand surrounding the place were too small to be McGivney's. So Liam had probably hidden his family here while he himself remained in Boston.

This was confirmed later in the morning when his wife and stepdaughter came out on the deck to breakfast. Gaerity watched them from the crest of a nearby dune. Here, behind an old fence, he'd buried the small suitcase he'd carried with him on the bus from Boston.

After eating, mother and daughter drove off in the Wrangler. This gave him a twinge of alarm until he broke inside by picking the door lock. They'd left their luggage behind, Kate's violin as well.

Yet they hadn't brought much with them to the cape, a bag apiece. Their stay would not be a long one. No wonder. The cottage reminded him of the abandoned mud-wall cabin in County Monaghan he'd been forced to use as a hideout while the Republic of Ireland police, at the bidding of the Brits, scoured the countryside for him. Cramped, stuffy, tawdry.

Waiting for their return, Gaerity strolled along the beach, going halfway to Woods Hole before turning around. He wasn't sure what to do next. This place was so out of the way. Not center stage like a bridge or a public square. No one would see, least of all McGivney. And that was the entire point of it, wasn't it?

But if he hesitated, another opportunity might not arise. McGivney and his squad were fully alerted by now. Gaerity had heard nothing about the device going off in Sergeant Franklin's flat. Too long now. Almost thirty-six hours since he'd planted it. Something had gone wrong.

Still, the loneliness of this place made his efforts seem insignificant.

Coming back onto the Falmouth shore, he was accosted by two young boys bearing plastic sacks full of live crabs.

"How much?" he asked.

Ten dollars a bag. A bargain, they insisted, one of them adding, "Everybody who comes here buys crabs."

"Oh very well, then," Gaerity said, "if it's the custom, what choice do I have?"

He hefted the sack over his shoulder, feeling its captives twitching against his back through the plastic, and ambled on toward the cottage. McGivney's family had returned, for the girl, Lizzy, was flying a kite. It was green, white, and orange. An omen, perhaps. The colors of the Irish flag.

He sat behind the fence, peering almost directly up at the kite. The bag of crabs added a touch of plausibility to his being there that had been absent before. He now added to it by shedding his shoes and rolling up his trouser legs to the knee. "There." Like T. S. Eliot's Prufrock, a shy fellow in middle age come to the tide's edge to contemplate death and his fear of women. As good a cover as any.

All at once, the kite swooped and started into a tailspin that sent it plummeting. It crashed into a fence a few yards down from Gaerity and hung there, the paper rattling in the breeze. He rose to a squat and went to it, standing erect just as Lizzy approached from the other side.

She stepped back, wide-eyed, but quickly found her tongue. "Who're you?"

"Who do you think I am?"

She had no answer to that.

"I'm the kite fixer. I appear magically all over the world at a moment's notice to save kites in distress." Gaerity took a butterfly knife from his jacket pocket. One more garage sale prize. He flicked it open. "Just minutes ago, I was in China, helping a lad with the most elaborate kite I've ever seen. It had dragon's horns and a tail a city block long. He'd crashed it into a star."

Her eyes riveted to the knife, she failed to smile.

Gaerity reached for the kite.

"Do you have to cut it?" she asked.

"Just the string, darling. It's so very much tangled,

don't you see?" He paused, staring at her, the knife jutting from his fist. "Do you mind if I ask you a thing or two?"

She shrugged.

He pressed his thumb against the blade. "When flying your kite, do you have a secret wish to see it crash? The consciousness of a child fascinated him. So pure, natural—yet, even at this tender age, the handiwork of misguided adults could be discerned. "Well then," he said, pressing the blade harder. "Do you like to blow apart dandelion puffs?"

She smiled.

"I thought so."

"Make little dams in the gutter and then smash them?"

Her eyes darted to his hand. "Ow. Does it hurt?"

He glanced down. His thumb was bleeding.

"Lizzy!"

Kate was running in her bare feet toward them. Gaerity cut away the balled-up mass of string. He retied the line before returning the kite to the girl. Finally, he pocketed the knife.

Kate stopped at a distance. Had she been crying, or was it allergies? "Lizzy, come here."

The girl, probably feeling that some thanks were in order, hesitated.

"Come here!" Shrill now. Frightened to death. Had Kate recognized him from that day at Saint Sebastian's? Gaerity didn't believe so, but she was certainly on full alert.

"Mom," Lizzy said, "this man helped me with my kite. He cut his hand. I got it caught on the fence. And he had this knife."

Kate visibly paled at her mention of that.

Gaerity took a few paces back from Lizzy to reassure the woman. "Just my fishing knife," he said, sounding as accentless as an American network broadcaster. McGivney would have no doubt told her to run from anything that even faintly resembled a brogue. "I didn't mean to scare you, madam. I know how worrisome it must be for parents these days."

Kate nodded, looking no less frightened. Lizzy had come to her side, and the woman wrapped a protective arm around her.

"Wouldn't happen to know where the Lindstroms' place is, would you?"

At last, she seemed to rouse from her fear. "Uhm, let's see, I've seen their sign. Keep on this road, second or third drive on the left."

"Appreciate it. Had a drink with them last night at the Willow Field Tavern and promised them some crabs." Gaerity winked at Lizzy. "I'm the local crab man as well as the kite fixer." He vaulted over the low fence. Smiling, he walked up to them, halted, and dropped the sack of crabs at Kate's feet. Time to see how keen her antennae truly were. "Actually, I don't make much of a living at this. Wind up giving away most of my catch to nice folks like the Lindstroms. Are you here for the summer?"

Kate took a moment. "Yes. My husband and I."

"Well, do enjoy." He sauntered on.

Lizzy quickly cried after him, "Hey, you forgot your bag."

Suddenly, Kate grabbed the girl by the shoulders, dragged her away from the sack.

Gaerity came back, chuckling. "By your face, madam, you'd think I was toting snakes around." He opened the bag, showed her the swarm of claws.

Kate smiled weakly.

"Taste better than they look," he said, moving on. His jaws tightened. He had his answer. At the very least, he would have to rig the device here in Falmouth. Kate would be even more on her toes in Boston. McGivney had her trained. No more American innocence. The surviving squad members would now be looking between their own toes for devices. Yet this didn't disturb Gaerity. It only made the challenge more interesting.

He actually went up to the Lindstroms' door and knocked. A fat blond woman answered, and within three minutes he had sold her the crabs for fifteen dollars. His mother had often said that her side of the family had some Tinker blood. Irish gypsies, who could sell sand to an Arab.

First darkness was always the most cloaking.

He waited for it before approaching the Wrangler. The windows of the cottage were golden against the dark sea. He slid his suitcase under the chassis, glanced around one last time, then crawled under.

He could hear Kate playing the violin within the cottage.

Dove coasted the Harley to a stop before his house. Rose-colored sunlight was just showing over the rooftops to the east. He walked up the driveway to make sure that no trip-wires were strung across it. Exhausted, he nevertheless made a full sweep of the yards and then continued the search inside.

Forty minutes later, he popped a Budweiser and fell into his easy chair. One of the photo albums lay open on the floor. He picked it, smiled at a snapshot of himself with Kate and Lizzy. Both of them were looking adoringly at him. Could he ever win that back?

Shaking his head, he flipped the page.

Instant pain. The bomb squad softball team. It had gone zero and eight in police league play, which had thoroughly disgusted Blanket. He'd played college ball on a scholarship and had expectations for the "Blind Bombers." But still, here he stood warmly beaming with one arm around Cortez and the other around Dove. Both the Cuban technician and Dove had grown up with soccer and found it unnatural to handle any kind of ball with their hands. Rita had been the best player next to Blanket and Maner. She was better than 'Bama if only because she didn't have fallen arches.

Rita.

Dove touched his fingers to her broad, homely face. They had rigged up catcher's gear for her out of bomb squad armor. She'd beaned a lieutenant from Internal Affairs who tried to steal second, knocked him out cold—

Dove snapped shut the book.

He closed his burning eyes. Most of the night had been spent in the state criminalistics lab going over the components of the devices they'd managed to salvage unexploded so far, the dummy rig from the trolley in Copley Square and the twin setup in Franklin's stereo system. Dove must have called every manufacturer of contact lens cases in the country, having security wake up the bosses. Finally an outfit in Atlanta recognized the model number to be one of theirs. For all the good it did. The company shipped to over two hundred retail outlets in the Boston metropolitan area. The identification technician had found a partial latent fingerprint on the egg timer taken from the trolley device. A computer-enhanced copy of it had been immediately faxed to the Washington bureau of Interpol. No return was received before Dove started for home, although Roarke had promised to call as soon as one came in.

Dove started to reach for the beer can, but then stopped. Too drowsy.

He dreamed of a softball game. He could smell the sun-warmed grass, hear the cheering and laughter. Blanket hit a single into center, ran for first, long arms pumping. His foot touched the base bag, and he vanished in a hot yellow flash. The smoke was still rolling away when Cortez doubled—and blew to pieces as he dived into second. No one said a word. And Dove himself felt powerless to stop the game. Rita went to bat and dropped a sinker along the first base line. She reached third, and the blast rocked the stands. Finally, it was Dove's turn. He'd never even gotten a clean hit, but now he homered. The ball flew out of sight. He tossed the bat aside and started around the scorched places that marked the bases. Home plate loomed ahead—

He startled, held his hands out in front of his face. Phone.

The phone was ringing.

He glanced at the mantel clock. It was twenty minutes after ten. "Crap." He had a stiff neck. Massaging it, he picked up the receiver. "Dove."

"Roarke, Jimbo."

"Yeah."

"It's Gaerity all right."

Dove sat up, rubbed his eyes. "Confirmation from Interpol?"

"Just came in. And we've got enough fingerprint comparison points to take it to court."

Dove tried to nurse a glimmer of satisfaction. But he just felt numb, fatigued. "What about reinforcements?" Dove had suggested that the department invoke some mutual aid agreements to bring in veteran bomb squad personnel from other departments. Even from the military, if necessary.

But Roarke said, "No dice on any outside help. But I've been authorized to borrow all our recent basic course grads from SWAT and Narcotics."

Dove rolled his eyes. But he was too spent to argue. "All right, Captain, I'm going to grab another hour or two of shut-eye, then hit the bricks again."

"You put your house on extra patrol, like I said?"

"Yeah," Dove lied. A cruiser driving by every hour or so wasn't going to deter Gaerity. An armored car could be posted at both ends of the street, and he'd still find a way.

Roarke asked, "How's Kate doing?"

"Fine. She's a real . . ." Dove stared off into space. ". . . trooper."

"Okay, guy. Be careful."

"You too, Fred."

Hanging up, Dove noticed that the answering machine was blinking. He was tempted to ignore it when he realized that Kate might try to reach him this way if she had any trouble with his cellular reception. He pressed the play button, took a swallow of warm beer.

The first two messages were from Sister Beatrice at Saint Sebastian's. Dove yawned.

The third call stood him right up out of the chair.

"Franklin was absent today because his brains slithered right out of a hole in his head. But *no*—it didn't come to that, Liam, did it? Well, don't think I'm angry. The master is never angry when his apprentice does well. I'm proud of you, boy-o. You kept your friend's brains on top of his neck. You recalled my predilection for the two-headed beastie . . ." Then, laughing, Gaerity broke into a ditty:

> *"From Carrickmacross to Crossmaglen*
> *There are more traitors than loyal men."*

Dove gnashed his teeth at the mention of the border town where Shiofra and the others had died.

"Now, Liam," Gaerity went on, "you're coming close to feeling what I felt that first year in Castle Gleigh. It's the utter helplessness that gets you . . . wouldn't you say?"

He sang again, another corruption of a traditional child's song:

> *"Ballybay for dynamite*
> *Monaghan for AN-FO*

Carrickmacross for gelignite
'Blaney for fuse and nitro.

"House has been awfully dark, Liam. Nothing sadder than a darkened house. I figure you told her everything—only that would've moved a brave colleen like Kate out. How'd she take it? Did she look at you as if you'd turned into a monster before her very eyes? Well, that's the truth of the situation, Liam. You *are* a monster. You can either deny it and go mad, or embrace it, just as I have. I knew you were of the fold the first time I laid eyes on you. Face of an angel but the heart of a demon. Say, how's this for an idea? You get me on the squad. One night I plant and you try to defuse them. The next night, make it the other way around. There's a completeness to that. It appeals to me. You too?"

Dove went to the window behind the chair, parted the curtains. Nothing moved on the street.

"And how about the squad? Have you told them about their wild colonial boy, Liam McGivney? Don't worry. I shan't be the first to tell. I'll leave that up to you. Meanwhile, must sign off. Never fear, I'll call again. So much to say. All that time in solitary, I suppose. May the road rise to blow up in your face." He laughed once more, then silence.

Dove picked up the machine and hurled it against the wall.

Gaerity bent over the Krups coffeepot. *Plup . . . plup.* A sickly green juice was pulsing in the little glass nipple atop the lid. "Oh that's very fine, very fine," he murmured to himself, taking the pot off the butane stove. He turned off the flame.

He walked through an open hatch and out onto the flying bridge of the *Dolphin Runner*. The moon had yet to rise, and the Inner Harbor was dark except for a few spangled trails of light off Logan's runways.

A buoy horn wailed mournfully. He poured the green liquid over the side, then returned to his makeshift laboratory.

Shortly after five o'clock, he'd made a second call to Liam, this time hoping to catch him at work. Thwarted again by modern conveniences. A recorded voice told him to press one for voice mail, two for his call to be diverted to the Boston P.D. communications center. He pressed one, then was instructed to punch in the first three letters of the squad member he wished to contact. D . . . O . . . V. No wonder the world was in absolute turmoil. It was being taken over by machines. He'd hung up after delivering his message, resolved to blow up the phone company at the first opportunity.

Now he removed the coffee filter from its cylinder and closely inspected the paper. As he watched, delicate emerald-colored crystals took shape. Barium nitrate.

"Oh yes," he said, breaking into song.

> *"We'll grow our own
> And blast our own
> In good old Tullaroan."*

He snapped a Baggie out of a box of them, placed the filter inside it, then added his freshest batch of barium nitrate to a drawer under the chart table. He'd suspended these Baggies by clothespinning them to rows of fishing lines. To allow them to dry proper.

"Harvest only that which is ripe," he said, taking one of the plastic bags already inside the drawer and pocketing it. "Now where's that bloody torch?"

Turning, he grabbed a flashlight and left the bridge. He made his way down darkened passageways and ladders to the engine room. Awful stench. Stagnant water lay under the bilge plates, and more of it dripping down all the time from the pooled rainwater in the salon directly above. Must be careful of stepping on corroded portions of the deck up there.

Gaerity took a six-foot-long wooden pole and crossed a catwalk to a tank. "Diesel" was stenciled in red letters on its big cap, which he removed. He plunged the stick down into the blackness, paused a moment, then drew it out. Four feet of its length glistened with fuel.

More than he'd expected.

Next he went to the engines. They were rusted, stripped of their injectors, and he could see directly down into the massive cylinders. He spun open a big valve above them. There was a gurgling sound, then a low rumble as diesel began flooding into the cylinders. He dug the Baggie from his pocket and laid the crystal-coated filter on the last cylinder in line.

Humming softly to himself, he watched the fuel rise and inundate the filter. After several seconds, the barium nitrate floated to the surface. Its little slick was as round and green as a lily pad. A seal of quality on some extremely high-quality ANFO. He grunted in satisfaction, then started back for the bridge.

"All things come to he who waits," he said, his voice echoing around him.

15

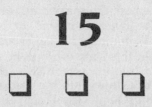

It almost seemed the voice of the Ryan Gaerity who would lead his confederates to a corner of the schoolyard and brag about his latest crimes. Striking the Union Jack that waved before the Presbyterian church and hanging the minister's cat in its place. Putting sugar in the gas tank of the constable's English Ford. "Sorry about your Manfred toy, lads," his voice was saying from the recorder, "but it's a peculiar Americanism to rely so much on technology. It's flesh, blood, and bone that sees you through the maze."

Dove hit the stop button.

No, there was something new in the voice. Something that went light-years beyond that juvenile pleasure in mischief and cruelty. Dove couldn't quite put his finger on it. Maybe an underlying rage, molten, that was rapidly dissolving Gaerity's rationality. He'd always been cruel—but calculating as well. In the old days, he would never have done anything that might accidentally derail his own cause. Like sitting back after a blast and phoning the peelers to gloat.

Gaerity, whether he realized it or not, was behaving as if this were his last job, ever.

And that worried Dove more than anything.

The briefing room door opened behind him. He heard it close again. Ordinarily, he would've ignored it, but now he twisted around in his chair for a glance. It was Franklin, yet it just as easily could have been Gaerity. In this state of mind he was capable of anything. The more outlandishly dangerous, the more appealing to him.

"You look like hell," Dove said, turning back to the tape recorder.

"Good morning to you too, Lieutenant. Sleep in those clothes?"

"Matter of fact, I did." Dove rewound the tape a few seconds, then replayed:

"... so much on technology. It's flesh, blood, and bone that sees you through the maze ..."

Franklin asked, "What's that?"

"Quiet a minute." Again, Dove rewound and played, listening intently, then backed the tape up one more time. "Came in shortly after quitting time yesterday evening."

Franklin straddled a chair, sat with his chin on the back. "Is that our boy?"

"Yes ... identifies himself on the tape as Ryan Gaerity."

"He sounds like he's off his fucking rocker."

"You can count on it," Dove said. "Listen to this—"

"... *bone that sees you through the maze* ..."

Dove clicked off the tape, looked to Franklin.

"What?"

"Didn't you hear it?"

"Sure, the voice."

"No, forget that," Dove said irritably. "Something in the background. *Listen* now."

"... *sees you through the maze* ..."

Dove could tell that Franklin had finally picked

out the mournful sound behind Gaerity's words. A moan, vaguely human.

"Foghorn?" Franklin asked.

Dove shook his head as he lit up a cigarette. Three packs since last night's dinner of clam strips and Pepsi. "Too soft. It's a buoy."

"So what're you saying—he's by the water? Boston's surrounded by water. There must be a thousand buoys."

"Not like this one," Dove said. "They use bells now, not horns. Except for the old ones down along the Inner Harbor. The owners of the tourist traps wanted to keep them. Think they give atmosphere." He reached for the telephone and depressed the intercom button. Roarke answered, smacked his lips as if he'd been awakened out of a nap. "Captain, it's Dove. Get down here. Finally, I've got something."

"Right away, Jim."

Dove's cigarette was giving him a watering eye. Taking it from the corner of his mouth, he recued the tape. He felt Franklin's gaze on him.

"What else do you have, Lieutenant?" the sergeant asked.

Dove looked up sharply at him, but said nothing.

"Good is good," Franklin went on. "But incredible is incredible. How'd you know there were two triggers in my stereo? That's pretty damn amazing, even for you. And if you weren't part of this squad, we'd all still be scratching our heads over what happened to McNulty." He paused. "But then, if it weren't for you, maybe there would've been no blast on the bridge—and Blanket'd still be alive."

Strangely, Dove thought of Gaerity's instructions of long ago in the event he was captured and interrogated. Maintain eye contact. Don't appear overly threatened. Remain composed, open, spontaneous. And, whatever you do, don't touch your lips with your fingers after lying.

Dove smiled as if confused. *"What?"*

"You heard me, man. He phoned you right after Durgin and Cortez bought it in the square. I saw your face. It looked just like it did right now when you were listening to the tape."

"Anthony, you may not realize it," Dove said mildly, "but what went down in your apartment left you mad as hell. It's all a predictable behavior pattern, okay? First, you're scared after being victimized like that . . ." Franklin glanced off into a corner of the room. "Then you get pissed," Dove continued. "Royally pissed. Some son of a bitch almost made you crap your pants. But where is that bastard? You don't know, do you? But your guts are still churning over this thing, right? You have to shit on *somebody* or explode. So who's handy? Me. Dove. The know-it-all prick who hauled your chestnuts out of the fire, who saw you sweating bullets."

"Bullshit," Franklin said, eyes hot.

Just when Dove had thought that he was making a small dent. He leaned back in his chair. "Oh yeah? Well, I can't count the times I've been through this." Then his own temper came to the surface. "And that's why I'm not knocking your insolent ass off that chair!"

"If I'm really out of line, Lieutenant—do it."

Dove ran his hand over his hair, smiled, then lowered his voice. "I suppose I deserve it. Stick around with dopers long enough, you start to think like dopers. Talk like them. I guess I've been around blasters too long."

"I don't know what you've been around, Dove," Franklin said. "You're the reason this shit's coming down."

"Do you know what you're saying?"

"Yes. So do you. And it doesn't have a goddamn thing to do with an acute stress reaction, the Stockholm Syndrome, or anything else—except you, James

Dove, and the fact that you're a fucking lightning rod." Franklin's hands plucked at the shoulders of his BDU uniform. "I've become a walking target just like the rest of these suckers. I need the truth, goddammit. Do you think I'm going to trust my fate to some stuckup bastard who doesn't even like me!"

Dove started to light a fresh smoke when he saw that another was still smoldering in the ashtray. "You'll get the truth. The whole nine yards. Soon enough. But for the time being, I'm asking you to do what's best for the unit."

"Best for the unit or best for you?"

Dove seized a handful of Franklin's shirt cloth and jerked him to his feet. "You're right—I don't like you worth a fuck!" he snarled, coming within an inch of smacking him. "But this uniform makes that irrelevant. I'll do everything in my power to keep you alive. And if you have any brains at all you'll make sure I'm around to do that. Shitcan me, Franklin—and Gaerity is all yours!"

The door clicked shut, and Roarke stood just inside the room, smiling uncomfortably. "What's up? Who's got what?"

"Lieutenant's got it goddamn all," Franklin said on his way out, smoothing his shirtfront with a hand. He slammed the door behind him.

Roarke approached Dove. "What's that all about?"

"Kid's just feeling the pressure. Like the rest of us," Dove said, hoping that the color had risen in his face. He turned on the recorder. "Check this out . . ."

Listening to Gaerity's gleeful voice, Dove realized that he had failed his second brush with the moral dilemma Ryan had given him. He'd come within a breath of squaring with Franklin.

But he hadn't.

Max O'Bannon failed to stand with the rest of the Fenway crowd as the white speck ricocheted off the

Green Monster. From the corner of his eye, he saw Mo Vaughn round first base and trot easily into second—but most of his attention was on the hot dog vendor who was trooping up the aisle, hunched with age, with a shapeless nose from a failed boxing career as a bantamweight.

As the crowd sat, O'Bannon sprang up from his aisle seat. "Hot dog!"

The vendor scowled. How he acknowledged a customer. He stopped, opened his hot case. "What're you doin' here, O'Bannon? They don't sell Bushmill's, and when the sun creeps over the stands you'll melt like the great lump of lard you are."

"Ah, grand to see you too, Boyle," O'Bannon said, sitting again. "Two dogs, four catsups, six mustards, and eight relishes."

"You want me to send for some horseradish and capers while we're at it?"

"Quit your bellyachin'. Is it a crime if I like 'em spicy? How're you doin'?"

"Feet are killin' me." Boyle dug beyond the first layer for O'Bannon's hot dogs. Moister that way. "But if they didn't hurt all the time I'd think somethin' was wrong with me. Four bucks, O'Bannon—and you're retired, so a peek at your badge won't do instead."

"Did I ever hit you up for a pop?"

"Does the devil have dibs on Protestants?"

"Well, if I did, it was an accident."

Boyle harrumphed. "Accident, he says."

"Sure," O'Bannon said, munching, "I thought you were just givin' me a freebie out of the kindness of your heart. Sit down there a spell."

"Sit down, he says. And get fired."

"I saw you sit down on top of your weiners for all of the All-Star Game in sixty-one—and don't deny it. It was a one-one tie in the ninth, and if it hadn't been for the rainout you'd still be sittin' here."

"All right, all right." Boyle checked over his shoulder, then eased down onto the step beside O'Bannon's chair. "You didn't have to resort to blackmail."

O'Bannon chuckled. "So . . . you still passin' the hat to keep the homefront in hot potatoes?"

"Workin' for Scotland Yard these days?"

"No, for meself. Say, you and the boys wouldn't be feedin' a wayward brother new to town, would you?"

"Damn you, Max—you didn't say I was in for a grillin'. Four bucks and I'm off." Boyle started to rise, but O'Bannon held him down.

"Easy, friend." O'Bannon rested the remaining hot dog in his lap, took a folded mugshot from the pocket of his polo shirt, and pressed it into Boyle's palm.

The vendor unfolded it, finding the fifty-dollar bill within. He studied the photograph for only a second before handing it back and pocketing the note. "Where'd you get that?"

"Still got my sources." Patrol had received them by the bushel, but O'Bannon didn't say that. "His name's Gaerity," he went on. "Ryan Gaerity. But I doubt he's socializin' under that name here in town. If you or the boys have done him any favors, you've only done the cause harm."

"When've you ever been concerned about the cause?" Boyle asked sourly.

O'Bannon grinned, then said in a hush, "Smile when you accuse me of somethin' like that, friend— or I'll send you up the aisle wearing that aluminum case of yours like a crown." He then shot to his feet and clapped as Detroit's pitcher overthrew first base and Vaughn loped for home. "That's it, lad!" Sitting, he lowered his voice again. "I pray every night for Ireland's freedom. One island, one nation. Catholic and Protestant in peace together under the green and orange flag. That's always been my dream. But I don't see how bombs will bring that about. Bombs bring the death of innocent children, and don't deny that the money you raise comes to that now and again, Timothy Boyle."

The vendor's mouth tightened.

"Gaerity's a whore of death," O'Bannon went on. "Killin' Boston cops right and left. Not to mention the Irishmen he murdered bustin' out of Castle Gleigh. But I'm willin' to let all that go for the time bein'."

Boyle looked worried. "What're you askin' for? A meetin' or what?"

"A meetin', if it can be arranged. Just his whereabouts, if not."

"I won't set him up, O'Bannon. I'm no bloody Judas. If you meet him, you'll come alone. No wire. And no revolver bulgin' on your hip."

"That his condition or yours?"

"Everybody's."

O'Bannon nodded after a moment.

"Armagh men eat like pigs," Boyle said, rising. "I'm out of fuckin' condiments. Back in a bit with more mustard for you."

O'Bannon started to unwrap his second hot dog, but then suddenly tossed it under the seat. Jimmy Dove would have a fit if he knew about this. But, God willing, he'd know nothing until Gaerity was collared. Going to the meeting without a handgun didn't really bother O'Bannon. His hands were still angry for what the man had done to his niece. His hands were strong with anger.

The inning ended on a strikeout. Clemens led the Red Sox back out onto the field. "Come on, Roger boy," O'Bannon said absently.

His mind was still on Gaerity.

Yes, this was the only way to do it. Keep Liam out of it. He'd suffered enough. O'Bannon remembered the first time he'd heard of Liam McGivney. It was at Shiofra's funeral. As they marched behind the casket, a friend of his brother's filled him in on what Gaerity had done in Crossmaglen. And how a boy in the same unit, a lean wisp of a lad who'd been fond of Shiofra, had tried to stop the sacrificial bombing. "Where's the boy now?" O'Bannon asked. Along the coast in County Down, hiding for his life, not knowing if he'd be killed by the Provos or the Brits. "Get him over to me," O'Bannon said. "Sneak him on a ship bound for Boston, and I'll find him a life." And so Liam arrived weeks later on the Battery Wharf, the saddest sight O'Bannon had ever seen, a teenager with an eighty-year-old stare. On duty at the time, Max pretended to collar him for vagrancy, then took him home to his wife for a needed bit of mothering. Emma had given Liam his alias. "Dove," she had said. "After all he's been through, he's still as gentle as a dove."

Boyle returned, his eyes cold now. "Let's see if this'll hold you," he said, giving O'Bannon a handful of mustard packets before moving down the aisle.

Among them was a slip of paper. On it was scribbled: *O'Dowell's Pub. 3 o'clock. Alone or else.*

16

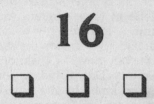

The buoy near the bow of the Moroccan freighter had a bell that clanged with each swell. But the buoy off the stern was equipped with the old-style horn. The ship, then, marked the eastern edge of the search area along the Inner Harbor.

Dove stood on the wharf in the shade of the superstructure, watching the swarm of patrolmen going from warehouse to warehouse. Franklin, who hadn't said two words to him since they'd left the bomb squad building, was talking to an old longshoreman on his coffee break. Dove strolled over to them. The stevedore was saying to the sergeant, "Sure, I knowed you two was dicks right off." His face had weathered to the texture of chamois. "All the dicks come in salt and pepper. Ever since that kid ..." He began snapping his gnarled fingers. "Oh ... big ... funny ..."

Franklin offered, "Cosby?"

"Yeah. And the white guy . . ." More finger snapping.

"Robert Culp?"

"Yeah. All black and white these days. Don't none of you guys make friends with your own kind no more?"

186

Franklin smirked at Dove. The first half-friendly gesture in four hours now. Then the sergeant took the mugshot from his inner jacket pocket and gave it to the old man. "Seen him anywhere down here on the docks?"

A full minute of scrutiny, a pensive sip of coffee, then: "You know, this kinda looks like the white guy."

"What white guy?" Franklin asked.

"The one you just said. The one used to be with Cosby."

Franklin rolled his eyes. "You noticed anybody—you know, street people, bums, whatever—sleeping in the warehouses?"

"Sometimes. But not recent. Cops run 'em off. They start fires in the buildin's to keep warm, you know."

Dove motioned toward the far end of the wharf. "All that down there looks pretty quiet."

"Yeah," the longshoreman said, "gamblin' ship company went belly-up. You know, after all the Indian reservations got in the business."

"Where's the ship?" Franklin asked.

The old man flung the last drops of coffee out of his lid and screwed it back on his thermos. "Just step around the dock office here. You'll see it. What's left of it. Sprung a leak on her last voyage, and they just let it go. She's sittin' on the bottom. Well, gents, it's two-fifteen, and the rules say I go back to work."

Dove asked, "Ever see anybody go aboard?"

"Just some guy on a bicycle once."

"Describe him."

"I dunno—a guy. I don't got eagle eyes."

Dove exchanged glances with Franklin, then they started down the wharf. Rounding the corner of the dock office, they saw the listing derelict.

"Call for backup?" Franklin said. "Plenty of blue-suiters in the neighborhood."

"No, let's check it out ourselves. If it turns out to be Gaerity, numbers won't scare him."

"What does scare him?"

"Nothing. He's where you think you want to be."

At two o'clock, Gaerity's cellular phone chimed. He applied his bicycle brake by reverse-pedaling and skidded to a stop. He looked around for police. A number of them had poured through the narrow walkway and onto the wharf a half-hour ago, forcing him to abandon the *Dolphin Runner*. Before leaving, he'd smashed up the gangway planking, making passage look almost impossible. "Yes . . . ?"

"Mr. Barry?"

"Speaking."

"It's Johnny Dunne, the bartender down at O'Dowell's."

Gaerity smiled. "Knew your voice at once, dear friend. I take it you have a message for me."

"Sorta. There's a cop who wants to meet with you."

"Cop?"

"Well, retired. Name's O'Bannon."

"Oh yes, I've heard of him. Any idea what he wants?"

Dunne hesitated, then said, "Well, he's made some accusations. Says you're this Provo named Gaerity. Killed cops and all. A real hard case."

Gaerity chuckled. "Oh, the stories. I will say this, dear Johnny. I've never killed a friend of Ireland."

"I understand," the bartender said gravely. "That's what we all figured. So we set some conditions."

"Such as?"

"Nobody comes armed. No wires. No setups. O'Bannon is finished in this town if he involves the P.D. anyway whatsoever."

"But won't he?" Gaerity asked.

"No, he's as good as his word. He's a tad soft on Northern Ireland, but he's okay otherwise."

"Very well," Gaerity said, "what time?"

"Three o'clock too soon?"

Gaerity took his bearings. He was a block away from Old North Church—he could see the steeple. "No. Tell Mr. O'Bannon I'll be there. And thank you for looking out for my interests, Johnny. I won't forget this."

"My pleasure. *Erin go bragh.*"

"Naturally." He disconnected. The only one of the timeworn sayings that rang true to him. Ireland till doomsday. The clock was ticking.

Must think.

It was a trap, of course. But with every trap came an opportunity to rush in and steal the bait before the iron jaws could be sprung. The bait here was Maxwell O'Bannon, originally of County Armagh, one of Liam's nearest and dearest pals.

Gaerity leaned his bicycle against the front bricks of a small coffeeshop and ducked inside. He took a table at the rear that had a clear view of the entrance and a peek through the windows at any sidewalk traffic. The police were now out in force looking for him. And, the world over, they tended to look for something only when they knew what it looked like.

"May I help you?" the waitress asked.

"Uh . . . yeah," he said in his best Boston accent, "how 'bout some coffee, black, and a bagel with cream cheese? Say, how long can I pahk on the street out here?"

"Two hours, honey."

"Thanks."

The question was: Did Liam know about this meeting? It didn't sound like his sort of approach. Too blunt. He would realize the dangers and take every possible precaution. He wouldn't agree to any conditions, knowing from the early days that there were no rules to this game.

Still, a little insurance was in order.

His coffee arrived. Gaerity winced. Awful stuff, coffee. Nevertheless, he took his cup with him down a gum-encrusted corridor to the pay telephone. Cambridge, he made up his mind. Draw off as much of the squad as possible from the downtown area. Dove, out of guilt alone, would respond to all the IED calls.

Checking the yellow pages, Gaerity went through the list of department stores, finally picked one at random, and dialed the security office.

"Store police," a pleasant-sounding fellow answered.

"You got a bomb, buddy. I'll give you a hint. It ain't in your desk. Everything else is fair game. Last time you sons of bitches fuck with me."

Then he hung up and went back to his table, pocketed the bagel, and picked up his check. He winked at the waitress on his way to the cash register.

Dove and Franklin stared at the gangway ramp. It looked as if the entire center of the span had rotted out. "I don't know, man," Franklin said. "Maybe we can roll SWAT to bring out a ladder."

"This could be Gaerity," Dove said.

"So?"

"Read the file—he always leaves himself a way in and out." Grabbing the pipe rail, Dove started heel-to-toe up the stringer beam.

"It's going to collapse," Franklin said. "You're going swimming. You'll get dysentery and all kinds of shit from that water, man."

"Shut up." Dove was halfway across when both his and Franklin's beepers came on. "Oh Jesus." He jumped onto the quarterdeck, then took out his cellular and dialed dispatch.

"Where is it?" Franklin asked, coming up the

stringer with one eye on the filthy water thirty feet below.

"Merriam's Department Store in Cambridge," Dove said. Then he told the dispatcher to have Captain Roarke give him a ring at once.

The call came in just as Franklin joined him on the deck. Dove jerked his thumb for the sergeant to keep watch on a nearby hatch. It was propped open. "Captain?"

"Yeah, Jim!" A siren was almost drowning out Roarke's words.

"Give us a few minutes, then Franklin and I will roll from the north end."

"Don't. 'Bama and I got this one. I want you two in town for anything else that might come up. This sounds like a tease. Disgruntled ex-employee trying to hurt receipts. Definitely not an Irish accent."

Dove fell silent for a few seconds. It didn't seem like Gaerity, but the bastard could pass himself off as anyone. 'Bama had been putting on a show of cheerfulness ever since he'd blown an emotional gasket in Franklin's apartment. But, actually, his improved mood might be one more sign that he was washed up. He might fail Roarke in Cambridge. Still, Dove saw no choice other than to say, "Okay, Fred—be careful."

"You too."

Dove put away his cellular, caught Franklin's eye, and said, "Let's see what SWAT taught you about searches."

O'Bannon found a parking space for his Bonneville well down the street from O'Dowell's Pub. He shut off the engine and sat a moment, thinking. A ray of afternoon sunlight slanted down through a tear in the ragtop and found his left hand. His wedding band glinted. "Ah yes, dear Emma," he murmured, "what're you sayin' about this? Setting out to kill a man. Well, he is no man, darlin'. He's a venomous snake, and you must take the hoe to a vermin." O'Bannon smiled. "Today's my day to play Saint Paddy and drive the serpents out of Boston. Will you bless that undertakin', Emma . . . please?"

O'Bannon twisted the band off his finger, pocketed it. *Till death do us part* had never made much sense to him. Sometimes she felt a closer part of him now than when they'd shared the same bed.

He looked around. Bad place to leave his car with a bomber coming to call.

Restarting the engine, he saw a red zone for a fire hydrant in front of the pub. Good enough. He drove to it, parallel-parked, and left his Retired Police Officers' Association membership card on the dash.

Then he went inside.

He halted just beyond the open door and stepped to the side, out of the square of sunlight that would make him an easy target.

Waiting for his eyes to adjust to the smoky gloom, he listened. He could hear the soft thud of darts striking the board. And the telly was going. A prize fight—that's right, a new middleweight from Galway was taking on Harlem's best.

Gradually, human shapes emerged out of the shadows. Three men sitting at a table. Locals, all of them. Two more men were playing darts. Both too short and squat to be Ryan Gaerity. The barkeep, a former officer of NORAID, the old cash pipeline to the IRA, turned from the fight and stared.

O'Bannon lit a fresh cigar, shook out the match, then said, "Bless all here."

Silence, but for the television.

O'Bannon slid onto a stool. "Double shot of Bushmill's and a Harp chaser. Johnny Dunne, isn't it?"

The bartender nodded, then grudgingly went to work. His eyes never roved around the place, which told O'Bannon that Gaerity hadn't shown yet. Johnny glanced over his shoulder at the screen just as the Irish fighter was knocked back on his heels, the sweat flying off his red hair. Only the bell kept him from winding up against the ropes. "You cockbite, Seamus," Johnny bawled, "keep your goddamn mitts up!"

"And fine glaums he has," O'Bannon noted before downing the whiskey in two quick gulps. "But the black boys have an edge in this."

"It's the nigger skull," a voice said from behind. "It's got fewer natural cracks in it than a normal fella's."

O'Bannon pivoted on the stool and smiled affably as he said, "Is that it then, lads?"

The three men at the table, one of whom had been the speaker, said nothing more.

Taking a sip of beer, O'Bannon peered out the front door. His Chevy looked undisturbed, but a bicycle was now tethered to the lamppost near it. He supposed that enough explosives could be crammed into the bike's frame to blow the Bonneville clear across the street. A little unsettling—that the rider had yet to enter the pub.

"You Yanks don't have tinkers," a voice said from beside O'Bannon. "But you still have thieves aplenty. Right, Dad?"

Gaerity was sitting on the stool beside him. Vicious eyes and an insincere smile. Face more gaunt than in his mugshot. Obviously, he'd slithered in through the back, just like the snake he was.

It was all O'Bannon could do to smile. "Aye, you're smart to lock it up like that."

"Black porter, Johnny," Gaerity said to the bartender before facing O'Bannon again. "Got the lock and the chain at a garage sale. Wondrous things, garage sales."

"Goddammit!" Johnny cried, foam gushing over the edge of the tall glass as he watched the fighter from Galway take a series of body blows that ended only when the black boxer grew too tired to carry on the attack.

Gaerity said, "Think our barman's got a bit of the legal tender riding on this one, Dad."

O'Bannon gave Gaerity's clothes a quick glance-over. He was wearing faded Levi's, a gray Harvard T-shirt, and a summer jacket. No apparent objects in any of the pockets. A dark line of dried blood showed on his right thumb. Scab from a cut of some sort. "Well, gamblin' can become a sickness, if you're not careful."

The cold, reptilian eyes fixed on O'Bannon. "Surprising, the things that become a sickness if you're not careful, Dad."

Then Gaerity grinned and slapped him on the back, letting his hand casually drop to Max's midriff. It amounted to a frisk on the sly, expertly done. "Now, Dad, let me guess what county you hail from."

"I'll save you the trouble—Suffolk County, South Boston, last bastion of workin' class decency."

"No, no," Gaerity said, pausing for a draft of porter, "there's lots of Irish in that voice. You grew up in the old country and don't tell me otherwise."

"What makes you think I grew up?"

Gaerity laughed, and O'Bannon thought that was the end of it. But then the man pressed, "Derry County?"

"Cold. Cold as the bloody Atlantic up there. I shiver just thinkin' of Ulster."

"Cavan?"

O'Bannon took a sip, shrugged. "Warmer."

"West Meath?"

"There you have it," O'Bannon lied. "Born and reared barefooted on the shore of Lough Ree." No use in confessing that he was from Armagh: Gaerity might make the connection with Shiofra.

The man didn't look convinced. "I once knew some O'Bannons down there. In the village of Kiltoom."

"Well, I'm from Glassan across the lake. And there are O'Bannons everywhere. A full page of us in the Boston phone book. Chalk it up to love. We take to it like birds to the air."

Gaerity nodded, then raised his glass and toasted, "May those who love us, love us. And those who don't love, may God turn their hearts."

"But if He can't turn their hearts," O'Bannon finished for him, "may He turn their ankles so we'll know them by their limping."

"You're okay, Dad," Gaerity said. *"Sláinte!"* He then held up his glass for O'Bannon to tap it with his own.

Yet Max hesitated. He was seeing Shiofra being borne toward the churchyard. A blustery afternoon with a broken sky. Her casket had looked so small under that sky.

At last he forced himself to touch his glass to Gaerity's.

"A hawk never soared on just one wing, Dad."

"Sure, set 'em up again."

"Johnny . . ." Gaerity pointed at their empty glasses. "So, O'Bannon, to what do I owe the pleasure of your company?"

"Suck me dead!" Johnny howled, slapping a hand to his forehead. His fighter was out cold on the canvas, and the black man was still bouncing around on the toes of his shoes.

"We warned you, Johnny," one of the men at the table said. "You can't bet on the white fella in this sport."

One of the television commentators was saying, "Flanagan is still out . . . the doctor has now entered the ring. If he's badly hurt, and we hope Flanagan isn't, it'll only add to the controversy surrounding boxing, I'm sure."

"Absolutely right, Marv," the other commentator jumped in, "there are those people who maintain that boxing is akin to murder, to killing a man in cold blood. Well, it isn't. The training these athletes—"

Johnny flipped off the TV in disgust.

O'Bannon saw that Gaerity was still waiting for a reply.

The man was a butcher, a mass murderer. He deserved to die and rot in hell.

Yet, now that the moment had come to send him down into the fires, Max wasn't sure that it was his place to do it. This, he suddenly realized, was what Emma would say to him. He'd left Ulster as a young man to escape kangaroo courts and summary executions. To get away from back alley justice. And he'd given his word to the gang of armchair rebels here at the pub that he would not involve the police. Yet wasn't that a small promise to break when compared to letting Ryan Gaerity walk free? "I've got a proposition for you," he finally said.

Gaerity hiked an eyebrow. "One I can't refuse?"

O'Bannon stood. "You've seen one too many gangster movies. I'll tell you all about it as soon as I visit the pisser. Watch me beer, will you? Need to choke the old snake."

"Watch your ankles, Dad," Gaerity called after him.

Dove and Franklin went through the hatch with handguns drawn. The main gambling salon tilted before them, the gaming tables seemingly poised on the brink of sliding off into the starboard bulkhead.

"Looks like a crooked joint to me," Franklin whispered.

Dove advanced over the mildewed carpet, carefully examining each table for cues of tampering.

Gaerity's trick in this kind of setting would be to leave something that begged to be handled. Dove thought he found it on the roulette wheel: the white ball was resting in the single-ought notch. Zero. Which was exactly how much Franklin was thinking when he reached for it, no doubt intending to give it a spin around the wheel.

Dove caught him by the wrist and hissed, "Think pressure release!"

The sergeant gave a sheepish nod, and Dove searched under the table. The wheel was clean. But something was missing. The ball rest that normally sat atop the spindle. Significant? He was left wondering.

"What do we look for?" Franklin asked as they moved on.

"Trip wires. Tight passageways. Dark. Natural place for them. And the file said Gaerity likes to improvise bazookas. Uses framing nails for shrapnel."

"The *file?*" Franklin was smiling doubtfully.

Dove's cellular rang. He was sure it was Roarke, already in over his head at the department store in Cambridge. "Dove."

"Jimmy."

"Max, let me get back to—"

"I got the bastard for you."

"*What?*"

"I got Gaerity cornered."

"Where?"

"O'Dowell's Pub. Just cover both doors to see which way he comes out, and it's an easy collar. He's not packin'. Just do it as he pedals off on his bicycle—that's how the unholy son of a bitch has been gettin' around town."

"Max, Max," Dove murmured, stunned. The old man didn't realize what he was up against. He hadn't cornered Gaerity; he was simply sharing the same cage with him.

"Listen, Jimmy—I kinda gave my word to the paddies here that I wouldn't call in the department. So make sure to take him down away from the place. It's a matter of honor, you see."

"Fuck honor, Max. Hang up right now and walk out."

"What're you sayin', boy?"

"Walk, dammit."

"And let Gaerity go free as a lark?"

"Exactly. Do it, *please*. We'll get him when there are enough of us to take him down safely."

"Oh Jimmy Dove," O'Bannon said, sounding offended, "d'you honestly think I'm that long in the tooth? I could still hold down a beat today, what if the civil service would let me. D'you think I'm ready for the convalescent—"

Then the line went dead.

O'Bannon stared at the receiver in confusion. He had stepped inside the men's restroom, threading the steel-jacketed telephone cord through the two-inch crack he'd left in the door. He opened it all the way, and a sparkle of glass came at his face. "Here's your beer, Dad," Gaerity said, striking him. "Got tired of watching it for you."

O'Bannon stumbled back against the toilet partition, blinded by white dots. His hands went to his forehead and came away wet with blood.

There was a click as Gaerity locked the door. "Do you think me a fool, old man?"

Suddenly, O'Bannon could make out shapes. He lunged for Gaerity, pinning him against the wall. The towel dispenser crashed against the floor as Gaerity flailed his arms and spun away. He came to rest against the urinal. "Do you think I'd forget Shiofra O'Bannon had family?" He threw a quick jab that caught O'Bannon in the mouth, loosening teeth.

"That I'd forget for a minute that we Irish are basically tribal—and vengeance is our favorite dish!"

O'Bannon lumbered forward, closing his big hands around Gaerity's throat. He squeezed and watched the man's eyes grow large in his face. A burst of joy. Shiofra's killer, gagging, his face turning purple.

But then Gaerity came out with a butterfly knife, flipped it open with a snap of his wrist, and slashed the side of O'Bannon's arm. O'Bannon fell back, holding the wound closed with his bloody fingers.

"What do the Italians say, old man?" Gaerity gasped, his chest heaving, knife held at the ready. "Vengeance is a dish best served cold. You almost did it. You almost had me convinced you weren't here to even the score!"

O'Bannon picked up the chrome towel dispenser and hurled it at Gaerity. As the man instinctively ducked, Max grabbed his wrist, bent it inward.

Gaerity grunted in pain, and the knife clattered under the stall partition and out of sight. But then O'Bannon was left off-balance for the roundhouse that followed. Again, his vision went to white. He hit the floor, and Gaerity began kicking him in the ribs. Little internal explosions as bones cracked and splintered.

O'Bannon could scarcely breathe, but he focused on the drainpipe. From the elbow of the trap, three feet of it ran straight down into the floor. Hands trembling as Gaerity went on kicking, O'Bannon grasped the pipe and pulled with everything he had left. Gaerity was now in a mindless rage. "Do you think I'm so stupid! Do you, old man!"

The fittings broke, and the steel pipe came loose in O'Bannon's clutch. Quickly, before he lost consciousness, he swung it into Gaerity's left knee.

The sharp crack of bone echoed in the tiled space.

The man collapsed but didn't cry out.

"You've gone and shattered my kneecap," he said

without emotion, sprawled on the floor. Then, wincing, he hopped up and stood over O'Bannon. "If you come to kill a man, never change your mind at the last minute."

Helplessly, O'Bannon watched Gaerity's shoe rear back, then start forward for his face.

17

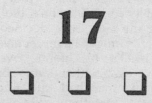

Dove ran along the wharf, holding his revolver to keep it from flopping out of his holster.

"Slow down, man!" Franklin called from behind.

"Can't!"

"Is it Roarke?" The sergeant caught up as they emerged through a narrow alleyway onto Commercial Street, where Dove had left his Harley. "Something go wrong up in Cambridge?"

"No." Hopping on one foot, Dove dug in his pocket for the key as he slowed for the bike. He straddled the seat and started the engine, but Franklin glommed onto the handlebars. The sergeant then depressed the brake lever with his left hand.

"What the hell's going on, Dove? Level with me!"

"Get outta the way."

"It's Gaerity, isn't it?"

"Yes."

"Scoot forward there. I'm going with you."

"Not this time. You used up all your luck the other morning."

Then Dove shoved Franklin's arms aside and accelerated off.

He knew that O'Bannon had given Gaerity the chance to set an elaborate trap. Gaerity, in turn, would give Dove no time to safely deal with it—not if he wanted to save Max. That would be the trade-off. Personal safety for O'Bannon's life.

Still, reaching the pub, Dove decided to circle the block once. Gaerity might have decided not to play it out at O'Dowell's, his lifeline over these past weeks. But Dove saw neither Max's Bonneville nor the bicycle the old man had said Ryan used. The neighborhood was quiet, the weeds along the cracks in the pavement wilted-looking.

Parking on the side of the pub, he unholstered and ran for the door. As much as he wanted to rush through, he took a moment to look it over before entering.

Except for the bartender, the place was empty.

"Where?" Dove demanded, gripping his revolver before him in both hands.

"Who the fuck are you?"

"*Where?*"

"I don't answer to nobody come in here wavin' a gun." Model citizen, all at once.

Dove advanced, checking under the tables and behind the jukebox. Then he reached over the bar and grabbed the bartender by the forelock. He yanked the man's face close to his. "You know who I am, Dunne—and if I have to take out my badge it's going six inches up your fat ass. *Where!*"

"Don't know," the bartender said in a low growl. "All I know is that I heard some noise in the head."

Dove let go of him. "How long ago?"

"Ten minutes, maybe."

Dove glanced down, then knelt and dipped two fingers into a blood spatter. It was just beginning to brown.

"Sure," he said, hurrying for the back. "You don't know a goddamn thing."

The men's restroom door was wide open. Beyond it lay a shambles. Dove stepped carefully through the mess, then stood on the sink to aim his revolver down into the stall.

Empty.

He began searching for devices. The crumpled towel dispenser. A metal trash receptacle. The toilet tank and light fixture over the mirror.

Nothing.

He picked up Max's tweed cap. Bloodied like most everything else in sight. The toilet partition had been heavily dented, and some plumbing ripped out of the floor.

Dove shook his head, feeling a jumble of anger, pride, and helplessness. O'Bannon had put up one hell of a fight. But he'd lost. Otherwise, blue-suiters from Patrol would already be here, and Gaerity would be handcuffed in the backseat of a cruiser.

"Damn you, Max!" Dove shouted. "Don't you listen to anybody!" He kicked the wall. Again. And again. He leaned his forehead against the tile wall and began kneading the Donegal tweed in his hands.

Something crinkled.

He looked down. A piece of thick, glossy paper was tucked inside the cap. He turned it over in his hand: a photograph of Ryan Gaerity and Liam McGivney in that long-ago Belfast schoolyard.

"I should've broken your neck then," Dove said.

Gaerity had drawn a small ink sketch in the corner. A manlike figure pierced with arrows. It made no sense to Dove. What was the bastard getting at? Was this Custer's Last Stand for the Bomb Disposal Unit?

He went out to the bar again and shook the bloody cap at Dunne. "If one hair on that old man's head is hurt, you're mine!"

"Dove, I had nothing to do—"

"Shut up!"

Dunne nodded, looking hangdog now.

"How'd they leave?"

The man started to hesitate, but then thought better

of it when he saw Dove's expression. "In O'Bannon's Chevrolet. Mr. Barry tossed his bicycle in the trunk."

"Barry?"

"That's what he calls himself. By the saints, you can ask any of the regulars."

Dove was heading for the front door when he froze. Saints. Saint. Arrows. Saint Sebastian's.

He ran for the Harley.

"Can you hear me, Mr. O'Bannon?" the voice asked. All civility.

Max's eyes were nearly swollen shut, but through the watery slits he could see a face in shadow. The day was getting late, and the sun was starting to go. Another day gone. Maybe not just another one. His last. So be it. His head was pounding; each beat of his exhausted heart came as sharply as a toothache. He could take only shallow breaths, or his ribs seemed to erupt into fire.

"Mr. O'Bannon?"

Max couldn't tell if he was sitting or standing. He was floating, maybe. Floating on a lake of flame.

"O'Bannon . . ."

"What?" he said thickly. His mouth was filled with a coppery taste. Blood.

"I want you to know that this isn't for coming to O'Dowell's to kill me."

Somehow, it struck O'Bannon as being funny. He started to chuckle, but the pain stopped him. Gaerity was in the mood for a parting chat. Irish spirit gone amok.

"I would've done the same had I been in your shoes, O'Bannon. No, I'm taking my pound of flesh for another reason. All you did for Liam. Sponsoring him over here. It had to be you to do that for him, right. Giving him a shot at the American Dream. A house on a nice street. A pretty wife and a secure job. He's had years of joy, thanks to Max O'Bannon. And for that you must be punished."

O'Bannon tried to spit on him, but there was nothing in his mouth except congealed blood.

"Something to say, old friend?" Gaerity asked.

"You want to destroy him . . ." Max felt his chin sink to his chest. He was powerless to lift it again. For the first time, he realized through his agony that something was fastened to his head. His chest too. "What've you got me wrapped in?"

"Something quite suitable for the occasion," Gaerity said. "Don't stand or jar yourself in any way—or they'll find your legs in Roxbury and your arms in Brookline. What about Liam and me?"

"You aren't a pimple on his dick. That's why you want him . . . dead. He's a fine, full man . . . and you're a pimple . . ."

Then the inside of O'Bannon's head went from gray to black again.

Decelerating around the corner, Dove was blinded by the glinting windows of the school. The flat rays of the sun were full on them, and he had to shade his eyes with a hand to scan the playground. He first noticed the statue of Saint Sebastian, realized it for what it was, then saw another human shape. This one was on the merry-go-round.

Max.

He was tied to a railing, his head sagging. Two sticks of dynamite were taped to his head like horns, and a straitjacket of plastique encased his chest. Wires bristled all over him: a morass of triggers.

Dove cut the engine and leaned the motorcycle against the chainlink fence. Drawing his revolver, he rushed through the gate—but immediately skidded to a halt.

Gaerity had to be nearby. He had to watch this.

Glancing up at the windows, Dove saw nothing but the same glare.

He holstered and started forward, watching for trip wires, disturbance of the ground that might mean Gaerity had planted a mine. He used an indirect path across the yard to the merry-go-round and approached O'Bannon from the side.

He saw nothing around Max's neck, so he checked for a pulse. Weak, shallow. Among the cakes of plastique he glimpsed a mechanical egg timer. Less than three minutes remaining. "Max?"

The bruised and swollen face twitched.

"Don't move a muscle . . . all right?"

O'Bannon's voice was almost inaudible. "Jimmy? That you?"

"I'm here."

"We alone?"

"Yes, he's gone. Nobody's here but us. Don't move."

"Is that the wind in the trees?"

Dove glanced around. The air was still, but he said, "Yes, a fine breeze."

"Like that sound. Reminds me of home. Don't have freshening breezes here . . . like home."

Gaerity had thrown in an anti-trembler device just for good measure. In a wooden block he'd gouged out a groove and dropped in a steel ball bearing. It tottered back and forth with every breath O'Bannon took. At each end of the groove was a triple-A battery. Probably just one of several sources of juice to ignite the blast. This also meant that Gaerity had remotely armed the device after walking away from O'Bannon—to keep himself from dying, had Max moved.

"What am I sittin' on, Liam?"

"Merry-go-round."

"You're kiddin'." O'Bannon made a sound. It

might have been a chuckle. "I'm wired to the hilt, right?"

"Yes," Dove admitted, fumbling for inspiration, his eyes filling. He quickly wiped them and frantically tried to think of a single measure that would cut to the heart of this Gordian knot. But he knew that there wasn't one.

Less than two minutes now.

"Somethin's making a sound like tickin'. That me too?"

"Max, I'm going back to my bike for some tools."

"No, boy—don't give him the satisfaction."

"What're you saying?"

"That's just what the snake wants you to try. Don't mean to question your talents, but I'm pretty well buggered—and you know it too."

"I learned from the son of a bitch. I can shut him down."

"By Christmas, maybe. Live to fight another day." O'Bannon struggled to open his left eye a little. "Ah, there you are, dear Liam. Tears and all. That's almost as good as goin' out with a priest. A friend's tears."

"Stop it. Don't even talk that way."

"Go on. Go get your tools."

"Don't budge," Dove ordered. "Are you listening to me?"

"Why should I?" O'Bannon rasped. "Have you ever listened to me? I told you to stay in Patrol."

Dove ran for his bike. Less than a minute. Look for the detonating devices. Blasting caps and such. Disconnect them from the dynamite and plastique. There'd still be a blast, but it would be far less than the full jolt of the explosives. Max and he might survive a lesser blow.

Dove tore the saddlebag off the Harley. He was hoisting it onto his shoulder and turning back for the schoolyard when he saw O'Bannon suddenly jerk his head upright.

"Max!"

"Forgive me, Liam."

The old man stood, seemingly into the midst of a greenish-yellow flash. Dove was thrown off his feet as the heat and roar came through the fence mesh. It rolled him across the sidewalk and flattened him against a parked car. Dust and smoke quickly followed, eclipsing the late afternoon sunlight. Dove buried his face in his arms as chunks of merry-go-round railing rained down, jangling against the asphalt, thudding against the roofs of the houses across the street.

Gaerity turned but didn't cower as the shattered glass of the classroom windows flew at him. He felt the shards bite into the back of his neck, nick his ears. But he grinned and pivoted for a look down through the smoke. The seat of explosion, the very heart of the blast, cleared first. He could see the merry-go-round, swept clean of its railings and, of course, O'Bannon. It had been folded nearly in two as easily as a pie tin.

Using a teacher's pointer as a crutch, he limped along the desks to one of the now jagged-edged windows.

Liam staggered to his feet.

Good. This was not meant to be the end of him. Just the beginning of the end. Gaerity had known precisely what the old man would do. He knew the type. Bombcraft was as much a study of human nature as of physics and chemistry.

Liam could be seen straining through the smoke for a glimpse of his friend. His dusty face was drawn, agonized. He swayed for a moment before stutter-stepping up to the fence and grabbing the mesh in clawlike hands. After a moment, his gaze swept up to the second-story window in which Gaerity stood.

He didn't step back into the shadows. He just stared back at Liam, his face blank.

"You watched!" McGivney roared, starting for the building. "You stayed to watch, you son of a bitch!"

Gaerity simply mouthed the word "yes," then about-faced and hobbled out of the classroom, his shoes crunching over the broken glass.

Something made him pause as Liam's voice echoed up from the vestibule in which the Madonna opened her plaster of Paris arms to all who entered: "I'll kill you, Gaerity!" He stood his ground a moment longer, savoring the thrill, knowing that Liam was after him with a revolver, then hurried for the far end of the corridor. Each step made his breath seize, so sharp was the pain of his broken kneecap, but he smiled. On IRA orders, he'd kneecapped many a poor fellow through the years, yet only now did he realize how intoxicatingly powerful that punishment had been. He even felt some of Liam's grief for the fine old man, and that too only heightened his sense of power.

He opened the sash window and climbed out onto the fire escape platform.

"Freeze!" Liam screamed as he swung around the stair newel post, his handgun glinting in the dimness. "Stop right there or I shoot!"

Still smiling, Gaerity started down the wrought-iron ladder. He was forced to jump the last eight feet to the ground. He tried to land with most of his weight on his good leg, but still the pain from his knee went through him like lightning. It left him with the sensation that he had no body, just an indomitable spirit that kept surging toward O'Bannon's Bonneville.

Liam screamed something more from above, but Gaerity lost it in the slam of the car door and the gunning of the engine.

Once more, he paused. This time, he waited before

dropping the automatic shift lever into drive—knowing full well that Liam was training his revolver through the Chevy's rear window.

Finally, he said, "It's a long shot on short nerve, Liam," and pressed the gas pedal to the firewall. He sped away, tires screeching on the three quick turns he made before blending into the downtown traffic.

18

Franklin spread the contents of the file over Captain Roarke's desk. It was labeled "Computer Codes," but inside were pamphlets on residential lawn irrigation systems and "building your dream loghouse in the Maine woods." Only one typed page dealt with accessing outside agency data bases. And nothing in that helped Franklin's specific need.

Finally, after ten fruitless minutes, he gave up and dialed the department's computer center. "May I speak to Jeffries, please."

"You're talking at him."

One of those people who never sounded like himself. He'd quit SWAT after developing head problems over accidentally killing a black hostage during a bank robbery call. Found himself a less stressful home in Support Services. "This is Franklin."

"Hey, what's happening, man?" Jeffries was also one of those white people who didn't quite believe that black people understood standard English.

"Not much." At least since Dove had vanished on the heels of O'Bannon's death, leaving Homicide to literally pick up the pieces. "Tell me—how do I access the Interpol main from one of the terminals over here?"

"Over here meaning SWAT?"

"No, I'm with BDU now."

"Really? You are *bad*. Wouldn't catch my ass in bombs right now. How many vacancies you got?"

"Too many," Franklin said curtly.

Then, abruptly, Jeffries turned all business again. "You can't do what you're asking."

"Why not?"

"Only one terminal in the whole department is empowered to plug into that system. And it's in Intelligence. Interpol's mainframe just isn't big and powerful enough to handle inquiries from twenty thousand law enforcement agencies in this country alone."

"Shit." Franklin checked his watch. It was two-thirty in the morning. Even if Intelligence were open for business, there was no way he could approach it with an inquiry about Lieutenant Francis James Dove.

Then Jeffries said, "Well, maybe there's a way . . ."

"Yeah?"

"Lemme try. Which terminal you at?"

"Captain Roarke's office."

"Oh, Christ. You'll probably have to disconnect his Nintendo first. Roarke phones me twice a week just trying to figure out his electronic mail." Jeffries sighed. "I'll phone back as soon as I have something."

"Thanks, guy—I really appreciate it."

Franklin hung up and strolled to the doorway. The main working area was darkened. Three of the desks had been swept clean of pads, pens, Rolodexes. They looked like green sarcophaguses. Franklin stared at his own cluttered desk and wondered how it'd look a month from now. Would the nameplate go into a cardboard box marked: "Personal Effects: A. Franklin"? He'd had to leave the room each time some-

body from personnel had appeared to do that chore.
It was just too creepy.

Roarke's phone rang.

Franklin hurried back to answer. "Yes."

"You got fifteen minutes. And if somebody's working late at Intelligence, my goose is cooked."

"Thanks, man. Bye." Franklin flew into the swivel
chair, booted up the screen. Scanning the instructions, he impatiently tapped the sides of the keyboard. Finally, he typed in under subject search:

DOVE, Francis James

Any typos? None, so he entered it.

Dove's date of birth would've been helpful, but
information like that was in Roarke's safe, and Franklin had decided to draw the line at misdemeanors.
Besides, if Dove was an alias, he no doubt would've
phonied his vitals as well.

Franklin's return came almost a full minute later:

Subject not found.

Sighing, Franklin sat back.

No, Dove would be slicker than that. And he'd
make sure that he couldn't be traced through any
possible American relatives. Half the Irish in Boston
had smuggled in a kinsman or two under the noses
of Immigration. Relatives were the way to ferret them
out of hiding. And if Interpol was on the hunt for a
fugitive, the investigators would lean on the kin first.

Franklin tapped his lower lip with a finger, then
typed:

GAERITY, Ryan

The computer asked him if he had a middle name
for the subject. No, he replied.

Still, within seconds, the screen went white with text. Franklin was leaning forward on his elbows to read it when a box appeared in the middle of the screen:

ALERT: Have you apprehended this subject or do you know his whereabouts at this time? Y N

Quickly, Franklin answered no. Otherwise Interpol would be telephoning Intelligence within minutes.

The text returned.

Criminal occupation: Terrorist.

"Tell me something I don't know," he said out loud.

Affiliations. Originally Irish Republican Army. Then a splinter group known as the Green Street Regulars. Doctrine that assassination, particularly by bombing, the most likely way to discourage British rule in Northern Ireland. Before going on to Gaerity's service with the Baader-Meinhof Gang and Libyan Special Intelligence Service, Franklin zeroed in on the Green Streeters. A list of terrorist operations sprang up. Bombings and snipings all over Northern Ireland. The last IED operation in the list was Crossmaglen, County Armagh, on May 1, 1971.

Franklin asked for the names of known members, then moved the cursor down them, hoping to find a Dove.

None.

Of the five names given, besides Ryan Gaerity's, four of the subjects were deceased. All on May 1, 1971, at Crossmaglen. The exception was Liam McGivney of Belfast. Present status unknown. No recorded living relatives. No entries after that date in 1971. Nothing. An empty bin. Possibly dead as well?

Franklin checked his watch. Only six more minutes before the terminal went down.

He went through Gaerity's activities with West German terrorists and the Libyans. Little of note. And no mention of an incident after Crossmaglen that might have involved James Dove, who joined Boston P.D. in the early seventies.

Then it hit him. O'Bannon.

One of the Green Streeters had been a Shiofra O'Bannon. Interpol listed the relatives even of deceased subjects, no doubt to widen the net to catch any surviving members of the gang, like Gaerity and McGivney.

"Whoa," Franklin said.

Shiofra had had relatives all over Armagh—and a Maxwell O'Bannon of Boston, Massachusetts.

"Shit," he said, "holy shit."

He made himself slow down.

What did this mean? Gaerity had murdered O'Bannon. So, quite obviously, there had been no love lost between the two. O'Bannon hiding Gaerity these past weeks was a longshot. No, Franklin decided, an impossibility. The old man had been genuinely upset over McNulty's death. O'Bannon had been a cop first, a mick second.

Yet he had been tight with James Dove. Word had it that O'Bannon had gotten him in the department.

There had been one Green Street survivor. Liam McGivney. Vanished. Fingerprint card on file with London bureau of Interpol. No photograph available.

"Lee . . . am . . ." Franklin was jotting down the name when a voice said from the doorway, "Excuse me."

The pencil squirted out of his hand, and he shot to his feet.

Kate Dove stood there, looking as scared as he felt. "I'm sorry," she said, "I—"

"It's all right, Ms. Dove. We're all just a little jumpy right now."

She nodded as if she more than understood. "Front desk let me in. Maybe I should've phoned up first."

"No, no. No problem." Franklin glanced at the computer screen. It had gone blank again. "May I help you with something?"

"Have you seen Jim?"

Franklin tried not to look worried. Dove had stormed out of an interview with Homicide that evening. There'd been no contact with him since. Franklin had figured that he was holed up with his wife and kid. Now this. "Uh, no, Ms. Dove, I haven't. He was pretty broken up over—"

"I can imagine," she said, saving him from having to finish.

Franklin steered her away from Roarke's office—no use having her tell Dove where she'd found him. He flipped on the lights in the working area. "Are you sure Jim wants you just strolling around town like this?"

"I'm not sure what Jim wants right now." Her expression turned desolate as she said this. But then she added, "Lizzy and I are staying with my aunt in Brookline. Would you mind telling him that if you see him first?"

"Of course," Franklin said.

She stopped beside Dove's desk, ran her eyes over a framed photograph of herself and her daughter. She was reaching for it when she shuddered.

"You all right, Ms. Dove?"

She pushed aside some papers and grasped one of Gaerity's mugshots. All but the eyes had been covered by other papers. "Is this him?" she asked, glancing to Franklin.

He nodded.

Turning, she rushed for the hallway.

But he stopped her at the door with: "Ms. Dove,

this may not be the time, but may I ask a quick question?"

She didn't answer, but neither did she continue on.

"Where'd you meet your husband?"

"Church," she said brusquely, then shut the outer door behind her.

Kate found him at dawn in O'Bannon's Jacuzzi.

His eyes dully tracked her through the gate, but he said nothing. After a moment, he slid his revolver under a towel.

She sat across the pool from him.

He was completely nude. The dawn sun was highlighting the gray in several days' stubble. There were dark crescents under his eyes. An empty fifth of Bushmill's lay in the planter, as well as innumerable broken bottles of Harps beer heaped against a far wall.

"Where are the bubbles, Jim?" she asked.

He apparently hadn't spoken for so long, he had to take a swig of beer first. His hand, when he lifted it from the water, was white and wrinkled. How long had he lain half-submerged here? "Max won the damn thing in a raffle," he said. "Never could get it to work."

"And what lesson do you take from that?"

"Don't gamble when you won't win in the end." Then he stared off toward Logan, a jet soaring into the golden haze. Despite all the evidence strewn around the yard, he didn't seem especially drunk.

"I heard about Max on the news. I'm sorry."

His expression remained blank.

"Jim?"

"Huh . . . ?"

"What've you been thinking that you needed that within reach?"

"Needed what?"

Her eyes shifted to a bulge under the towel.

She expected him to deny her accusation. But he didn't. He just cupped his hand, filled it with water, and rubbed his face. "I have been thinking . . ." A strange, airy quality to his voice now. ". . . that America has always been a mirage to us Irish. Go west over the sea to Amerikay and leave the past behind. A new life. There's no such thing. Just the same old litany of blood and betrayal in a new setting."

"Do you regret having come?"

"Oh yes," he said with absolute conviction.

That hurt her. "Why?"

"For the harm I've brought those I love. I should've known that when you come from the gutter in Belfast your fate is sealed. Best to accept it and not try to flee. Oh, you might have a good time for a while in the New World, but eventually you turn a corner and there it is—the Banshee, crooning death for you and those closest to you." He hoisted his bottle. "*Sláinte.*"

"You don't believe that."

"Oh Katie, I'm too beat to believe in anything." Then it visibly came to him. "What the hell are you doing in town?"

"Does it matter?"

"What d'you mean?"

"You've obviously given up. Sitting with a bottle in one hand and a gun in the other, waiting to feel sorry enough for yourself to pull the trigger."

"Oh, bullshit."

"The hell it is!"

For the first time, he exchanged stares with her.

"Besides," she said, lowering her voice. "He was down there."

Dove sat up slightly. "How do you know?"

"He was in Falmouth, dammit. Helping Lizzy with her kite. He was standing three feet from her with a knife in his hand!" And then she plunged into the pool, clothes and all. She was more angry from seeing Dove like this—trying to get blind drunk to forget what could be neither forgotten nor undone—than from remembering Gaerity with Lizzy.

She slapped him.

"Kate—"

"He was trying to get my daughter, and you're throwing in the towel on me!"

Then, catching him unawares, she grabbed his hair and plunged his face under the surface. He came up, spluttering for breath.

"Do you think blowing your brains out will keep him away from Lizzy and me? Do you think he means to quit anytime before we're all dead?"

She reared back to strike him again, but he caught her hand in mid-flight. He started to say something, but then words failed him and he just shook his head. He was doing it again. Sliding back into self-pity. She could watch it happening.

"I don't care what you did back in Ireland," she went on. "Ancient history. As far as I'm concerned, the records are sealed. Just like that bullshit you laid on me about your juvenile offenses in Somerville. I'm chalking it up to peer pressure and a shitty upbringing." She paused. "What I do care about is Gaerity. You find him, James Dove. You brought him here—you find the son of a bitch. Meanwhile, I've got no place to hide, so I'm going on with my life."

"Katie, you can't," he said miserably. "You've got to get away from here. Away from me."

"Neither. I have a performance at Hatch Shell this evening, remember? It's Fourth of July. My goddamn job is on the line. And then I love you, whatever the hell your name is."

Then she climbed the steps out of the water and kicked his beer over.

19

A patrolman was still posted at Saint Sebastian's, more to guard the damaged building while over fifty windows were reglazed than to protect any remaining evidence. Homicide had come and gone, probably for good at this point. "Hey, Lieutenant Dove," the blue-suiter asked, stepping out of his parked cruiser, "what you doin' here?"

Dove put the kickstand down on his Harley. "Looking for a stick to shove up somebody's ass."

The patrolman chuckled, but clearly had no idea what he meant. "Remember me? Hedison? I went through your basic course a couple years ago." He showed all ten fingers. "Still in one piece."

Dove did his best to smile. "Good."

"Happy Fourth of July, Lieutenant. If you need anything, I'll be in my car listenin' to the Sox game."

Dove shouldered his saddlebag of tools. "Who's winning?" The blue-suiter told him, but he'd forgotten by the time he crossed the schoolyard to the buckled merry-go-round.

There, he took a moment and stared up into the sky. It was still white with heat, although dusk was fast approaching. Late this morning, after crawling out of the Jacuzzi and shaving, Dove had gone downtown and taken possession of Max O'Bannon's few remains. Barely enough weight to be felt in the casket. But, as executor of the will, he saw that it was put aboard a freighter bound for the port of Belfast. Max had wanted to be buried in Armagh. The same cemetery in which his wife and Shiofra lay. Under an Irish sky.

"Done," he said to himself.

Kate was right. Ancient history. He had his own family to save now.

Dove turned and went to the sandbox. Kneeling, he studied the charred and splintered redwood two-by-eight that had faced the blast.

"No," he said, rising, "not the way to go."

He already knew what kinds of explosives had been used. Linking them to magazine thefts in the metropolitan area would lead nowhere fast.

He strode into the box, began sifting the sand with the side of his shoe. Privacy. Gaerity needed privacy in which to work. He would trust no one to know about this place, especially any of the alcoholics at O'Dowell's. Homicide had leaned on the bartender and the regulars pretty hard and come up with nothing, according to the reports Dove had read over lunch and a pot of strong coffee.

Leaving the sandbox, Dove went to the swing set. He probed the melted rubber of one of the seats, then suddenly tossed the prongs back into his bag. No time for this kind of investigation.

Transportation.

Yesterday, Traffic had recovered Max's Bonneville, abandoned and stripped, near Suffolk Downs Racetrack. That had led Homicide to speculate that Gaerity was operating out of East Boston or even one of the towns up the coast, like Lynn. Not entirely unreasonable. One of the dicks had gone so far as to determine that Lynn Harbor had the old style horn buoys.

But Dove still believed that Gaerity was holing up in the Inner Harbor area. Max had said that he was getting around on a bicycle. The River Street Bridge, Copley Square, Dove's own house in South Boston were all a haul from Lynn on a bike. If he'd gotten down to Falmouth, as Kate claimed, it hadn't been on two tires.

The sun was throwing long shadows. Before the schoolyard was lost in twilight, Dove scanned all around.

Something glinted above the gate. Something on the backside of Saint Sebastian. For an instant, Dove thought that the statue had been scuffed by shrapnel off the merry-go-round. But no. The steady gleam was silver-colored, not bronze.

He ran to the gate, dropped his saddlebag to the ground.

"What is it, Lieutenant?" the patrolman asked, bailing out of his car again.

Ignoring him, Dove scrabbled up the chainlink so that his eyes were level with Saint Sebastian's robe. Something was imbedded in one of the bronze folds. Something silver-plated. "Toss me a standard screwdriver out of the bag."

"Comin' right up," the patrolman said.

Dove pried the object out of the statue, turned it over in his hand.

"What's that, sir?"

"A ball rest."

"Pardon?"

"Goes on top of a roulette wheel spindle."

"Like gamblin'?"

"Yeah." Embossed on its base was a dolphin leaping above some stylized waves.

"What's it mean?"

"Bicycle," Dove said, climbing down.

"What's that, sir?"

He stared right through the patrolman, seeing the

Dolphin Runner, hearing the old longshoreman tell him about the bicyclist he'd seen on the quarterdeck.

Kate was absolutely right. He'd been too preoccupied with the past.

"Entropy," Gaerity said, then downed a slug of whiskey straight from the bottle.

All was in place.

Did that mean that everything was finished? Gaerity was beginning to suspect so. There was a bit of choreography to dance out, but all the steps were fixed on the path to inevitability.

"En . . . tro . . . py," he repeated, rolling his tongue on the syllables. Energy and matter on the verge of degrading to the ultimate state, that hushed inertness which every living thing secretly desired to join. So, when he tried to see beyond this evening, he saw nothing. Or nearly nothing. An unbroken landscape of snow. A featureless plain of sand on the bottom of the ocean.

Was tonight the end?

It felt like the end. He was tired, and no place the world over seemed to beckon him.

He took another jolt of Bushmill's, then swiveled around in the captain's chair. He gazed through the bridge windows at the Moroccan freighter that had brought him to Boston. Her mast lights were just coming on against the nightfall. Tomorrow she would sail—*with or without you*, as her Libyan skipper had said.

Gaerity tried to visualize himself sneaking up the accommodation ladder, being spirited under decks by the crew.

But he couldn't.

At last, after a lifetime of frenetic effort, of endless struggle, he seemed to be at the center of all things. And that center was a dark void. Yet the old man, O'Bannon, had made an interesting point. Liam

McGivney was a fine, full man—and how could there be a pure void if such men existed? Men like that filled voids, made a mockery of entropy. The young McGivney had been like a god, utterly fearless. *My God, he did things I myself feared to do!*

All at once, Gaerity raked everything off the chart table with his forearm. "You could've helped me tear it all down, you headstrong bastard!"

The tragedy of this was mythic in scope. God lamented the fall of Satan because he was the one other force in the universe capable of understanding Him, His works, His triumphs and torments. And so it had been for Gaerity when Liam McGivney had suddenly opposed him in Crossmaglen.

"Damn you to hell!"

He stood and began ripping the Kerr jars off the beam, lids and all. He hurled them against the far bulkhead. They broke, splattered yellow and red and green in a wide fan across the deck. He was reaching for another when he heard a creak on the stairs.

"Not a minute too early," he whispered, "and not a minute too late."

Dove had gone five steps up the staircase when instinct made him halt. He could hear Gaerity carrying on in the bridge—perhaps drunk, perhaps only feigning it as he belted out the lyrics to a U2 song. He was also smashing glass.

But that wasn't what had made Dove stop.

He knew that Ryan Gaerity would never leave the entrance to his lair unguarded. The narrow stairway up to his Belfast flat had bristled with devices.

Lowering himself onto his chest, Dove peered up the carpeted incline into the light spilling down from the open bridge door. He saw it at once—a strand of filament cloaked with spider webs. It stretched into a shadowy recess on one side of the stairs. There, something tubular lurked. A homemade bazooka, one of Gaerity's more obvious devices—which made Dove all the more cautious as he rose and continued up the stairs.

He kept the door in sight over the barrel of his revolver.

Above, Gaerity went on singing, slightly out of tune, words slurred. "I Still Haven't Found What I'm Looking For."

Dove went no farther than the threshold.

Gaerity was in the captain's chair, turned away from Dove and facing the city lights. He broke off his song and calmly said, "Not to worry, Liam. No infrared beams at the door. They're passe, you know. Come in and make yourself at home." Slowly, he glided around in the chair, giving Dove a start: he was wearing the black hood of the IRA. Dove had forgotten how chilling eyes looked in the oval slits.

"Bring back memories, Liam?"

"A few."

Gaerity laughed. "A few, he says."

Gingerly, Dove stepped onto the bridge deck.

"Oh-oh," Gaerity abruptly said, "didn't you hear it?"

Dove froze in his tracks. He'd heard nothing but knew better than to move.

"You didn't hear it, did you?" Gaerity asked incredulously. "After all my schooling, here you bumble in like a Boston gumshoe with donuts in his ears. Well, keep coming, Liam, and we'll talk about the first thing that pops up."

Dove glanced down at the deck tiles. One of them was a slightly different color and texture.

"That's right, Liam. You've gone and cocked the trigger on our bouncing friend. Stand fast. This too shall come to pass. And please don't point that vile thing at me."

But Dove kept his revolver trained on the hood.

"Well, are you ready to go?" Gaerity asked.

Dove kept silent, thinking. To his chagrin, he realized that he was in the same fix he'd put Franklin's basic class through. How demented was Gaerity? Was he willing to die if Dove tested the Betty? No doubt, much of the man's boozy jocularity was a put-on. Gaerity could drink phenomenal amounts and keep a razor-sharp mind. But there was something else in his voice, his eyes, his airy mannerisms that wasn't being faked. Gaerity was beyond fear.

"Where would I be going, Ryan?" Dove finally asked.

"To hell."

"For what?"

"For what, he says." Gaerity snorted, then whipped off the hood.

Dove had had a glimpse of him in the school window, but that had been at a distance. Close up, he looked sunken-cheeked, sad, desperately unbalanced.

Gaerity said, "I seem to remember a lovely spring day down in old Crossmaglen. I'd gone there with a troupe of friends to entertain the British. But things happened. They went awry, and the performance was ruined."

Dove said, "I'm done feeling guilty."

Gaerity wiped the back of his neck with the hood. "My God, how you've grown." Then he smiled. "You know, dear Liam, there's another possibility that may have escaped you all these years ..."

Dove wondered if he might be able to dive backwards through the door. He could never beat the detonation, but if he were tumbling down the stairs the injury might be limited to his legs.

"Don't even think of it," Gaerity said, reading Dove's eyes. "I boosted the propellant charge. Liftoff and detonation will be virtually simultaneous." He steepled his fingers under his chin. "Back to Crossmaglen. Aren't you even curious about this possibility?"

"No."

Gaerity pretended to pout. He was completely gone, Dove realized. "Why not?"

"It already occurred to me."

"Really . . . when?"

"Recently, I've thought of little else."

"And what'd you come up with?"

"You went down to Crossmaglen meaning to kill Shiofra and the gang. You had a timer on the device."

"And what makes you believe that?"

"It's standard practice with a remote. Backup if something interferes with the frequency. But that wasn't the clincher."

"What was?" Gaerity asked, still smiling.

"You didn't have time to depress the button before I was on you. The timer kicked in before you could use the remote." Dove paused. "You'd already made your decision back in Belfast. They were all doomed simply because they trusted you."

Gaerity asked, "But why would I ever do such an awful thing to my own comrades?"

"You despised them. They'd become mirrors of yourself, and you'd grown to hate them as much as you hate yourself."

Gaerity appeared thoughtfully surprised. "Never looked at it that way."

"Goes without saying."

"Well, if I'm so terrible, I think I should die. Kindly step off the trigger. Wake up old Betty and let her take us by the hands into the dark."

Furtively, Dove glanced around. He needed a piece of furniture or something to shield him from the blast. The chart table, upon which Gaerity was now resting an elbow, was too far away.

"What're you thinking right now, Liam? Don't try to punish me with silence, not after all these years.

You don't know how I've looked forward to this little chat. Something wrong?"

Dove's hand was starting to ache from gripping the revolver too tightly. He eased his grip slightly.

"Are you thinking of your wife, Kate? Fair Kate with the flaming hair. And your pretty little step-daughter?" Gaerity then brought down both shoes and stomped the deck.

Dove felt the vibrations pass under him. He flinched, despite himself, which seemed to make Gaerity do it merrily again.

"Throw me the gun, Liam. Unless you're as ready to die as I am. As long as Betty sleeps, the possibility remains that you can defeat me . . . right? If she goes, all is lost—and Kate and Lizzy may begin mourning as soon as your detectives scrape us off the bulk-heads. You're sweating, Liam."

Dove didn't have to be told. A small trickle went down his neck from his hair. He couldn't decide if it felt hot or cold.

"Speak," Gaerity implored.

"I can die in peace if I know that you're going with me—and they're safe."

"Yes, you could. But something precludes that."

"What're you talking about?"

Gaerity started to reach for the television on the floor beside him, but stopped when Dove raised the revolver to eye level. "Easy, Liam. May I just have a go at the telly?" After a moment, Dove nodded, and Gaerity turned on the set. An old black-and-white Sylvania. "If the newspaper is correct, we should see . . . ah, here we go . . ."

The camera was panning a crowd. People were rising from their lawn chairs and picnic blankets. Dove recognized MIT across the twilit Charles River. Then his heart sank as Hatch Shell came into view. On stage was the Pops, striking up the National An-

them. Somehow, he'd hoped that Gaerity would believe that Kate and Lizzy were still on the cape.

"What've you done?" he asked, his voice sounding
small in his own ears.

"Only the inevitable, Liam," Gaerity said. "Only
the thing you set into motion the instant you turned
against me at Crossmaglen."

The camera zoomed in on the sections of the orchestra. Percussion. Woodwinds. Then Dove held his
breath as he saw Kate, her expression intent as she
swayed to the rhythm, violin under her chin.

"I imagine little Lizzy has a very good seat, what
with Mama part of the show. Children do so love
fireworks. I think we all do, deep down. I can almost
see the flickering lights."

Dove bit the inside of his cheek to keep from pulling the trigger. He'd never felt an urge so strong—
to pump all six bullets into Gaerity's smug face.

"Do it, Liam," he said with a sickening grin. "Confirm all that I believe about you."

Dove had to do something. The urge was over-
whelming. He clicked back the hammer so that only
a slight amount of pressure on the trigger would
drop the firing pin against the primer.

Finally, the moment passed. No report. No smoke.

"So it goes," Gaerity said. "You still want to save
them. We both know what that entails. Keeping me
alive till you learn what devilry I've been up to. The
gun, please, Liam—or I'll take the secret that might
save them to my grave."

Dove couldn't move.

"The gun!" Gaerity cried.

Dove eased down the hammer, then lofted the
piece over to Gaerity, who no sooner caught it than
he chucked it out a porthole. "I hate guns," he said,
sitting back again, interlacing his fingers behind his
head. "Which of my clues led you here?"

Dove took the roulette ball rest from his pocket.

"Oh," Gaerity said, looking disappointed, "the most obvious one."

"How'd you get down to Falmouth?" Dove asked.

"Bus. Only rabble seem to ride the bus in this country."

"Why didn't you kill Kate and Lizzy there?"

"Is that what you think this is all about . . . killing?"

Dove didn't know what to say.

"Do you really want to understand this thing, Liam?"

"Yes, I do." Dove said this as softly as he could without whispering.

"Do you have any idea what it feels like to be betrayed by someone you held as dear as a brother?"

Dove dropped his voice slightly more. "Why should I have mattered more than the others?"

It was working. Gaerity rose and limped forward, closing half the distance between them.

"*Why, Liam?*" he echoed. "The rest were chaff. You were the one with imagination. With a sense of personal loyalty, I thought. Do you have any notion what the two of us could've accomplished all these years?"

"The bloodshed and terror?"

Gaerity frowned, took another step forward. "What? Speak up."

Dove repeated the same words at the same level of sound.

In frustration, Gaerity came on another pace. "I'm trying to—"

Dove seized Gaerity by the neck, yanked him close, and fell backwards. He buried his face against the man's shoulder as they slammed together onto the deck. Two blasts, nearly simultaneous as Gaerity had promised, filled the bridge with smoke—the Betty's propelling and detonating charges.

Then silence.

Dove locked gazes with Gaerity. He looked for signs of pain or shock, but saw neither. Just a faint amusement that was confirmed when Gaerity scrambled up onto his knees and half-turned, laughing, to wave his arms through the confetti that was falling to the deck like snow.

"Did you think to make a bomb blanket of your old comrade, Liam?" he asked. Then the cords in his neck stood out as he cocked a fist and shouted, "I am the mentor!"

Dove tried to turn his face, but it was too late. He took the blow on the mouth, tasted blood immediately. As the shock faded, he rose from the hips, groping for one of Gaerity's legs. But a kick to the ribs sent him sprawling again. An agony of breathlessness. He squirmed across the deck, tried to sit himself up against the bulkhead.

Gaerity was standing at a service sink. He took a Silly Putty container from an egg holder and opened it. "I've saved my best little beastie for you." He poured a glistening substance down the drain. "Bombs away. Mercury, Liam—off to tip the scales of Justice."

Dove tried to rise, but he still had no legs.

"Time's up," Gaerity said, hobbling across the deck at him.

Dove grabbed his ankle and overturned him. But not before Gaerity snatched the handcuffs off the back of Dove's belt. He lunged forward to get them back, only to grope helplessly in the air as Gaerity snapped one of the bracelets around his left wrist.

Dove threw a roundhouse with his right that glanced off Gaerity's jaw. The man came back at him with an elbow, bashing Dove in the nose.

Sneezing blood, he blindly tried to keep Gaerity from pulling his left hand up by the cuff. He flailed with his free fist and shoes, but realized that Gaerity was slowly drawing the other cuff up to the bulkhead handrail. The ratchet was starting to close around the pipe when Dove jammed the toe of his Oxford into it.

Gaerity let go of the cuff and whirled to strike Dove. He was drawing back for a quick jab when Dove drove his heel into the man's left kneecap.

"Damn you!" he howled. Then he staggered and went down on all fours.

Dove leaped onto him, and together they skidded through the doorway, stopped only by the friction of the carpet. He punched Gaerity twice in the face before Gaerity wrapped him in his arms and rolled off the landing. They tumbled freely down the steps—until Dove realized what Gaerity had in mind. The bazooka. Dove tried to muscle him around so that Gaerity was between the muzzle and himself. But their fall was so chaotic that Dove had no idea who was in jeopardy until one of them hit the trip wire and the flash dazzled all around them—at that instant, he felt icy needles bite into his left foreleg.

"Christ!" he cried in pain as the two of them came to rest at the foot of the stairs. A half-dozen framing nails were protruding from his calf.

Gaerity hollered in triumph, "Eye for an eye! Leg for a leg!" Then he closed the crook of his arm around Dove's neck and tightened it like a vise.

Dove's fingertips found the nails.

"Right now, dear Liam," Gaerity said breathlessly, "the mercury's dripping out of the third deck overhead . . ." Dove clawed at the nails, ripping them out of his flesh while Gaerity went on throttling him. ". . . into an old toilet. From there—"

Dove, growing light-headed, gouged at Gaerity's eyes. He must have raked one of them, for Gaerity backed off, making guttural sounds.

Lunging again, Dove grabbed him around the waist. They rolled down the tilting deck of the salon toward the stagnant water pooled against the starboard side, knocking over gambling stools as they grappled.

Then Dove felt the deck plate lurch beneath them.

Gaerity shoved him back, almost into the water, and scrambled up the sloping carpet to safety.

Dove tried to do the same, but the rotten deck began collapsing beneath him. A cloud of rust flew up, choking him, and chunks of plate could be heard clanging against metal surfaces far below.

He was sinking into the ever-spreading hole.

"Thirty feet to the engine room deck below, Liam," Gaerity said nonchalantly. "With any luck, you should arrive about the same time the mercury does. It will light a fuse that winds up into a lovely mix of barium nitrate and diesel. Getting the picture?"

Dove tried to grab the water-soaked carpet above him, but it shredded apart in his hands.

Cross beams. They had to run under the deck, somewhere.

Sinking ever lower atop piles of putrid-smelling carpet, he felt all around with his legs for a beam. He found one—and wrapped his hands around it just as the entire plate groaned and tumbled into the darkness below. His injured leg was burning with pain. But he continued to hang on his arms, fighting for breath and a purchase on the slick beam as water drained in a torrent onto his bowed head. When it was gone, the last drops echoing down in the bilge, Gaerity's head appeared over the edge. He snicked on a butane lighter, waved the flame back and forth as he looked past Dove. At last, he said, "Thank God—thought for a moment you'd flooded out my little project. Care for a hand?"

Dove knew he couldn't hang on much longer. Yet he couldn't bring himself to ask for help.

Gaerity's smiling face was ghoulish in the glow of the lighter. "Oh come now, Liam—you don't want to fall from grace a second time . . . do you?" He paused. "By now the mercury is spinning around a most marvelous toy I bought at Saint Sebastian's. A roller coaster for marbles. Are you ready for a hand now?"

Dove gnawed on the inside of his cheek.

"Very well, Liam. In that case, let me lend you a foot."

Gaerity rose from a crouch and stood on the edge. His shoe came down on Dove's right hand. He used the heel to slowly grind harder and harder.

Dove saw the open bracelet dangling off his cuffed left wrist. He flung it upward, but only slapped Gaerity's shin with it on the first try.

Gaerity sniggered in confusion, lifted his shoe off Dove's hand. "What the devil—?"

The second try closed the ratchet around the man's ankle.

Dove let go of the beam and plunged. He dropped about two feet before Gaerity came down hard against the beam. He tried to find his balance, but Dove swung up a leg and shoved him over the opposite side.

Gaerity bellowed as his head fell six feet and stopped with a neck-snapping jolt.

The handcuff chain was draped over the top of the beam with Gaerity's ankle on one side and Dove's wrist on the other.

Inverted, Gaerity suddenly laughed. "Didn't get much of a look at this beam, did you?"

Dove strained for a glimpse.

"It's corroded, you damn fool!" Gaerity said.

Thirty feet below, Dove could see the small flame of the butane lighter atop one of the bilge plates. Diesel cylinders. A strong smell of fuel and barium nitrate.

His wrist was killing him. It felt as if his hand was going to pop off his forearm at any second.

"Here we are," Gaerity said giddily, "joined as one again!" He started to sing:

> *"When boyhood's fire was in my blood,*
> *I read of ancient freemen,*
> *For Greece and Rome who bravely stood,*
> *Three hundred men and three men!*
> *And then I prayed I yet might see,*
> *Our fetters rent in twain,*
> *And Ireland——!"*

Then a horrible sensation of sinking made Gaerity fall silent and Dove shut his eyes. The rust-weakened beam was gradually bending under the weight of both men.

Dove began fumbling with his right hand in his trouser pocket for his keys. His tiny chrome handcuff key.

"Don't fight it, Liam. We were meant to go together. I only wish that you could see the trigger from here. Trigger to beat all triggers. The Stradivarius of triggers!"

At last, Dove came out with his key ring. He was bringing it up to his eyes when Gaerity kicked his hand.

The keys sparkled as they fell onto the bilge plates below.

"Once again, you disappoint me, Liam."

Dove reached down and punched Gaerity squarely in the face.

But it only made the man shriek with laughter. "You're going to hell with me, boy!"

The beam gave another few inches, then stopped once more. Rust chips sprinkled down into Dove's uplifted face. Then he thought he was imagining something unbelievable, a human figure standing above in the semidarkness of the salon.

"Franklin?" he asked, astonished.

"Yeah . . . what the hell are you doing?" the sergeant asked, thumbing on his flashlight.

"We're handcuffed together," Dove quickly said, squinting. "Get that damn thing out of my eyes and find something to cut the chain."

"No!" Gaerity roared, starting to rock back and forth in an obvious attempt to bring down the beam at once. Dove tried to hold him steady, but the man only swung more furiously. "Don't do this to me, Liam!"

The beam dropped a half-foot.

Franklin reappeared and set his flashlight on the deck. He had a fire ax in his right hand. Offering Dove his left, he said, "Grab hold!"

Dove did so, and Franklin brought the blade down onto the chain. At that second, Gaerity was trying to jackknife himself up so he could latch on to the beam. He was looking directly at Dove as he began to fall away. Almost at once, a look of quiet resignation came into his eyes.

His body thudded against one of the cylinders and was left sprawling over a catwalk.

"Jesus Christ," Franklin said, pulling Dove up. "Was that one crazy fucker or what?"

"Run," Dove said, although he had no breath for it. "This whole ship's set to blow."

20

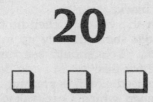

Gaerity couldn't move his legs. He tried a few times to wriggle his toes, then quietly accepted the fact that his lower back was broken. But his hands were still his. He used his fingertips to explore the bloody gash in the back of his head, then pressed with all his remaining strength.

The pain sharpened his mind again. Cleared his vision.

Turning his face, he saw that his butane lighter hadn't burned out yet. It was casting wavering shadows around the engine room.

A soft plopping noise made him smile through his pain.

Silvery beads could be seen spangling down through the light. The mercury was dripping from the compartment's overhead into a plastic funnel, filling the other half of the Silly Putty egg. This he had propped upright in one of Lady Justice's pewter scales. As he watched, enraptured, the scale began to dip under the weight of the quicksilver. The kitchen match taped to the scale's underside began slowly sinking, and then the red-tipped head scraped the cinder block Gaerity had positioned next to the statuette.

The match flared, and the spot of fire touched the end of the fuse he'd looped ever so precisely over the top of the block.

"Oh, entropy . . . yes . . ." Then he tilted his head back so he could shout directly up into the hole in the salon deck. "You should see this, Liam! You should be here for this!"

The flame rasped down a graceful arc of fuse to the bilge plate on which Gaerity lay. As it inched near, he raised his hand, tempted to slap it dead. His final temptation. But then, smiling again, he cried upward, "You'll never make it, lads! All things must degrade to nothingness! You, me—all things!"

He folded his hands over his chest and let the flame creep past him. It reached a junction, branched off along four trails of homemade napalm—Ivory Soap flakes and gasoline—and raced up into the cylinders.

Franklin reached the gangway first. Turning, he glanced back across the quarterdeck and saw Dove limping toward him. "What happened to your leg?"

"Run-in with a bazooka," Dove said. "Go first, go!"

"No, man, you're hurt!"

Dove gave him a shove just as the entire ship shuddered, the radio mast swaying as if in an earthquake. Licks of orange flame shot out of the hatches. The bridge windows disintegrated, showering the weather decks with glass. Franklin felt himself being picked up. For a split second, he thought that it was Dove, shoving him again. But no. It was the blast overpressure—hot, enormous, invisible—swatting him over the side. From the corner of his eye, he could see Dove pumping his arms and legs in midair as if trying to reach the wharf. Franklin himself failed, splashing down into the water. Filthy, oily tasting. He stroked upward before his plunge bottomed out, kicked wildly, and finally broke the surface.

The sky directly above was a crackling orange.

Dove burst into view, gasped, and began swimming frantically for the wharf. Franklin was confused by his urgency. They were already wet.

Then the harbor seemed to ebb beneath him.

Thrashing around, he watched, mesmerized, as the entire ship reared, drawing up a huge swell of water around the keel. The midsection split, disgorging more flame, and the two halves of the *Dolphin Runner* plowed downward again. Franklin ducked under the foaming surface. He was breaststroking when the returning wave picked him up and carried him along like flotsam. He was washed headfirst onto the wharf, then slammed onto the planking as the wave broke. Receding, it tried to suck him back into the harbor and the fires now completely encircling the ship. He grabbed a piling and hung on.

Dove was trying to save his Harley. No good. It went over the side and sank. The lieutenant was knocked prone. He dug his fingers into the crack between two planks and rode out the withdrawing wave.

Franklin saw that the water pooled all around them on the wharf was being pocked with blast debris. He threw his arms over his head. Dove walked over, seemingly oblivious to this deadly hail, and demanded, "Where's your car!"

"Commercial Street. Get down, man!"

Dove crouched for a moment, but then the heat of the spreading fires drove them around the corner of a warehouse.

"Your car!" Dove cried. "Lead the way!"

"Let's have a look at that leg first."

"Car!"

"What's the rush? The motherfucker's dead!" Franklin felt himself grin. "We got him!"

"Too late," Dove said, momentarily taking his weight off his bleeding leg. "It's not over."

"How can—"

"He planted something before we got him!"

"Shit." Franklin supported Dove under the arms, and they set off across a loading yard that was dotted with small fires set by flying debris. "Where?"

"Hatch Shell."

Franklin was opening the driver's side door to his Mustang when Dove snatched the keys from him. "Say what?"

"I'm driving."

"Bullshit."

But Dove pushed him back and climbed in behind the wheel. Franklin ran around the front end and rapped on the glass for Dove to open the passenger door for him.

For a moment he thought he was going to be left behind.

But then, wincing, Dove reached across the seat and sprang the latch. He swiftly punched the pedal to the floor. Swearing, the sergeant dragged his left leg inside the car, slammed the door, and belted himself in.

Dove was doing eighty by the time they passed the Coast Guard base. "Easy, man!"

The lieutenant just stared straight ahead, his hands white on the steering wheel.

"Lucky I found you, huh?" Franklin asked.

"You were following me," Dove said, going into a four-wheel drift as he made a sharp left onto Washington Street. A foot patrolman blew his whistle from the corner.

The sound quickly faded behind them.

Franklin braced his hands against the dash. "Dispatch said you were out on the wharf. I remembered the ship from the other day. Put two and two together."

"I didn't tell dispatch."

A trolley was locked by traffic in the intersection with Sudbury.

"Stop, dammit!"

But Dove barreled on. At the last possible second, the trolley crept forward, leaving just enough space for the Mustang to streak through.

Franklin shouted, "Are you out of your goddamn mind!"

"We'll see," Dove said. So quietly it gave Franklin a chill.

This year, the Pops' program had been shortened so that the fireworks wouldn't come too late for the smaller children. Kate glanced down into the front left seating. Lizzy had leaned her head on Lannie's shoulder. She yawned. Too young for Tchaikovsky. Kate was relieved that *The 1812 Overture* was coming to a close. The conductor was sweating like a pig. She only hoped that none of it would fly off onto the first violins when he went spastic for the finale.

A crump sounded from behind the shell. It was closely followed by a shrill scream that made the adults sit upright in their seats and the children plug their ears with their fingers. Even Kate was caught off-guard. The hair stood on the back of her neck as suddenly a shower of white-hot sparks blossomed over the Charles. The airburst was reflected by the dark, still waters. The next was green, and then a red one that disintegrated into pinwheels that didn't go out until they fell into the river.

The crowd came to its feet, cheered.

The music ended. The conductor turned and bowed limply, although the throng's attention was now on the aerial display. Kate looked for Lizzy's reaction. She and Lannie were standing on their seats.

Lizzy was chewing on a finger, delighted.

*   *   *

Dove ignored Franklin the first time he asked.

His mind was on the fireworks exploding on the far side of Beacon Hill. The perfect way for Gaerity to disguise a rocket. Dove could visualize the speck of fire wobbling up into the night sky, the hushed expectation of the crowd as it looped back in on itself and started toward the ground again—directly at them. The nervous muttering and then screams as it screeched down on their heads.

"I *asked*—what's the takedown here, Dove?"

"We'll see."

"What d'you think he did?"

"No idea. Too many ideas. You have any tools in this wreck?"

"Yeah, my saddlebag's in the backseat. And it's not a wreck."

"Night's young," Dove said, speeding down Mount Vernon Street toward the river.

Several rockets went up at once, exploded, then winked out. The show was over. Dove rolled down his side window, listening for one final detonation. Smoke was sifting over the oval seating area below the shell. Had Gaerity's device already gone off?

No, Dove decided with a glance. The crowd wasn't running. It was calmly breaking up, people streaming out of the river park, toting ice chests and folding chairs. Looking forward to the rest of the holiday.

A blue-suiter held up a white-gloved palm to keep Dove from turning onto Storrow Drive.

He told Franklin to flash his badge through the windshield as he accelerated across the lanes and bounced over the opposite curb into the staff parking lot.

"Watch the car, dammit!"

"Fuck the car," Dove said.

Franklin gave up with a loud sigh. At least he

wanted one concession before things got hairy again. "You said thanks to me, didn't you?"

"No. Thanks. Now we're even."

"Not quite, Dove. There's something we're going to discuss when this is over—"

Bailing out, his wet clothes squishing, Dove hobbled to the back of the Mustang. He stepped up on the bumper and then onto the car roof. "Kate!" he shouted. "Kate O'Bradaigh!"

No answer.

He climbed down over the hood. His left leg, already swelling massively, buckled as his shoes hit the pavement, but he got up right away and ran as best he could through the lot.

Reaching the Wrangler, she thanked and paid Lannie for having babysat Lizzy. The teenager then split off with her equally vapid boyfriend, who promised to drive her home right away.

"Thank God that's all a couple of years off," Kate said under her breath, helping Lizzy into the front bucket seat and locking the door. Sleepy-eyed, the girl pressed the side of her face against the window and drifted off at once—her jaw slid open and her breath misted a pulsing spot on the glass.

Kate started to check over the car, but then made herself stop.

She wasn't going to live that way. Life became a prison without walls if you feared everything.

Getting in, she resolutely inserted the key in the column and cranked over the engine. It gave off its familiar throaty rumble. The muffler was going bad. Add that to the list, which now included a weak air conditioner and a broken emergency brake. She glanced at the odometer. A milestone was coming. Another four miles and the Wrangler would have gone 100,000 miles. And now even the odometer was breaking down. The last three numbers in the sequence were jiggling crazily.

She backed up and squeezed into the line of cars heading for the exit. Approaching Storrow Drive, she had to hit the brake pedal hard because of the inattentive driver in front of her. The bassoonist.

"Figures," she muttered, checking on Lizzy. The jolt hadn't awakened her.

But the pedal might need looking at. Kate had heard a resounding twang as she'd eased up on it. Like something metallic unraveling.

"See it?" Dove called to Franklin, who was searching the opposite side of the lot.

The sergeant held up his hands in apology.

"Christ." Dove stepped up onto another bumper and scanned all around. Maybe he should head home, try to meet her there. But he wasn't sure if she might be staying at her aunt's in Brookline.

Then his gaze was drawn to the rear lights of one particular vehicle. They were pulsating—a short in the electrical system. It was the Wrangler. Dove jumped down and ran for it, his leg now so stiff and swollen it felt like running on wood.

Flickering lights. Those had been Gaerity's words when talking about Kate's part in the celebration.

"Stop the Jeep!" Dove shouted at the motorcycle cop who was in the intersection, directing traffic. "Hey!"

But the street noise was too much, and the blue-suiter waved Kate on.

Her shorting rear lights were already heading up Embankment Road when Dove reached the traffic cop. He whipped out his sopping wallet and showed his badge. "Dove, bomb squad. Need the bike."

The whistle fell from the man's lips. "What's your—?"

But Dove had already mounted and started the engine. He clamped down on the throttle and sped off.

His best hope was that she'd get snarled in another long line of cars. But she knew all the shortcuts around Boston Common, and by the time he'd crested Embankment Road she was moving eastward at a fast clip.

The brake lamps had quit entirely by now.

"Don't hit that pedal again, baby," he whispered, hugging the center line, forcing oncoming vehicles to swerve around him.

The next signal ahead went from yellow to red. Dove held his breath as she slowed. One slight tap of her foot and the Wrangler would become a fireball.

Pulling alongside, he forced himself not to shout. Once startled, she would instinctively brake.

She glanced sideways, and he motioned for her to roll down her window.

She did so, after glancing ahead at the light, which had turned green again.

"Don't brake, Kate!"

"What?" she asked, slowly accelerating again.

"There's something in the car! No braking!"

"What do I do? Emergency brake's shot!"

"Take your foot off the gas too. And downshift!"

There was a clunk of old gears as she tried. But it was useless at the speed she was going—the Wrangler had started down the east slope of Beacon Hill. It was no Everest, but Gaerity had no doubt planned on this descent to force her to lay on her brakes.

"Get Lizzy to open her window!" Dove shouted over the wind. "Then have her crawl in the back!"

Kate gave a firm nod, but Dove could see the fear in her face. The Wrangler was gathering even more speed as it dropped down toward the State House.

Dove fell back, then rounded the Jeep and sped up on the passenger side. Lizzy waved from the backseat, and he offered her a quick smile. Hopefully reassuring. Then, still gripping the handlebars, he stood on the Harley's seat. He prayed that his left leg wouldn't give out. Not now.

Then he leaped.

Slamming against the roof, he groped for the roll bar and caught it just as he began to slide backwards. The lower half of his body was dangling over the side, but he was secure for the moment. There was a crash to the rear as the bike skidded off into a darkened storefront, but Dove kept looking forward.

The light at the next intersection was against Kate, and the traffic was heavy.

Lizzy was screaming.

"It's all right, honey!" Dove lied. Then he swung his legs through the open window and lunged inside, banging the back of his head on the armrest.

"What do I do, Jim? Kate asked, her voice high and thin. "The light's red. Horn?"

"No," he said. That might bring into play Gaerity's backup trigger, if he'd installed one.

"Mom, stop!" Lizzy cried.

Dove twisted around on the seat so that his shoes were jutting out the side window and his face was against Kate's right knee. "Move your legs over." Horns blared on both sides of the Wrangler as he felt the stem of the brake. His hand froze. A pipe bomb.

"Hang on!" Kate warned, swerving wildly.

Dove withdrew his hand, gnashed his teeth together to keep from biting his tongue. She straightened out,. but he was sure that she was now doing at least fifty miles an hour.

"Hurry, Jim! We're coming on gridlock!"

"Flashlight!"

"What?"

"Toss me the flashlight from the glove box!"

She tapped his back with it, and he grasped blindly over his shoulder. The batteries were weak, but he had enough of a glow to see the copper filament that wound down from the dash. The movement of one of the gauges up there had cocked Gaerity's metal spring trigger that connected to a needlelike firing pin.

Gently, he reached for the spring, but a pothole bumped his fingers away. "Easy, Kate!"

"Then you drive!"

Taking in a deep breath, he clamped the top coil of the spring between his fingernails and began stretching. He kept eyeing the bomb that lay only inches from his face. Any hint that ignition was imminent, and he'd shove as much of his torso as he could between it and Kate.

At last, the firing pin popped free.

"Hit the brakes, Kate!"

Her foot came down with a vengeance. The brakes shrieked, and he braced one more time as the Wrangler skidded sideways to a smoky halt. He kissed Kate's ankle.

"What the hell're you doing?"

"Get out," he ordered, crawling back onto the seat, "everybody out right now."

The three of them were sitting on the curb around the corner from the Wrangler when a line of cruisers approached a few minutes later. Franklin was in the lead one. He'd bailed out and started for the Jeep when Dove cut him off. "Leave it be till Roarke gets here. I disarmed one, but we can count on two from Gaerity."

The sergeant frowned. "Don't trust me to sweep it?"

"Not at all. Your clothes are wet. Couple drops of water could collapse a circuit."

Franklin stared at him a moment longer, then said, "I'll buy that."

"What else are you buying, Anthony?" Dove knew full well what he was asking. But he wanted this over. One way or the other.

Franklin looked to make sure that Kate and Lizzy were out of earshot. "They okay?"

"Bit nerved . . . but okay."

Franklin took two cards, stapled together, from his inner jacket pocket. Still wet from the harbor. They almost fell apart in his hands, but he gave them over without a word.

Dove turned the top one into a streetlight, then said, "So? It's a copy of my fingerprint card from when I hired on."

Franklin nodded. "Look at the other one."

It was from Interpol. A photostat of prints taken nearly a quarter century before in Belfast from a Liam McGivney, who'd been detained for suspected IRA affiliation. Dove didn't have to check to see that the classification numbers on both cards were identical. "Here," he said, "give 'em to Roarke. Tell him whatever you want."

Franklin gazed off, the skin stretched tight over his jaw muscles. Then he ripped up the copies, walked over, and stuffed the pieces down a storm drain grate. "It's a long way to Tipperary," he said on his way toward the Wrangler.

"I'm not from Tipperary, Anthony," Dove said.

"Then it's a long way to Somerville." Franklin began whistling the old tune.

Dove went back to Kate and Lizzy. They looked up at him, their eyes still glassy. "Let's get one of the blue-suiters to give us a lift home."

"What about the Jeep?" Kate asked. "Didn't you say you wanted to go through it for another bomb?"

"Changed my mind. Leave it for the squad. I just want a good night's sleep." He held out his hand to her.

Smiling, she accepted, and he brought her to her feet. But on the stroll across the street, she said, "Dove?"

"Yeah?"

"Get my violin out of the Wrangler."